PRAISE FOR FICTION RIVER

"The *Fiction River* series is a wonderful mind-expanding read."
—*Astro Guyz*

"The stories in this anthology are reflections on the inner conflicts of the human heart. Superhero stories should be human stories after all, and that is always worth your time."
—*Tangent Online* on *Superpowers*

[*Fiction River*] is a worthy heir to the original anthology series of the 60s and 70s. ... It's certainly the top anthology of the year to date."
—*Amazing Stories* on *Fiction River: Unnatural Worlds*

"[*Fiction River*] is one of the best and most exciting publications in the field today."
—Keith West, *Adventures Fantastic*

"Readers will find many impressive voices, both familiar and new."
—*Publishers Weekly* on *Fiction River: Past Crime*

FICTION RIVER SPECIAL EDITION: SPIES

An Original Anthology Magazine

EDITED BY KRISTINE KATHRYN RUSCH

Series Editors
KRISTINE KATHRYN RUSCH & DEAN WESLEY SMITH

Fiction River Special Edition: Spies
Copyright © 2018 by WMG Publishing
Published by WMG Publishing
Cover and layout copyright © 2018 by WMG Publishing
Editing and other written material copyright © 2018 by WMG Publishing
Cover art copyright © ooGleb/Depositphotos
Cover design by Allyson Longueira/WMG Publishing
ISBN-13: 978-1-56146-071-7
ISBN-10: 1-56146-071-0

"Foreword: Spies to Die For" © 2018 by Allyson Longueira
"Introduction: Spying on the Editor" © 2018 by Kristine Kathryn Rusch
"Spy in the Sky" © 2018 by Tonya D. Price
"Meeting at the Rise and Shine" © 2018 by Kristine Kathryn Rusch
"Highpoint" © 2018 by Michael Kingswood
"Through the Eyes of a Dog" © 2018 by Angela Penrose
"Cat and Mice" © 2018 by Jamie McNabb
"Our Man in Basingstoke" © 2018 by Sabrina Chase
"Night Flight" © 2018 by Jonathan Kort
"End of the Line" © 2018 by David H. Hendrickson
"The Florentine Exchange" © 2018 by Dayle A. Dermatis
"The Message" © 2018 by C. A. Rowland
"Not What You'd Expect" © 2018 by Leah Cutter
"Turkish Coffee" © 2018 by Johanna Rothman
"The Path" © 2018 by David Stier
"Trafficking Stops" © 2018 by Lisa Silverthorne
"The Spy Who Walked into the Cold" © 2018 by Ron Collins

CONTENTS

FOREWORD

Spies to Die For

Out of the blue, my 8-year-old daughter announced she wanted to be a spy. When I asked her why, she said it was because she thought it would be fun to be sneaky and not get in trouble.

An oversimplification of spy craft, of course, but evidence of how pervasive spies are in our culture.

No one wants to be spied on, but we love the romanticism of spying on others.

A paradox to be sure.

But really, espionage comes in many forms and for many reasons.

When editor Kristine Kathryn Rusch proposed this topic, I was intrigued. Kris always edits powerful volumes, and I couldn't wait to read the contenders.

I was lucky. As an editor for the same workshop where she put together this volume, I got to read them all and mock-edit my own volume (as we editors do in the workshops). Let's just say I don't envy her having to choose from that pool of stories. As the actual editor, she had to fit her choices within a strict word count limit (I know, because as the publisher, I'm the one who set the limit). My mock volume would have gone way over word count.

Because of the nature of these stories, I can't tell you much more or I might ruin them. But I can tell you this: these spies come in all shapes and sizes. And the stories offer perspectives you might not expect.

Kris did an amazing job of organizing these diverse stories into a very powerful volume and it was a pleasure to reread them again in this order.

Enjoy.

—Allyson Longueira
Lincoln City, Oregon
July 17, 2018

INTRODUCTION

Spying on the Editor

Sometimes I just want to call anthologies that I edit *Stories Kris Likes*. It would certainly be easier than the hours I spend noodling with the table of contents, trying to make an anthology flow.

If I called the anthology *Stories Kris Likes*, then there doesn't have to be an order. Readers would understand that the only thing linking the stories is my taste.

After spending four hours tonight ordering and reordering and re-re-reordering the contents of *Fiction River Special Edition: Spies,* I almost gave up and went for the *Stories Kris Likes* order.

But, these aren't random stories that I like. These stories were written to my specifications. I had asked for stories about spies. I wanted different tones, different cultures, different time periods. I was afraid I'd get Bond-James-Bond stories (and really, the man is not a spy. What spy walks around introducing himself?) or some *Americans* rip-off or something.

What I got was a wide variety of tales with a wide variety of spies. The tone goes from satire to serious, from touching to brutal, from light to oh-so-very-dark. And not every point of view character is human either. Even though I asked that there be no fantasy or sf, I did end up with an *Animal Farm*-ish satire that even references

George Orwell. I choose to believe the non-human protagonist story is not fantasy, but who am I to judge? (Except that I do, and did, because I'm the editor. Ah, well.)

What links these stories, besides their wide variety of spies and spying, is their willingness to look at the world in all its messiness. The stories don't flinch from the effect that secrets have on those keeping them (or those who are victims of them).

The other thing that links the stories is their entertainment value. Even as I reread them, I couldn't put them down. Even when I knew what was going to happen. The writing is compelling, the characters more so, and the situations memorable.

The writers in this volume outdid themselves.

What screwed me up the most is that normally, I have tentpole stories—one at the beginning, one at the end, and one in the middle. I knew I had to end with Ron Collins's spectacular "The Spy Who Came in from the Cold," not just because it's powerful, but also due to the length. I like ending with a nice weighty piece of fiction. The moment I read this story, I knew it would close out the volume.

Just like I knew that Tonya D. Price's "Spy in the Sky" would start the volume. That strong story does a lot of things that the other stories in the volume do—it has an unusual protagonist, an unusual setting, and a lot of tension.

But that middle tentpole? The one that reaches out and grabs readers (who read in order) and keeps them moving forward? Well, I had a lot of choices. Lisa Silverthorne's "Trafficking Stops," which is too brutal to use as the opening story, would have been a great choice, except there's nothing else like it in the volume. Just like Sabrina Chase's "Our Man in Basingstoke," which shares a tone with a few other stories (and a pitch-perfect voice) but is (again) unlike anything else in the volume—and was too light to start the book, considering, well, Lisa's story. And Ron's, and Dave Stier's and a few others that I can't cite here without ruining them for you.

Most of the remaining thirteen stories could have been tentpoles. I finally gave up on the idea of a middle tentpole at all. The stories are so strong, I think any one of them could pull you through. So, pick your own middle story. That's the only area where I defaulted to the *Stories Kris Likes* template.

I'm pleased to share these spy stories with you. As always, I suggest you read the stories in the order presented, so you can flow from mood to mood, balancing the dark with the light. But dip in out of order if you want.

If you dare.

And enjoy!

—Kristine Kathryn Rusch
Las Vegas, Nevada
June 11, 2018

SPY IN THE SKY

TONYA D. PRICE

When I think of spy stories, I think of stories set during the Cold War. I grew up reading those stories, because I grew up during the Cold War. But those stories were always filled with grim-faced men in suits, having conversations about things that I (as a younger person) barely understood. The action happened toward the end and usually involved dark, rain-filled streets, and lots of diving in and out of doorways.

Tonya D. Price's story, "Spy in the Sky," is set during the Cold War, and the story does have its share of grim-faced men. But there's also a lot of sunshine and an unexpected protagonist and a lot of historical accuracy.

Tonya has written for Fiction River *before. She has several stories upcoming, and you'll find more of her work in* Fiction River: Hidden in Crime. *Her short fiction has also appeared in a variety of anthologies and genres. Tonya has an MBA from Cornell University and is also the author of the nonfiction book series, Business Books for Writers (www.BusinessBooksForWriters.com). Her most recent publication released in April 2018 is* Completing the Writer's To-Do List.

For "Spy in the Sky," Tonya channeled her childhood. In 1962 Tonya lived a mile from Wright Patterson Air Force Base. She spent 12 days in her basement with her mother, brother, and four neighborhood families during the Cuban Missile Crisis while the military fathers stayed on base. As a civilian, only Tonya's father could return home in the evening.

She writes, "We have a short memory when it comes to history. This story is a reminder of those days in hopes our children are never forced to relive them."

October 19, 1962

Sixteen-year-old Roberto MacAllister threw the first punch, catching his classmate square in the jaw. The bully fell like a sack of cane to the floor. The crowd of St. Mary's schoolboys pushed each other to get out of the narrow hallway as the bell rang for the second class. Footsteps sounded like a stampeding herd of cattle on the tile floors.

Stefano grabbed Roberto by the arm. "Run. Quick, before the priests catch you."

Roberto was small but fast. He ran out the front door into the midday sun. Shouts from inside the school called his name. Despite the heat, Roberto raced across Jose Marti Avenue, then cut between two Royal Palm trees lining Jose Marti Avenue. Two years ago, on the first anniversary of Batista fleeing Cuba, Roberto's father had run into the jungle in hopes of escaping Castro's Directorate of Intelligence. There was no disgrace in fearing the DI, his father had told him. It was just being smart.

Roberto circled the roots of three mangrove trees along La Sagua Rio then risked a quick look back toward the center of town. He saw no sign of Michael or Father Pedro. Roberto didn't feel very smart.

He feared capture. Fidel was big on education. The PNR policemen dealt with truants with cane beatings. Roberto had tangled with them once before when he ran away from the boarding school. As the son of an executed traitor, he risked much worse than a beating if the police caught him skipping classes.

He should have known better than to throw a punch at Michael, whose father commanded the local Defense of the Revolution Committee in Sagua La Grande. Michael's beatings would have been nothing compared to what might await Roberto if jailed. He should have held his temper in check. This weekend, he was supposed to find out if he could fly to Miami with three other boys as part of Operation Peter Pan. Father Pedro described it this way, You will be safe in Florida. You already know everything I can teach you about rockets. There you will learn much more. The path to your dreams does not lie in Cuba, my son.

Now, he might have lost the chance to go to America. His mother would be so disappointed. All she talked about was getting him to freedom. If he missed the plane, he would never fulfill his promise to his father to go to MIT. Roberto would be forced to live his entire life in Cuba as the son of a traitor.

Wiping the sweat off his face with his blue school bandana, he loosened his tie and rested a moment. Sweat made his arms stick in the sleeves of his school jacket and shirt. He pulled them off along with his shoes and stuffed them into his backpack. Shirtless and barefoot, he wouldn't look like a schoolboy, but blend in with the *niño callejero*. The orphans who lived on the streets knew him. He often gave them food. They would not betray him.

The heat of the October sun on his bare back took the strength from Roberto's legs. He left the path along the river and walked east into the forest. He knew these woods. He would be safe here. But for how long?

Fear kept him going, but after climbing the lime cliffs outside of town, he stopped to rest. From this point, he could look over the forest to the south or see the Bay of Sagua La Grande to the north. If any of the Revolution Committee followed him, he would be able to see them before they saw him.

Lured by the midday heat and his long hike, Roberto fell asleep under the shade of a cedar tree.

A sharp pain in his side woke him with a start.

"*Vstavay.*"

Roberto shielded his eyes from the sun. Two blonde men stood in front of him. They wore checkered shirts like common farm workers, but he had no idea what they had just said. He did recognize the language: Russian.

"*Auf standen.*" The man kicked him and pointed a rifle at Roberto's head.

"Spanish, not German. Speak Spanish," the second man said, in Roberto's own language.

The first man sighed, and in broken Castilian Spanish he motioned with the tip of his rifle. "Standing up."

The second man, who stood as tall as the first man, had a face burned so red Roberto thought he must be in pain. The second man held a calculator and a notebook, not a rifle. In perfect Castilian Spanish he asked, "What are you doing here?"

Roberto stood. "I got into a fight with another boy at school and ran away from the priest. I didn't want to get a beating."

To his surprise, the two men laughed.

5

The first man shook his head and in his broken Spanish said, "Go home. No one is allowed here. If we catch you here again, we shoot you. Understand?"

The second man took a step toward Roberto, and for a minute he appeared about to grab him, but the man just pointed down the path toward Sagua. "Go on, get out of here while we are in a good mood. Don't tell anyone you were here. Don't tell them what you saw. And don't come back."

"Yes, sir." Roberto scrambled to his feet. "I will say not a word."

He slipped and fell over his own feet.

The two men laughed.

Roberto picked himself up. As he stood, he noticed a convoy of trucks following a new road at the base of the cliffs. Behind them marched three columns of white men in the checkered shirts and cheap pants of farm workers.

The first man took a warning step toward Roberto. "Go, now, boy."

Roberto ran down the path along the top of the cliff. Once out of sight of the soldiers, he looked to his right. In the bay, he saw ships. Not the usual fishing boats but large cargo ships with Russian lettering.

He didn't know what was going on, but something big was about to happen.

With no place else to go, Roberto went to visit his friend Pepeto, who worked in his family's cantina on the outskirts of Sagua. A steep overhung canvas covered an open-walled room to allow the breeze and to provide relief from the sun. A crowd of men in checkered shirts stood shoulder to shoulder around a worn mahogany bar. Most were white, with blonde hair. Roberto knew all of the townsmen. He didn't recognize any of these strangers.

"Roberto!" Pepeto called from behind the bar. He waved with

both hands. "Come. We are in need of help. My father will pay. Come, quick."

In the middle of the open room, a dozen men sat side by side on both sides of a narrow table.

Roberto did not need the money, but before he could refuse, Señor Cruz, a former freedom fighter with a thick mustache, came up from behind him. His hand clasped Roberto's arm. "Thank you for helping. We have never had so many customers before. In the kitchen. You can wash the glasses."

The thought of arguing never occurred to Roberto. For the next three hours, he scrubbed glasses and washed ashtrays full of cigar butts. Relief came when Señor Cruz entered into the back room.

"Roberto, thank you for your help today. The crowd of Russians has died down." He looked upward. "Here, take this plate of Arroz Moro and go have something to eat."

Roberto took the black beans and rice and went to find a table in the open bar area. Only a few Russians remained. One was the man with the clipboard.

"Hey, truant," the Russian motioned Roberto close. "Come over here."

At first, Roberto thought of just running out of the cantina, but the Russian had slid off his stool and stumbled toward Roberto, lurching to the right and left as he came over. He finally fell into a chair at the table.

"Tell me, mal'chik," the man waved a near empty bottle of Vodka at Roberto, "did you make it back to school?"

Roberto didn't answer but took a big bite of rice.

"Ah-ha!" The Russian laughed loud and long. "You need to study hard. Through education, you can rise above this..." he looked around the small bar, "pig pen, if you want to amount to something. Tell me mal'chik, what do you want to be when you grow up?"

Roberto didn't like the man. "What is this word, mal'chik, you keep calling me?"

The Russian took another swig from his bottle. "Mal'chik? It just means boy. Not an insult."

Drunks could turn mean in the space of a breath. Roberto, who had been taught to honor those older than him, answered the question, which seemed harmless enough, but he didn't trust the man. "I want to be an astronaut and go into space like Yuri Gagarin."

The Russian blinked several times. He put down the bottle. "What are your math grades?"

Roberto smiled. "The highest in my school."

The Russian nodded. "High math grades are good, but..."

Roberto blurted out, "The highest of anyone who has ever attended my school."

The Russian smiled. He turned and called out to Señor Cruz, "Bring me some paper and a pencil, por favor."

When Señor Cruz brought the paper and pencil, the Russian took them and began writing furiously. "You don't speak Russian?"

"No, but German, English, Spanish, and Latin."

The Russian looked up from his writing long enough to frown. He gave a quick look around the room. "You learned all these in school?"

Roberto hesitated before admitting, "My mother is half-German, half-Cuban." He said nothing about his American father.

"Good. Good. German is a good language for a rocket scientist to know. Almost as good as Russian." The Russian finished, turned around the paper, and said, "Solve this equation."

Roberto read what the Russian had written. "A spray combustion model?" He picked up the pencil and began to work on solving the equation. When he finished, he handed the paper back.

The Russian read through the work. When he finished, he no longer slurred his words. "My name is Sergei Albertovitch. I am the head of Propulsion Engineering at the Moscow Aviation Institute." There was an intensity in Albertovitch's eyes that scared Roberto. "You are going to be my prize pupil. What class are you in school?"

The night before Castro's men arrested his father, Roberto had promised he would find a way to go to the United States and attend MIT. Not for a minute did he want to go to Russia to study. He had told the lie to impress the Russian. His mother always warned him his pride would be his undoing.

"Come, come, mal'chik, which school do you attend?"

Unable to think of a way to avoid answering the question, Roberto told the truth. "St. Mary's Secondary School."

Albertovitch raised one eyebrow. Apparently, he knew the school's reputation as the best science school in Cuba. "Which class?"

"I'm a senior."

"Good!" Albertovitch clapped his hands. "You graduate in the spring. Excellent. I will arrange for you to come to Moscow. You will learn Russian in the meantime." He turned his vodka bottle upside down. One drop fell to the table. Standing up, Albertovitch shouted, "More vodka!"

What a strange man. Roberto watched as Albertovitch opened the bottle Señor Cruz brought him. "May I ask, why are you in Cuba, Señor Albertovitch? We have no rockets here."

Albertovitch twisted around to stare at Roberto. At first, he seemed angry, and Roberto feared he might have made a big mistake asking such a personal question. The Russian brought a finger to his lips. "Not here. Go home now, mal'chik."

Roberto got up to take his plate back to the kitchen. Albertovitch reached out to take Roberto's arm. "Leave it here. Come back tomorrow. After school. I will be waiting for you. We will have your first lesson."

Today was Friday. "Tomorrow is Saturday. We have no school."

"Excellent." Albertovitch waved him off. His eyelids were only half open. "Come in the afternoon then."

Father Pedro sat in St. Mary's small chapel, his head bowed as he prayed. Roberto stood in the doorway, crossed himself, then entered, taking care not to make a sound as he closed the double doors.

He waited for the priest to raise his head before walking up toward the plain altar. He kneeled again, bowing his head to the simple cross and communion table at the front of the room.

Then he took a seat on the pew beside the priest.

Father Pedro said nothing for several minutes. Roberto folded his hands, closed his eyes and pretended to pray, but no words came to him. He wondered how his father had felt in prison, waiting to learn if he would live or die.

Roberto waited now to see what would happen to him for hitting the son of the head of the Revolutionary Committee.

Unable to stand the suspense any longer he opened his eyes to find Father Pedro watching him.

"You ran because you were afraid."

Roberto nodded.

"I understand. I have talked to Miguel's father. He laughed when he heard you had struck his son. He said Miguel wouldn't tell him what started the fight but whatever it was; a good revolutionary always defends his honor. Was this a fight of honor, Roberto?"

Roberto nodded but said nothing.

"The other boys said Miguel said things about your father."

Roberto took a deep breath but still said nothing.

"It is dangerous for you to defend the honor of your father, Roberto. Do you understand that?"

"Yes, Padre."

"Good. Where did you go today?"

"To the lime cliffs."

"I will pray over your punishment tonight and let you know in the morning how you can make amends for fighting, and running away from school."

"I understand." As a boarding student Roberto had no other adult he trusted for advice, and he needed advice now. "Father, I saw Russians today. Many Russians."

Father Pedro sat back down. He looked not at Roberto but faced the cross on the wall in front of them. "How many?"

"More than I could count. Trucks too."

"What type of trucks?"

"Dozens. They were driving to the limestone cliffs."

Father Pedro smoothed his frock over his knees. "I have heard stories from villagers living on the outskirts of town that for months many men have arrived."

Roberto leaned close. "They found me on top of the limestone cliffs and told me to tell no one and not to come back." He waited and when Father Pedro said nothing continued. "I went to see my friend, Pepeto. He works."

Father Pedro raised his hand in the air. "I know Pepeto. His father, Señor Cruz owns the cantina at the edge of town."

'Yes, that is the one. The cantina was so full of Russians that Señor Cruz told me to stay and help them washing glasses. He gave me dinner as compensation."

Father Pedro laughed. "Then I suppose telling you to go to bed with no dinner is not an effective punishment tonight."

Roberto hung his head down and tried his best to look sorry. "No, Father." He continued with his story. "There is something else. I talked to one of the Russians. I told him I wanted to study rocket engineering in college. He says he is the head of Propulsion Engineering at the Moscow Aviation Institute, but he wore clothes like a farmer, not a professor. He must be lying but he gave me a propulsion equation to solve, and when I got it right, he said he wants to teach me Russian and engineering."

"Well." Father Pedro sat back in his chair. He put the fingertips of both hands together. "That is quite some story."

"Father, why would a missile expert be in Sagua La Grande dressed as a farmer?"

"That," Father Pedro said, "is exactly what I want to know."

"Should I go, Father? To see the Russian?" On the one hand, Roberto wanted to know everything he could about rockets and space travel. On the other hand, the Soviets scared him.

"Did he tell you to come and see him again?"

"Yes, tomorrow after church. At the cantina."

"Good." Father Pedro stood up again. "Go to your room. Get the assignments you missed from the other boys. I expect to get your homework tomorrow morning, even though it is not a school day."

Father Pedro started for the door. He stopped and turned back to face, Roberto. "Do not tell anyone else about your meeting with the Russian. These are dangerous times. You can never trust Castro or the Russians. Remember that."

October 20, 1962

After Mass, Father Pedro found Roberto in the hall. Father Pedro leaned close. "Say nothing, but walk with me."

They walked out of the school.

They reached an old wooden bench positioned to watch the boats in the bay, under a big belly palm tree. The heat of the sun had brought out the aroma of blooming Butterfly Jasmine along the river. Father Padre stopped and sat down. "Roberto, I knew your father very well. He was an intelligent and brave man."

Clouds moved in from the east blocking the sun. The sudden change in temperature caught Roberto by surprise. "You knew my father?"

"Yes. We worked closely together...on a number of...projects."

"I didn't know that." What kind of projects had the two worked on together? Was Father Pedro trying to tell Roberto he too was a spy?

Father Pedro smoothed his cloak over his knees. "Are you afraid to meet with the Russian again?"

A breeze blew in from the water causing a nearby flag to whip back and forth. The metal clasp clanged against the tall pole. "No."

Father Padre turned and gazed at Roberto as if trying to make a decision. "Truly? You are not scared to see the Russian again?"

"Only that I might have to go to Moscow. I promised my father I would go to school at MIT."

Father Padre laughed. On the bay, a Soviet ship sailed by. "Do you see that ship?"

"Yes, it is a Soviet vessel."

"Correct." Father Padre watched the ship sail by for a few minutes. He didn't look at Roberto but continued to look at the Russian ship. "The Soviets say they have agricultural equipment on board their vessels. Do you believe you saw farming equipment when you were on the cliff?"

"It is hard to say. I saw a convoy. The canvas sides were up. Inside were men. There were a couple of flatbed trucks with what looked like tractors. I guess they must be for the farms."

Father Pedro pulled out a cigar and sniffed it. "Why do you think your Russian friend was on the cliff if he were a rocket scientist?"

Roberto had wondered the same thing. "Well, rockets are impacted by the wind. He might be taking measurements or installing equipment to provide meteorological readings."

"Yes. I think that might be true. You know Roberto, Cuba is a small island caught between the Americans and the Soviets. Both see us as weak. But the Soviets are here, and they invade countries and take them over."

The priest lit his cigar. He puffed several times until the leaves caught. Then he took a long drag. After he had blown the smoke out toward the bay, he continued. "I have heard rumors since July that the Soviet ships have been arriving every few weeks. Some of the villagers say that the ships have brought construction equipment and much machinery to Cuba. If that is true, we could find ourselves in the middle of a battle between the U.S. and the Soviets. If the two countries start shooting missiles at each other, they may well destroy each other, but what is true is that they will destroy Cuba."

"What do you need me to do, Father?"

On the bay, the Soviet ship blew its horn as it neared the dock.

"I need you to meet with your Russian rocket scientist and find out just what the Soviets are doing in Sagua La Grande."

He reached into his robe and withdrew a tiny miniature camera no more than two inches long. It looked just a real camera with a lens smaller than a Mexican silver dollar. The little camera even had a brown leather case with a snap on top. "Take this. You have used a camera before?"

"Yes." Roberto didn't tell Father Pedro that after his father's arrest his mother had found the same camera under their mattress. But where did Father Pedro get his?

"Good. This camera works like a real camera. See this button beside the lens? Push this to take the picture." The single click was loud for such a tiny camera.

Father Pedro rolled the dial with two fingers. Then he reached back in his robe again. This time he pulled out a small box no more than an inch by two inches. He looked around.

Roberto followed Father Pedro's lead. There was no one in sight.

"Hold out your hand by your side. Palm up."

Roberto obeyed and Father Pedro, holding his hand upside down dropped the small carton in Roberto's palm. "Film. Five rolls. Do not let anyone know where you got this. Lives are at stake, Roberto. Do you understand?"

"I do."

"If you are caught, you will be charged as a spy. They will torture you to find out who you were working with."

"I'm a boy. I went out of curiosity."

"I don't think so."

Roberto thought for a moment. "I work for the Americans as did my father."

Father Pedro hung his head down as if in prayer. "They will believe you. And they will kill you for it."

"Then," Roberto tried to look brave as he imagined his father had been. "I will not get caught."

Father Pedro looked back at the bay. "Once you have taken the pictures to show what the Russians have brought to Cuba, go to the mangrove just outside of town by the river. There are three trees together."

"I know the place."

At the base of the middle tree, you will find a string attached to a jar hanging between the tree roots. Put the camera in the jar and lower the jar back in between the roots. That way if you are caught, I can still retrieve the camera and the photos. After you return the jar, get to a phone and call me. Let the phone ring three times, then hang up. Afterward, go straight to the airport. Talk to no one. Say nothing to your friends. Your life will depend on it."

Roberto knew better. Everyone at the school knew how close he was to Father Pedro. Both of their lives depended on silence.

And his success.

When Roberto entered the cantina, Albertovitch waved to him. "Come here. I brought you some books. They are in German so you should be able to understand them."

After they had completed an introductory lesson on thermodynamics, Albertovitch called Señor Cruz over and ordered a bottle of vodka. He had several drinks in quick succession. "You know you catch on very quickly. I'm impressed."

Roberto remembered Father Pedro's advice to keep quiet. "Thank you."

Albertovitch continued to drink. The more he drank, the more he talked. "Say, Roberto, have you ever seen a missile?"

"No. Just in books."

Albertovitch threw back his head and emptied his glass. As he poured a refill, he poked Roberto in the arm. "How would you like to work with me on real missiles?"

"Great, I'm a bit worried about Moscow though. It is cold there."

"No, no." Albertovitch laughed, then leaned forward and whispered, "Here. In Sagua La Grande."

For a moment Roberto thought he must have misunderstood. There were no missiles in Sagua La Grande.

Albertovitch laughed louder and slapped his leg. "You don't believe me? Come, come. I'll take you right now."

"Now?" Roberto began to wonder if this man were sane. Perhaps he was just a drunken fool, and his talk about being a propulsion expert was just the bragging of an alcoholic. "You work on missiles at night?"

Albertovitch looked at his watch. "Yes, we should go now. Come mal'chik, let's go see your first real missile."

The storm grew worse as they walked through the forest. Palms leaned so far to one side and then the next Roberto feared they might topple over.

"This cloud cover is good. No planes overhead." Albertovitch covered his eyes to shield them from raindrops as they walked into an opening in the forest where men in checkered shirts and cheap pants secured tarps covering various types of equipment.

Men shouted orders in Spanish and Russian as the storm intensified. Hurricane season lasted another month. Roberto turned his face away to breathe as an unrelenting wind howled through a small grove of mahogany trees.

Underneath the cover of a few palm trees, the Soviets had hidden dozens of tents. Roberto couldn't count how many men the camp held, so he counted groups of tents. There were ten groups, each with over one hundred tents. Over ten thousand Soviets were just outside of Sagua La Grande, and no one knew.

The Soviets wore civilian clothes, so Roberto didn't look that out of place. Still, Albertovitch appeared to grow nervous as they walked through the camp.

"Here, here." Albertovitch pulled Roberto over into a large tent. "Get inside."

Albertovitch relaxed a bit once they entered the shelter, but he still kept looking at the doorway. He leaned close to Roberto. "Do not talk. I think it is better if you just listen."

The tent held several crates, all closed. Soviet workers stood around various types of equipment, none of which Roberto had seen before.

Albertovitch stopped in front of a crate that Roberto estimated to be nearly 72 feet long. This one was open and inside, Roberto saw his first missile up close.

"Are you excited?" Albertovitch reached out to give the weapon an affectionate pat.

Excited wasn't the word for Roberto's feelings. His stomach had tightened into such a knot he found breathing a chore. "Are you sure it is okay for me to be here?"

Albertovitch looked around. "We don't tell anyone, right?"

"Right." Roberto's hand brushed against the camera in his pants pocket. If these men found the camera, he would see his father soon in heaven. It was a small consolation, and although Roberto had never admitted as much to Father Pedro, he wasn't sure he was a believer.

Numerous lamps placed around the tent. "There is so much light. Where do you get your electricity?"

Albertovitch smiled as if he had received a compliment. "We built our own power station!"

Several men came over and began to talk to Albertovitch in Russian. Roberto couldn't understand them, so he just studied the missile.

He had only seen a missile like this in a magazine, but he was sure this was an SS-4. The kind the Soviets liked to use in their military parades.

The SS-4 was a medium-range ballistic missile. Thermonuclear. If he could sneak a photo, he would have the proof nuclear missiles were in Cuba.

Missiles that could be used in a world war.

Roberto reached into his pocket, nudged the camera lens to the hole in his pants and pressed down on the tiny button next to the lens. There was a distinct click.

Behind him, a man said in Spanish, "What is your name? Who are you? What are you doing there?"

Four men were closing in on Roberto.

Albertovitch came to his side. He began arguing with three other men in Russian. After several minutes of what sounded like an angry exchange, the Russian said, "It is okay. I have told them that you are a progeny and are studying at the university with me next year. We should go now. Do not look back at them."

Roberto tried to act normal, but decided scared to death was probably a normal reaction for a Cuban teenager caught in a Soviet secret camp.

He followed Albertovitch outside. The rain came down so hard the drops hurt when they struck bare skin. A large mahogany tree that had toppled over in the storm blocked a flatbed truck carrying barrels of wire.

Albertovitch took hold of Roberto's arm. "Be careful. The men told me that a hurricane is coming. We do not have much time to return to town."

In the forest, Roberto heard creaking. Albertovitch pushed him forward. "Keep going; you are hearing trees falling."

Only a hundred yards more and Roberto would be back on the familiar trail to Sagua La Grande.

Behind him, Roberto heard a voice in Spanish. "Stop. Stop that boy."

Five Cuban soldiers ran up and raised their rifles, blocking Roberto's way to the path and out of the camp.

"What is this boy doing here?"

Roberto stood in the rain. At first, he didn't recognize the man pointing at him and then he did. Miguel's father. The head of Sagua La Grande's Revolutionary Committee.

Albertovitch extended his hand. "I am Sergei Albertovitch. I am in charge of the missile installation. This boy here is a protégé of mine. He..."

Miguel's father pushed Albertovitch aside. "This boy's father was executed by Castro for being an American spy. Are you the idiot who brought him here?"

Roberto took a gamble. "I cannot help what my father did, but I am a loyal Cuban citizen who wants to be a Soviet astronaut. Professor Albertovitch is helping me become a committed Communist."

An argument broke out between the Russians and the Cubans. Roberto stood in the rain, listening to the pounding of the ocean waves, the screaming of the wind and the creaking of the trees as the men's voices grew angrier.

A tremendous explosion drowned out all the noise. At the far end of the camp, the jagged light of a lightning bolt ignited a white fireball of sparks and flame.

Every lamp in the camp went out.

Roberto could hear men shouting at each other, but under the forest canopy, he could not see.

And, he realized, no one could see him.

So he ran.

He ran as fast as he could off the path and into the dense forest. He tripped over stumps. He felt brush scrape his skin.

He put his arms in front of his face, and he kept running until he tripped and fell into the mud.

In the dark, he heard voices shouting his name.

His fingers felt not ground beneath him, but smooth, jagged roots. He had reached the mangrove trees.

He should be able to see the lights of Sequa La Grande, but he could not see a thing.

Electricity must be out in the city as well. On his hands and knees, he climbed over the mangrove's roots until his fingers felt the smooth bark of the tree trunk.

He crawled to his right over more roots, tracing the manacles as they widened until he reached another tree trunk.

He repeated the exercise again, but this time, when the roots became thinner, he found no others. He must be at the third tree.

In the distance, he heard a rifle shot.

He had come too far to back down now. It is okay to be afraid, his father had told him. It was okay to be afraid, but his father had still carried out his mission.

Roberto climbed back over the roots until he reached the middle tree. He plunged his arms into the water around the roots at the foot of the trunk. On his fourth try, his fingers found a string. Pulling on the string, he raised a small glass jar.

Roberto put the tiny camera in the jar. He screwed the lid back on and lowered the jar back into the water. He hoped the rain had not ruined the film or everything he had risked would be in vain.

He had completed his mission. Now, no matter what might happen to him, the world would know that the Russians had nuclear missiles in Cuba.

Roberto crawled on his hands and knees until he found the path leading back to town. A path he had traveled hundreds of times since entering St. Mary's.

Afraid of being followed, Roberto didn't go to the school but instead went toward the cantina. In the town the people had boarded up their windows, but the light from candles shone through the cracks. Roberto found the cantina. He pounded on the door. The wind howled so loud he doubted anyone could hear him, but after a few minutes, Señor Cruz opened the door.

"Roberto? What are you doing out in this storm? Don't you know there is a hurricane going on?"

"I was lost in the woods. May I come in?"

He didn't need to ask for Señor Cruz was already pulling him into the kitchen that connected to the outdoor bar, then guided him into the back room where the family lived.

Roberto thanked him for his hospitality. "May I use your phone."

Señora Cruz opened a mahogany chest decorated with deep carvings. "The phones are not working in town. The storm must have blown down the telephone poles." She took out sheets and a blanket. "Here, you will sleep on our floor tonight. Tomorrow, in the daylight you will be able to see to return to school."

October 21, 1962

Roberto didn't sleep. He listened to the storm until the sound of the rain quieted to a soft patter. Rising quietly, he tiptoed out the door, through the kitchen, and into the dark street. He followed the road toward the airport.

In most parts of the world, the sun rises is such a way that there is a faint light that gets brighter during a period called dawn according to Roberto's geography books.

Not in Cuba. The night is dark, and then in a sudden burst, the sun appears, and there is light. Only on rare occasions, is there a brief period of the dim light called dawn.

God must be looking out for him Roberto decided, or perhaps the hurricane was to blame, but as he walked through town on his way to the airport, dawn broke, allowing him to see the debris on the ground.

Many of the Royal Palm trees that lined the boulevard had fallen. He climbed over them with ease, even with his short legs.

The streets remained empty.

Soon, though, the sun would appear, and everyone would be outside. The soldiers and Revolutionary Committee members would be working to clean up the damage.

Roberto needed to get off the street before someone saw him. In the forest downed trees would make walking hard, but here in the open he could be spotted.

The sun reached its peak as Roberto stood at the edge of the woods, in sight of the small airport on the outskirts of Sagua. The only way to enter the airport was to walk through the gate. After a quick prayer and appeal to his father to give him courage, Roberto left the cover of the forest and walked down the road.

"There he is."

A truck with four Cuban soldiers honked its horn. The men shouted for Roberto to stop or they would shoot. Roberto ran. He ran as fast as he could for the gate. Inside the gate, he recognized Father Pedro waving his hands.

He expected to be shot with every step he took. As he reached the gate, he did hear gunshots, but to his amazement, he was not hit.

Father Pedro ran up to him and pulled him toward the airport entrance. Roberto knew he didn't have much time before the soldiers caught him. "I couldn't call you, Father. The phone lines are all down."

"It is okay, Roberto."

"The package is safe."

Another man wearing a fedora and dressed in a black business suit came up to them. "Is this the boy, Father?"

"Yes. This is the one."

Roberto thought he must be in trouble. Was he about to be arrested?

The man extended his hand. In English, he said, "Roberto MacAllister, on behalf of the United States, I want to thank you for your bravery. Follow me."

Father Pedro ran with Roberto and the American through the airport, down a corridor. They came to an exit door and ran out onto a runway. A Pan America plane sat on the tarmac, its propellers turning.

Roberto stopped running. "Father, what is going on?"

The American pushed Roberto forward. "This is an Operation Peter Pan flight. We are taking you to Miami, Roberto, where you will be safe."

Safe? Did that mean the Americans would protect him from the Russians and Castro?

Inside the plane, Roberto saw children, mostly teenagers, in every seat. The door closed. A young woman in a uniform smiled at Roberto. "Please sit down and buckle your seat belt. We will be taking off immediately."

Taking off? But he hadn't seen his mother. He hadn't said goodbye to her. What would she think when she found out he had left Cuba? Too much had happened too quickly. Roberto tried to breathe but couldn't manage more than short gasps.

Father Pedro put his hand on Roberto's shoulder. "Here, Roberto, sit. Take a few deep breaths. You are safe now. You can relax. He pointed to the aisle seat. On the other side of the aisle sat the American.

Father Pedro sat back in his seat. "When the storm hit, I knew you couldn't call, so I came to the airport and asked the Project Peter Pan to hold a seat for you on this plane to Miami. You are going to the United States where you can study. Like these other kids. I have been working with this project for two years to get students out of Cuba and to the U.S. to study."

The American leaned over across the aisle. "Roberto, Father Pedro tells me you were in a Soviet camp?"

"Yes." Roberto watched Cuba disappear under a cloud. He was still thinking of his mother. She would be relieved to learn he had escaped. She had prayed for so long they might return to her country. But he would miss her. "I saw many Soviet soldiers and Cuban soldiers. And I saw an SS-4 missile."

"You are sure?"

Roberto didn't hesitate. "Yes. I've seen them in magazines."

"Then it is true." The American shook his head. "We've heard rumors from villagers a while, but Washington hasn't believed us."

"I took a picture of the missile." Roberto turned toward Father Pedro. "I put the camera in the jar under the mangrove tree. Just like you said."

The American unbuckled his seat belt. "Excuse me. I need to go to the cabin and get a message to headquarters. I have to tell them to get that jar and then get the goddamn U-2s in the air."

Father Pedro smiled at Roberto. "You did well, Roberto. Do you still want to be an astronaut?"

"I think," Roberto thought for a moment and realized he was very sure of his answer. "I want to be a spy." He looked out the window at the blue sky above him and the clouds below him. "And an astronaut."

Father Pedro laughed. "A spy in the sky. Your father would be very proud."

The Americans and the Soviets could still start launching missiles. The danger wasn't over, but Roberto knew he had done what he could. Just like his father.

MEETING AT THE RISE AND SHINE

KRISTINE KATHRYN RUSCH

In January of 2018, I vowed I would have a story in each upcoming Fiction River *volume, but a life crisis and a move from the Oregon Coast to Las Vegas upended that goal. I won't have a story in all of the volumes, but I will have one in as many as I can.*

I thought I wouldn't be able to finish a story for Spies. *I wanted to write a story under my pen name, Kris Nelscott, but all of my research books were in another state. Then, one morning, I went to a diner in Vegas after dropping Dean off at the airport. The opening line of "Meeting at the Rise and Shine" came to me, and I wrote the story right there.*

The story is set in 1984. I was working as a journalist in 1984, and the news and fears of those days are as familiar to me as the back of my hand. I haven't really tried to write much set in the 1980s. I generally poke around the 1960s with my Kris Nelscott name, most recently in a novel called Protectors, *but I suspect, as comfortable as this story felt, there's more 1980s tales hidden deep inside me. Time to get them out…*

N owheresville Nevada. The diner was funkier than Susan expected. Memorable, which was a bad thing. She didn't want memorable, for anything.

She wasn't memorable. She'd like to say she cultivated her unmemorableness, but she hadn't. Being a middle-aged female in 20th century America meant she was de facto forgettable. A little spread in the hips, a few lines in the face. Hair went from mousy brown to mousy brown with even mousier gray.

She'd never really been pretty, but in her twenties she could pass for it, with the right amount of makeup and a good style. Now, the same makeup made her look even older, like someone's mother. Someone's grumpy mother, at least today.

And she was grumpy. She'd put a finger on the map, picked the town, saw the name of the diner—The Rise and Shine—and figured it would be standard 1950s diner updated for the 1980s. Instead, it was some kind of destination for weirdos.

Pointed alien faces covered the windows and the menu. Someone pasted expensive 45s to the yellow walls, and all around them, graffiti. Deliberate graffiti. The Rise and Shine let people write on the walls, and people, in their own inane way, wrote stupid stuff, like *Bruce Was Here* and *Thanks So Much For The Good Food!*

It didn't help that she was the only one here. The dumpy 50-something waitress was fawning on her, calling her "hon" and asking too many questions.

"You just drivin' through, hon?" "You like a little more coffee while you're waiting, hon?" "Looks like your friend is late, hon."

Looked like her "friend" saw this place out in the high desert scrub on the edge of town, and drove on past. She wouldn't blame him if he had. She almost had, and not just because she had been surprised by how visible and memorable this place was, but also because she was having second thoughts.

Her gigantic purse, which looked appropriate for a woman her age, was stuffed, not with makeup, a book, and a gigantic wallet, but papers. Papers she copied painstakingly, late at night.

The last time the unbelievably good-looking photocopy repair guy showed up at the lab, he had shown her how to reset the internal counter, so that the machine wouldn't keep track of how many copies it made. In fact, he'd shown her a lot of tricks for that gigantic loud machine.

She'd planned the repair guy's appearance too, sabotaging the machine almost weekly, so that someone would show up regularly to fix it. She wanted the thing to have a reputation for screwing up, but not such a bad reputation that they replaced the machine (as was part of the contract).

The unexpected bonus was that the repair guy was gorgeous. Black hair, a little too long, beautiful fingers that should've been touching a woman not the inside of a machine, broad shoulders that suggested an athletic past (or present).

Of course, he didn't give her the time of day—not in the way she wanted. He treated her like the office manager everyone assumed she was, not the scientist hired by a manager who got fired not three weeks later partly because he made "unusual" hires.

The problem with government hires, even new and "unusual" ones (like women and blacks and Asians), was that government hires were almost impossible to fire. And the union, which was running into all kinds of trouble under Reagan, kept educating people on how to keep their jobs, even if they didn't do their jobs.

Susan clutched her purse on her lap, feeling those papers like a weight. She was the definition of disgruntled employee. Only she wasn't just disgruntled with her job. She was disgruntled with herself and being on the near side of forty, with no kids, no husband, and a job where she got no respect at all, no matter how hard she worked.

She was disgruntled with her world. The Bulletin of Atomic Scientists' Doomsday Clock was now set at three minutes to midnight—meaning her colleagues thought Reagan was bringing everyone to the brink of nuclear holocaust.

She had been nervous about it since his election four years ago, and now there was talk that he was going to bomb Nicaragua to stop the Sandinistas. He'd already attacked Grenada, that tiny Caribbean country that no one knew the U.S. had troops in, and he had done it just to prove a point to the Soviets, making the world even more dangerous.

And for the past two weeks, weeks before the election, the chatter at the lab was that Reagan would bomb Nicaragua just to prove how tough he was.

Tough and crazy. There were obvious signs of dementia, and that scared her even more. A country run by a man whose brain was going, whose advisors had an agenda that had nothing to do with real people, and everything to do with their wealthy backers.

She still didn't know what they all would gain by waging war on various countries south of the border, but she suspected it had something to do with the military-industrial complex—the very thing that Eisenhower had warned about when he left office in 1961, back when she was just going into college, back when she thought she would actually get an MRS, and she ended up with a PhD in physics instead

—fighting and clawing for every single advantage, even after being told that men deserved the spot that she had, that she was in their way. Even after her thesis advisor had stolen her work and published it as his own. Even after her complaint to the university had become A Big Deal. (*Listen, hon*, the Dean of Students had told her. *You can fight us, or you can accept that the world is harsh, and this is your first lesson in the harshness.*)

She was getting tired of the harshness, which was why she was here, with all her photocopies. Why she'd had a surprisingly good omelet while she was waiting for the "friend" who would probably never show. Why she had risked her entire career to...what?

Prove to the world that the U.S. was reckless with its nuclear weapons? Show everyone that there had been accidents at nuclear facilities in the past few years, that there had actually been near-meltdowns, that entire facilities were no longer usable? That people had *died?*

To what point? Who would care?

And even if someone cared, what could they do? Complain to the very government who had put them in danger?

Her stomach twisted, and her fingers tightened on her gigantic purse.

And who was she, after all? Just a woman who would be going back to her job, helping build the very weapons she was terrified of.

But, as she had planned to tell her "friend," she was terrified of those weapons because she understood them. Because she knew what would happen to anyone and everyone who got near the weapons.

She knew what was going to happen to her, if World War 3 actually started. The bombs would hit the facility where she worked, just like they would hit all the other facilities that the Soviets knew about.

She was going die in the first wave, which was probably okay, considering nuclear winter. Considering the way that the U.S. (hell, the world) would be unlivable.

Considering...

"Mallory?" The voice was male and too close to her right ear.

Susan jumped, then remembered. She was using her mother's first name, not her own.

She looked up, saw him, and winced. He looked more out of place than she did. Buttoned-up pinstripe suit with vest, red tie, flare pants and expensive shoes, an outfit no one in this part of Nevada wore. Too dressed up, too modern for here. The locals, if they wore suits and ties, looked like refugees from the 1960s Egghead society.

"Pretty conspicuous," he said, looking around, judging her.

Judging the place, just like she had.

She shrugged.

"What have you got for me?" he asked as he slipped into the seat across from her.

Of course, the waitress beelined over to them.

"Hey, hon," she said, clutching the order pad. "This your friend?"

He looked decidedly uncomfortable, his cheeks flushed. Susan would've thought that someone who was the Southwest reporter for a big East Coast paper like the *Times* would've known how to dress. Would've known that he looked East Coast, looked out of place, looked...

"No," Susan said, surprising herself. "We're not friends."

She tucked the purse next to her, felt the thickness of the papers. He wasn't even looking at her. He was looking at the menu as if it were trying to poison him.

So what was she trying to do? The list of facilities, the catastrophes that happened, the plans for some of the new weapons, what would this overdressed guy do with them?

Would publishing make a difference?

She'd been trying to answer that question in her mind for weeks now. She'd been studying what happened five years ago, after *The Progressive* published an article on how to build a hydrogen bomb. All that had done, as far as she could tell, was let their enemies know how easy it was to build a bomb. What would happen when this jerk from *The New York Times* published her leaks? Protests, worries, fears, and still that crazy president would do what he wanted whenever he wanted.

The jerk from the *Times* was ordering toast, for God's sake. And coffee. With such a look of disdain that even she was offended.

The waitress left, shaking her head just a little, and Susan stared at him.

"So," he said again, "what've you got for me?"

"Nothing," she said.

That flush grew in his face. "Nothing? Looks like something in that purse of yours."

She nodded. Then half-smiled at him. Said, "Rumors. That's all I can give you. Rumors that Reagan is thinking of bombing Nicaragua."

"Latin America is not my beat," he snapped. "Nuclear secrets are."

Her breath caught. Was he that much of an idiot?

Clearly, he had no idea what was at risk, or he wouldn't have said that out loud, here, in this conspicuous diner in Nowheresville, Nevada, where they were the only two customers and the waitress was eavesdropping because she was bored.

"Well, then," Susan said. "So sorry I wasted your time."

She grabbed her check, stood, and felt...regret? Relief? She wasn't sure.

She had tried to be a spy, tried to make her country better, but this wouldn't do it. This would just muddy the waters, make everyone worry even more, and what could anyone do?

What could she do?

Then she realized: *she* had a choice. She could decide how to act. She'd already done the tough stuff, photocopying everything, hiding what she had done from the security cameras and the copy machine itself. Getting information she thought regular people needed.

Regular people who could make choices. They could decide whether or not to elect officials who supported this stuff. They could decide to disassemble the military-industrial complex. They could decide to get rid of the weapons that helped her make her living.

If she made a choice to keep this stuff quiet, then she was denying all those regular people their choices.

"You got a car?" she asked.

"How else do you think I got here?" He didn't have to be so damn sarcastic.

She really disliked him. She had a hunch that the feeling was mutual.

"Did you roll the windows down? You're in a desert, after all."

His eyes narrowed. He was assessing her. Then he looked over the diner, with its yellow walls and paintings of aliens and the oldies on the jukebox, with the empty booths and the bored waitress, and the cook, leaning out of the serving window, watching everything.

Even this jerk had to realize how conspicuous he was. No one would remember her, but they would certainly remember him.

He handed her his keys.

She took them, not even asking which car was his, because that was obvious too. He had the only other car in the parking lot, the brand-new silver 1984 Volvo rental that looked as out of place as he did.

She didn't even say thanks. She walked out of the diner into the cool dry morning air, the sun intense against her skin even though it was October.

She walked to his car, reflecting that intense sunlight off its eastern flank, and opened the trunk. His black suitcase was there, with an airline tag on the handle. He had flown in and come directly to her, which explained just how stupid he was.

She left the trunk lid open because it hid her actions from the people inside. Then she opened the driver's door, pulled all of her papers out of her purse, and set them upside down on the seat.

They looked like a dissertation, like the way her dissertation had looked when she had left it on her advisor's desk chair fifteen years ago. She hadn't known then what he would do with it. She hadn't known that he would steal her ideas and her life's work.

This jerk wasn't going to steal anything from her. If he published, he would be condoning her theft.

A wave of dizziness hit her. She clutched the car door, catching herself. She almost snatched up the papers, terrified someone would be able to trace these papers to her. But she had no idea how.

She was on vacation, after all, and there was no way to track her. Besides, she would be in Las Vegas in a few hours, and partying conspicuously. There, she would try to be memorable—even though she doubted she would succeed.

But she'd save her receipts. She'd make sure that if anyone asked, she would tell them she had had a lot of drunken fun and lost a lot of money and contemplated marrying a guy (whom she would describe, using the photocopier repair guy as her base) but changed her mind at the last minute, deciding it was too much of a cliché.

And no one would think twice about what she told them, because no one thought twice about her. Mousy brown hair, invisible, the kind of woman whom no one saw as a threat.

She closed the driver's door, then walked back, and had a passive-aggressive moment, thinking about locking the jerk's keys in the trunk. But that would make him even more memorable, even though he really didn't need help in that area.

She kept the keys in her right hand. Then using her left, she slammed the trunk.

She walked back inside, handed him the keys, said, "Enjoy your breakfast."

He caught her wrist. "You're not going to give me context?"

The waitress stood at attention. The cook leaned forward, suddenly looking tough.

Susan realized they were thinking the jerk was an old lover, boyfriend, husband, someone who wanted to hurt her. Maybe even the lawyer for an ex. And she'd let them think that.

She looked down at her wrist, at his manicured fingers (who knew men did that?), and then glared at him.

"You don't need context," she said.

"I think I do," he said, making himself even more conspicuous.

"Then you're dumber than I thought." She tugged her arm slightly.

He still didn't let go.

"If you don't let me go," she said quietly, "I'll scream. And they will help."

She nodded at the waitress and the cook, who were watching intently.

The jerk released her wrist as if it were on fire. "I may not use any of what you gave me, then, without context," he said.

"Your decision, not mine," she said, glad she had given him the wrong name. Glad she had come to Nowheresville, Nevada, glad she had used pay phones in other towns to make the long-distance calls to the *Times*, glad he knew next to nothing about her.

She rubbed her wrist. It was actually sore. She would have bruises.

But, in that sore hand, she still clutched her bill. Passive-aggressive. What the hell. She slapped the bill on the table, so loud that they had to have heard it in the back.

"You're buying," she said loudly. "Have fun."

Then she turned her back on him and headed for the door.

A piece of good graffiti, scrawled with a black Magic Marker, caught her eye.

Wake Up.

Drink Coffee.

Punch The Day In The Face.

Maybe she liked this place after all. Maybe she liked the sentiment.

She would decide later. After she read tomorrow's newspaper.

After she saw if the world had changed.

HIGHPOINT

MICHAEL KINGSWOOD

Modern spy stories are all about tech and, to be honest, I worried that I wouldn't get one. I worried needlessly. Michael Kingswood gave me the very type of story I had envisioned when I put out the call for this anthology.

Michael Kingswood is a twenty-year veteran of the U.S. Navy submarine force. He primarily writes science fiction and fantasy, and is best known for The Pericles Conspiracy, *a first contact novel, and the* Glimmer Vale Chronicles, *a sword and sorcery fantasy series. He is currently working on a Space Navy series, the first of which is scheduled to be released in mid to late 2018. He can be reached at michaelkingswood.com. He also has a weekly podcast and YouTube channel, "Story Time with Michael Kingswood," where he shares excerpts from his work.*

About this story, Michael writes: "I have no knowledge or experience in spy craft, and only very small exposure to the intelligence community. But during my Navy career I saw overhead imagery on a number of occasions during briefings. When Kris sent out her vision for this anthology, I had a hard time coming up with an idea that interested me, or that I thought I could pull off well, involving a traditional spy. But then I thought back to some of those briefings I'd received and the imagery in them, and I wondered what it might be like to be one of the people whose job it is to analyze those images. Then I wondered if there was any way an analyst like that might have to take a more active role in events? The story just flowed from there."

J eremy Levin frowned at the image on his screen. What was that?

He leaned forward, squinting, and rolled the scroll wheel on his mouse to try to increase the magnification. It didn't budge.

A quick glance at the lower right corner of the display window made his frown deepen. It was already zoomed in as far as it could go. Jeremy leaned back into the cheap faux-leather of his semi-movable office chair and crossed his left arm over his chest, then began tapping at his lips with his right index finger as he thought things through.

The image on his workstation's display was black and white and extremely high resolution, but zoomed in as it was, it had begun to pixelate. Still it was easy to pick out the medium-range ballistic missile transporter erector launches (TELs) behind the heavy lift trucks that towed them. The guard towers surrounding the encampment, the barracks, and the communications antennas were also easy to discern. But what in the hell was that, halfway behind the barracks building? It could have been a vehicle of some sort, or maybe a stack of crates, but it was arranged in almost exactly the right angle to put it out of the field of view of the reconnaissance satellite that had taken the image.

It was damn annoying.

"What's wrong, Jeremy? Our pals over there doing something bad?"

The cheerful, alto voice drew Jeremy's gaze away from his screen, and his frown faded away immediately. Sarah always had that affect on people. She was average height and a bit dumpy, but not actually fat. She wore her black hair up in a bun, and had on a light green blouse over khaki pants that were perhaps just slightly too tight about the thigh. A faint fruity fragrance surrounded her, and, of course, like always, she was smiling ear to ear and her dark, slightly angular eyes were twinkling merrily.

It was really hard to be grumpy facing that smile.

Jeremy shrugged, the cloth of his short-sleeved white-collared shirt rustling slightly against his chair. "Not really." He waved his hand toward the almost indiscernible object. "I just can't figure what that thing is."

She stepped into his little cubicle area and leaned in close to his screen. Her smile faded slightly; a scowl on anyone else. Then after a moment, she shook her head and straightened. "Me neither." Looking back at Jeremy, she brought her smile back to full brilliance. "Can't be that big a deal though, right?"

Jeremy shrugged again. "Dunno. Probably not. Still..." He let the thought go unsaid, and she nodded with understanding.

"I hate not being able to answer Truman's questions too." Their

Department Head was not nearly as classy as his Presidential name-sake had been. When his people didn't have the information he needed, it could sometimes get ugly. She looked at the digital clock that was mounted up on the wall past the next row of cubicles over from Jeremy's. "When do the images from the next pass come in?"

He switched tabs on his workstation, calling up the satellite ephemeris data, and did a quick conversion in his head. "Four hours from now." His eyebrows rose when he looked at the footnotes to the ephemeris tables. "And it's a Mark 3."

Sarah clapped him on the shoulder. "Well. You'll know soon enough then."

He sure would. The Mark 3 was the newest bird, with twice the resolution as the Mark 2, in both visual and infrared. It also followed a steeper orbital track than the Mark 2, so its angle of view ought to line up quite a bit more nicely to identify that strange piece of equipment.

Jeremy's growing smile slowed as he considered that the Koreans knew their overhead times as well as he did, maybe better. There was a good chance that if whatever-it-was was important they would move it, to keep it out of view. If they could. And if they remembered to.

Communists were not exactly known for their exactness and competence, after all.

"Here's hoping," he said, and Sarah chuckled.

She turned and left Jeremy's cubicle, and he tabbed over to the next image he had to review.

The hours passed quickly, as they tended to when Jeremy became engrossed in his work. Sifting through dozens of images, noting features of interest for deeper analysis later, and then going back to do that analysis is not for everyone, but Jeremy had quickly found an aptitude for it when he joined the Agency. And, amazingly enough to his initial superiors, he found he liked it.

Occasionally, part of him felt guilty for being a professional, and legal, Peeping Tom of sorts. But only occasionally, and really that was a silly comparison to make—but thanks Mom for making it. After all, he had seen a few highly redacted after action reports from oper‐ atives in the field who had used the information he gleaned out of these images to do important things, and save the lives of his countrymen.

It made him feel good, knowing he played a hand, however small, in that.

He didn't notice lunch time had arrived until Sarah gave him a nudge. He stood, taking a minute to stretch, and reflected that his trousers were getting a bit tight as well. Maybe he ought to think about joining a gym or something.

When he returned to his cubicle, an electronic beeping greeted him. His timer.

Jeremy glanced up at the clock and a shiver of anticipation went through him. The Mark 3 images of the Korean site should be ready for review.

He sat and pulled his chair in snug to his desk, slipped his access card into the card reader built into his keyboard, typed in his person‐ alized pin code...

And found nothing. Just the files for the images he had already reviewed and set aside for later review. But the imagery application was devoid of anything new.

Frowning, Jeremy pulled up the ephemeris table again. Sure enough, the Mark 3 had overflown the site on schedule, so the images should be there. Maybe the data processing and distribution system was backed up. Or maybe weather had moved in, obscuring the site from overhead eyes. But there should have been a flag in the system for the former, or an email or other notice for the latter, and there was nothing.

"What the hell?"

Jeremy pulled out his access card, locking his terminal, then pushed back his chair and stood. He took a moment to look overtop the grey fabric cubicle partitions surrounding his workstation and the rest of the analysts' bullpen, as they called it. Three rows of six identical cubicles, all manned by people like him: men and women who were for the most part introverted and detail-focused, not particularly athletic, and, he admitted, not the snappiest of dressers. All of his colleagues had their heads down, leaning into their terminals, all of which were covered by special screen protectors that would obscure the displayed image from any angle except from almost directly in front of the monitor. Only the break area at the end of the room, next to Truman's office and the main entrance, broke the monotony, and then not by much. It consisted of an old white fridge next to a nondescript linoleum table upon which sat a coffee maker and a small chest of drawers that held grounds, filters, and some assorted snacks, and finally the lockbox where everyone would put their contributions to cover the cost of the things they took. And, of course, there were the pair of large flat-screens mounted in the back corners of the bullpen, one tuned to Fox News and the other to CNN.

Couldn't have a command and control space or an intelligence analysis center without the news on.

That would be sacrilege. Or something.

No one else seemed to be voicing any chagrin over the imagery. That made his frown deepen. Of course, there was a good chance no one else needed to access the Mark 3 imagery; the Korean ICBM site was his baby, and his alone. But still...

He walked two cubicles down to Sarah's workstation, and found her happily poring over imagery of the latest Russian destroyer.

"Hey Sarah, you having any issues with the Mark 3 imagery?"

She turned in her chair, a much nicer unit than he had; she had sprung for the cost of it herself after Truman assented in light of her back issues. Sarah shook her head. "No, but I haven't tried to access it. Why?"

Jeremy shrugged. "I've got no data from it at all. It's weird."

She raised an eyebrow at him, and he flushed.

"Never mind. It's probably just overcast conditions." He sighed and looked down the line of cubicles toward the closed and cypher-locked door out and, catty-corner to it, the door to his boss' office. "Truman would know, I guess."

Sarah winced, but managed a light-hearted chuckle. "Have fun with that."

"Thanks."

Truman always kept the door closed when he was in, and there was no window looking into his office. He had made it abundantly clear that there would be hell to pay if anyone had the gall to burst in without knocking, which led the grunts in the bullpen to joke that he spent the day jerking off to old images of Stalin. He was that kind of "leader." It was a funny joke, but Jeremy never gave it any credence. Truman simply got too much done for him to be wasting time back there. It never seemed to matter how many memos, analysis reports, or raw images the bullpen forwarded to him, or how many taskers came down to him from on high; he always—always— had the admin forwarded before its due date, and Jeremy had never seen an error in his work.

Or at least, no errors that he couldn't blame on a subordinate.

So much as he disliked the man, Jeremy had to admit a grudging respect for Truman. Which didn't mean he wanted to see him any more than absolutely necessary, which was to say at the morning bullpen briefings and when Jeremy had to present a report that was on its way up to Higher.

So it was with a fair amount of trepidation that he rapped the requisite three knocks on Truman's door, then opened it and walked in at the curt, "Come!" from his boss.

Truman was about sixty, with salt-and-pepper hair that seemed too thick to be true. He always wore a suit and tie, alternating between the same five each week, on the same days of each week. Today, Tuesday, he had on the pinstriped charcoal grey with white shirt and American flag tie.

Never a surprise from Truman, at least not in that sense.

Jeremy's boss was seated behind a standard-issue government desk that might have been pine or maple unless you looked too closely. The wall behind the desk was covered with pictures and plaques that Truman had accumulated over the span of twenty-five years in Naval Intelligence followed by another fifteen at the Agency, surmounted by his pride and joy: a picture of him shaking hands with Margaret Thatcher, a big shit-eating grin on his face.

The rest of the office was normal intelligence-drone decor: a four-drawer high security GSA safe in the corner, a bookshelf on the right-hand wall with all manner of binders and manuals crowding the shelves, a laminated, small-scale map of the world against the wall opposite the shelf, with various places of interest marked up in dry-erase marker, and a pair of simple wooden chairs in front of the desk.

The place was chilly, at least five degrees lower than the bullpen, and had an antiseptic smell to it, as though Truman had been spraying an odorless air freshener at regular intervals. But he didn't smoke, and Jeremy wouldn't bet whether he had ever touched a drink, so he couldn't imagine what Truman would be trying to cover up with that.

Truman looked up from the paperwork he was working on as Jeremy approached his desk. His brow furrowed and he regarding Jeremy for a moment before grunting and nodding toward the chair on his left. "What can I do for you, Mr. Levin?" His voice was deep and gravelly, his intonation completely neutral as though he didn't really care what Jeremy needed or wanted.

Jeremy cleared his throat, not moving toward the chair. "Have you received word of an outage in the Charlie-orbit Mark 3 bird? It was supposed to make a pass over my Korea site, but no images have come through and there's nothing on any of my feeds as to why."

Truman's expression hardened. For a second, Jeremy thought he was going to kick him out of the office. Instead, he set the paperwork down and rotated his chair to the left, toward his desktop terminal. He tapped the screen to life and entered his login information, then after a few seconds, scowled.

"Well it's right here," he said, and spun the monitor so Jeremy could see what he was looking at. The imagery cache application was open, and, sure enough, there was a note attached to his pass. A casualty in the Yokosuka communication relay station, estimated time of repair thirty minutes from now.

Jeremy's mouth fell open. "Wha—?"

He didn't get to finish. "What the hell are you wasting my time for, Levin? You get kicked in the head this morning or something?"

"That wasn't there—"

"Shut the hell up and get out of my office." Truman shook his head in disgust and glared daggers at him until Jeremy had gone.

He walked back to his cubicle in a confused daze. That material condition flag had not been there before, he was certain of it, and it had been long enough since the time stamp on the flag that it should have been posted an hour ago.

So what the hell?

"Ouch," Sarah said as he drew near the cubicle. She had been leaning out of hers to watch his approach. "Looks like that didn't go so well. Everything ok?"

Jeremy shook his head. "Casualty in Yokosuka."

"It wasn't flagged."

"It was. I guess I missed it."

She shook her head and made a low whistle. "Yeah, that had to hurt. Sorry." It looked like she really meant it, too. She wasn't just screwing with him. Sarah flashed him a smile that Jeremy supposed was meant to be comforting then slipped back into her cubicle.

Back at his workstation, Jeremy called up the imagery application, and sure enough the material casualty flag was up, clear as day. The time stamp was the same as it had been in Truman's office. So why the hell hadn't he seen it before?

This was too weird. He opened up the help function on the application and started looking through the troubleshooting procedures, trying to find a FAQ or common problems page. But it wasn't like the application was from Microsoft or some other big-name software house. This was a specialized application, made specifically for the Agency by a firm Jeremy had never heard of. Consequently, the troubleshooting documentation sucked.

He closed the help file and stared at the screen for several moments before he realized he was tapping his lips again.

It occurred to him there was one thing he could try. But he had only seen it done once, and it was risky; doing it without authorization technically constituted a security violation, and could result in him being reprimanded, if not worse. And he was fairly sure he was going to make GS-12 in two months. A reprimand could screw that all up.

Screw it. He went back to his queue of waiting images and began to sift again.

Ten minutes later, he was just on his second image. His mind wasn't on it, but on the issue of the casualty flag. He couldn't get the nagging mystery out of his head. What the hell had happened there?

Screw it.

Moving quickly so he couldn't second guess himself, he opened a command-line interface window, and switched to the network root directory.

There he paused for a few seconds. The rational part of his mind told him to drop it, back the hell off. This was going to get him into trouble.

Instead, he typed the coded command the cyber security guys had shown him, back almost two years ago during an extremely short-lived cross-functional training session. The high-ups had thought that training the various departments in some of each others' skills would make everyone in the Agency more well-rounded, and better able to tackle an emergent series of taskings.

Not a bad idea, but it hadn't lasted long. Too much to do, too little bang for the buck. The program was quickly scrapped.

But Jeremy still remembered the routine to pull up the network-wide keystroke log interface system, so he supposed it wasn't a complete waste of time.

A half hour passed like two minutes, and Jeremy had it.

He was right. The flag had been inserted late, only a couple minutes before he went to Truman's office. And, weirdly, it didn't look as though it originated from Yokosuka.

Jeremy felt like he had been frowning all day, and his grimace just grew deeper. If Yokosuka hadn't put in the flag, who had?

He entered a couple more commands, and felt like his heart had stopped in his chest.

"Holy shit," he said.

The flag had originated from within the Headquarters building. That wasn't normal at all, and it sent a shiver down his spine.

Three commands later, he had the workstation location that had issued the flag. Terminal—

"Holy shit!" The man's voice—Yohan's Jeremy thought—was filled with shock, fear even. It carried through the room without effort and roused Jeremy from the near-trance he had been in while running this down.

He gave a jerk and straightened in his chair. What was—?

"Oh my God!" A woman now, Stacey. "They hit Guam!"

What???

Jeremy shoved his chair back and leapt to his feet, spinning so he could see the closest TV monitor.

The anchorman looked taken aback. He was speaking, but the volume was down and Jeremy couldn't hear it. But BREAKING NEWS was in bold beneath him, and the scrolling ticker said something about explosions on the island.

The other analysts were standing up, one and all looking at the news monitors in various degrees of disbelief. A general murmur of confusion and growing unease spread through the room as people started talking with the colleagues next to them. It felt as though everyone was about to lose it.

"All right, cool down, people!" Truman's authoritative voice cut through the noise of voices, and all eyes turned to him. He had moved out of his office and now stood beneath the CNN TV. His face was more grave that Jeremy had ever seen, and that was saying something. He held a printout in his left hand, which he raised in front of him. "We just received a HIGHPOINT SOLAR FLARE message."

The bottom went out of Jeremy's stomach. "Oh shit," he murmured. SOLAR FLARE meant—

"There have been nuclear detonations on Guam, at Andersen Air Force Base and the Naval Base, at Kadena Air Base on Okinawa, and in Misawa and Yokosuka." His eyebrows rose. "Artillery has begun to fall in the outskirts of Seoul and all along the DMZ. It looks like this was a decapitation strike to remove our ability to respond while the North Koreans push south."

"Nukes?" True fear was Yohan's voice as he repeated Truman's words.

Truman nodded. "No indication of how they were delivered," his eyes came to rest on Jeremy, "but there are only a few possibilities."

Jeremy nodded understanding, and immediately dropped back into his seat. Turning back to his monitor, he began to mouse over to the imagery application. He needed to see if he'd missed anything about the ICBMs, some indication they were readying to launch. Something—

Before he had moved the mouse more than a whisker, he saw the terminal code on the keystroke log. He recognized it. He had helped the tech guys troubleshoot it just last week.

It took him a second to get back to his feet; his knees had gone like rubber. But he managed, and he looked over at the cubicle in question.

It was empty.

He cast around wildly. Truman was still talking, and Jeremy's colleagues were gathering in a loose semicircle around him. All except—

Jeremy turned toward the main entrance door in time to see it click shut.

Crap.

He probably should have just called security. In fact, the back of his mind screamed at him to do that. But he couldn't be sure, and with everything going on right now pulling security off on a wild goose chase would be idiocy.

He hurried across to the door and pushed it open, then stepped into the corridor beyond.

It was your typical government office building corridor. Painted walls that were just a bit too yellow to be white, black flashing along the wall-floor interface. White tiles with black speckles that were supposed to look like marble but fooled no one. Recessed fluorescent lighting in the ceiling. Pictures of Agency things every few feet along the walls. No windows.

A single figure hurrying away from the bullpen in the direction of the stairwell down to the first level.

Jeremy hurried to catch up. "Sarah!"

She stiffened at the sound of her name, and that should have confirmed it in Jeremy's mind. But when she turned to face him, her usual smile was on her face, though much reduced from the tension that shone clearly through her eyes. "Hey."

"You ok?" He stopped in front of her, and she nodded.

"Just heading to the—"

He didn't see the knife until she had buried it hilt-deep into his belly.

An involuntary exhalation that sounded halfway between gasp and moan left his lips, and he was shocked to feel no pain. He had always thought getting stabbed would hurt. But this was just—

And then it hit him, and he all but doubled over in agony.

"Sorry," Sarah said. Then she said something else in a language Jeremy didn't recognize, pulled the knife out, and turned to hurry toward the stairs.

Jeremy slumped back against the nearby wall, and found himself sliding down to the floor. It was like his legs had no strength.

Wetness was spreading across his belly, and down his waist into his legs, and he was beginning to feel uncomfortably cold.

And the pain...

Another groan came out of his mouth as he watched her hurry away. He reached out, futilely, to try to grab a body already thirty feet away, and couldn't figure out why he didn't get ahold of her.

Then his eyes alighted on something in the wall halfway between himself and the stairwell doors. It took a few seconds for Jeremy to put together what it was in his head.

The security call box.

Every corridor had one, and it could be either intercom, loud-speaker, or panic button. He just had to get to it.

Pushing himself back up to his feet was the hardest thing he had ever done. It hurt like a son of a bitch, and he lost his strength halfway up twice. But eventually he made it. Mostly. He had to lean against the wall for support, but at least he was up.

Sarah was long gone, but that didn't matter. Get to the call box.

He stumbled forward a step. Then a second.

Then a third.

He lost count a few steps later. The call box was all, and it seemed to swell to fill his vision. So close...

He thought he heard a scream behind him, but everything was fading out except for that call box. It was his entire world; the only thing that mattered. That, and the horrid pain in his belly.

Jeremy stumbled into the wall again. His legs were going again, and there was no way he could get back up.

And, frankly, most of him didn't want to. He longed for the blackness that was encroaching on the edges of his vision, for the oblivion it promised, and the end to the pain.

But he had to hit the call box.

One last surge of strength, and he flung himself at it.

Before the entire world went black, he felt something solid beneath his fingertips and then, far away, he thought he heard the wailing of an alarm.

———

Jeremy awoke to painfully bright light, but he found he didn't mind. It sure beat not waking up at all.

He was in a hospital room, that much was obvious from the medical instruments surrounding him and the utilitarian furnishings and decor. That was to be expected, he supposed.

What wasn't expected was the sight of Truman, sitting on the visitor's chair next to his bed and looking like he hadn't slept in days.

"Welcome back," Truman said, and his voice was as strong as ever. If it wasn't for the fact that he hadn't shaved and he had bags under his eyes, this could be just any other morning, from the sound of it.

"How long was I out?"

"Three days," Truman said, and Jeremy blinked in surprise. Truman had on the same charcoal suit and American flag tie he had been wearing the last time Jeremy saw him. Had he been at Jeremy's side that entire time?

No, that would be inconceivable.

"You gave us a bit of a scare, but the docs say you'll pull through fine."

That was good. But—

Jeremy tried to sit up, but found himself restrained, both by the massive bandages across his abdomen and by straps around his forearms. "What the hell is this?"

Truman raised a hand, and Jeremy stopped talking. "Docs didn't want you pulling out the staples while you were out. I'll get the nurse in here."

"Ok. But...Sarah?"

Truman's face hardened. "Didn't make it out of the building. Guards found her in the ladies' room on the first floor with her wrists cut, and a gash to the femoral artery in her left thigh." He shook his head. "She didn't want to take any chances of being saved."

Jeremy's jaw dropped open and he knew he was gaping, but he couldn't help it. He shook his head. "Why?"

"You know she's half-Korean, right?"

Jeremy nodded.

"Turns out that's half NORTH Korean. How the hell the background checkers missed that..." Truman shook his head. "Gonna be hell to pay."

"She did something to the imagery feed, put in a fake—"

"We know, we know." Truman tried to make a smile that Jeremy presumed was supposed to be calming, comforting. He failed miserably. "She boned us hard. Inserted a worm to take down the theater-wide ICBM launch monitoring birds, another one to disable the imagery download subsystems, and then manually inserted the maintenance flag when she realized one had not been generated by the automatic system."

Jeremy whistled softly. He had figured that was the case, but still...to hear it...

"We got the Mark 3 back online and did a pass over your site yesterday. The missiles are gone, launched. And that shape you couldn't figure out? Well, it—"

"How did you know about that?"

Truman just looked at him, and after a second, Jeremy deflated a bit. He had marked the images specifically to draw attention to that object, whatever it was. He waved for Truman to continue, and he did.

"Turns out that was a storage container. Carried the nukes, looks like." He leaned forward. "It's one of ours."

"What??"

Truman nodded. "Like I said, they boned us hard. Operatives and moles all over the place, causing havoc. And in the meantime, the ROKs have been pushed back almost to Inchon again, and the Chi-Coms took advantage of the situation to launch an attack on Taiwan."

"Son of a bitch."

"Yep. We've got a lot of work ahead of us." Truman stood, and his knees popped loudly.

Jeremy studiously avoided commenting, or doing anything that would indicate he had noticed.

"But for now," Truman said, not missing a beat, "you focus on getting better." He extended his hand and shook Jeremy's, then added, "Good work, Jeremy."

Jeremy wasn't certain, but he thought that was the first time Truman had ever called him by his first name.

It wasn't much, but it buoyed his spirits. And he felt sure he was going to need that encouragement, to face the troubles ahead.

THROUGH THE EYES OF A DOG

ANGELA PENROSE

Not every spy works for a spy agency or a governmental organization. Some spies work for corporations, trying to get dirt on their competitors. I have a fondness for corporate spy stories. And in this day and age, corporate spy stories are also all about tech.

I had hoped for a great corporate spy story, and Angela Penrose provided it. Angie worked for a Silicon Valley tech company for almost a decade, and spent another decade working in the computer game industry. She's known a lot of techies, with their competitions and feuds and rivalries.

In addition, she's a Fiction River *favorite. Her work has appeared in seven volumes of* Fiction River *so far, including* Hidden in Crime, Recycled Pulp, *and* No Humans Allowed, *with more stories to come.*

She's also a dog person. As she writes, says this is "one of the few times when the writer being a dog person actually is *relevant to the story."*

The first thing Shawn noticed pulling up to the gate was the sound of barking. It was hot enough that he had his Honda all buttoned up and the AC blasting, but he could still hear the dogs even before he stopped in front of the wrought iron gate.

At least five or six dogs, all mixed breeds in a wide variety of sizes, were bouncing around on the inside of the gate, barking and poking their heads through the bars.

Then Shawn saw another dog, some kind of Retriever mix, tied to the outside of the gate by a rope attached to his collar. The Retriever was thin and ratty, and he was tugging against the rope like he wanted to get away from all the other dogs.

At least that explained what had the inside gang all fired up.

Bushes grew thick and green through the bars of the fence to either side of the gate. He could just see the occasional ornamental spearpoint capper poking out through the top of the hedge. It extended to the right and left of the gate, into the distance. Shawn peered through the bars, wondering whether the barking dogs would attract any attention from inside, but the tree-lined driveway curved a few dozen yards in; the landscaping blocked any view of the estate.

That made sense. Al and Dina Corcoran were known to be protective of their privacy. They couldn't go anywhere in public without being mobbed by paparazzi or fans or techies with great "investment" opportunities, so when they were at home, they wanted the rest of the world completely shut out.

Shawn stopped right next to the security panel, sleek and shiny, standing on its post just to the left. He rolled down the window, grimaced at the blast of heat, and pressed the big, white button.

A moment later, a fuzzy male voice said, "Can I help you?"

"Shawn McCay, I have an appointment."

"One moment, please."

Shawn waited a few seconds, then said, "And, uh, there's a dog out here. On the outside, I mean. Tied to your gate."

There were several seconds of silence. Shawn amused himself imagining various things the security guy might be muttering to himself with the intercom off. Finally the fuzzy voice said, "Hang on, I'll be out in a minute."

"No prob," said Shawn. He rolled up the window and basked in the cool breeze from the AC for a few moments, then shut off his engine. Might as well get started, right?

He got out of the car and the dogs inside the gate exploded with renewed excitement—barking, yapping, yelping, baying... One of the dogs, a Shepherd mix, was growling, hackles up and everything, but the others were bouncing around like they wanted to play.

The dog tied to the gate whined and twisted, pawing at its collar.

"Hey, buddy," said Shawn. He kept his voice high pitched and quiet, approaching the dog slowly. "It's okay, no one's gonna hurt you, buddy. Come on, calm, calm..."

He got down on his knees, glad he'd worn jeans and a polo instead of the slacks and dress shirt he'd considered.

"Come on, that's it, it's okay." He ducked his head and held a fist out to the ratty looking Retriever. Up close he could see that the dog needed a bath. Specifically a flea bath; most of his fur was light enough that he could see the fleas moving around.

"Bet you're real uncomfortable, huh? We can take care of that, get you some dinner?"

At the word "dinner," the dog perked up, cocking his head at Shawn.

"Oh, you know that word, huh?" Shawn smiled and moved his fist closer to the dog's head. The dog sniffed it, keeping a wary eye on Shawn, sniffed again, then gave him a lick.

"Good boy! Yeah, we're gonna be friends, aren't we?"

The voice from the intercom, unfuzzed, said, "You got him?"

Shawn looked up and saw a guy in his forties approaching the gate, dark blue slacks and short-sleeved button-down. His hair was cut short, but not buzzed, and he was in ridiculously good shape. Pretty clearly security, although not armed, or at least Shawn couldn't see a weapon on him.

"Maybe," he said. "Let me try." He turned his attention back to the dog and said, "Okay, we're buddies, right? How about if we get you untied, then we can go inside..." He looked up at the guard and said, "We're taking the dog in, right?"

"Yep," said the guard. "We have a whole collection." He waded through the bouncing crowd of dogs inside the gate, getting happy barks and licks as he went. "You can pass me his rope if you want, I'll take him up while you drive in."

Shawn carefully petted the dog, starting with a chest scratch, then moving up one shoulder, across the back of his neck, then went for the ear scritchies. The Retriever relaxed and whined at him, his eyes half closed.

"Yeah, I bet you're itchy. We can fix that, don't you worry." He looked up at the guard and said, "I can take him, if you'll take my car to wherever it's supposed to go? The key's in the ignition."

The guard cocked his head at Shawn, looking a lot like the Retriever had a minute earlier. Shawn suppressed a grin. He added, "I'd just put him in the car, but I don't know if he gets carsick. And I don't have a crate with me—if he doesn't have good car manners, he could jump down under my feet. I just paid this thing off, don't want to wreck it yet."

The guard smirked and nodded. "Sure, makes sense. Just follow the driveway. Mr. and Mrs. Corcoran are waiting for you. I'll let them know you're bringing a dog." He tapped the radio hanging from his belt.

"They might not want this guy in the house till he's had a flea bath," Shawn said.

"Roger." The guard unlocked and opened a pedestrian gate a crack, blocking the barking pack with one leg while Shawn untied the dog's rope from the larger gate.

"Come on, buddy, let's go inside. How are your leash manners? Kinda non-existent, huh?" He held out a hand in front of the dog, trying to lure him to follow, patted his thigh, but nothing worked. The Retriever was stressing out again, tugging and twisting, trying to escape the rope leash.

"All right, it's okay, come on..." Shawn reeled the dog in, then picked him up. He probably weighed about forty pounds—likely a good fifteen or so less than he should, but some groceries would fix that. After a startled yelp and squirm, the dog settled down in Shawn's arms, giving his neck a lick.

"There you go, good boy. Let's go make some friends, how about it?" Shawn took a breath and strode up to the gate, carrying the skinny Retriever in through the seething horde of bouncing dogs.

The Retriever got tense and whined some, but otherwise behaved while being carried. Shawn trudged up the drive to the house, which turned out to be a good quarter mile from the gate. Carrying the dog would've slowed him down on its own, but avoiding the dogs bouncing around his feet made him step carefully, so he had plenty of time to look around while walking up the drive.

Past the curve near the gate, which Shawn decided was only there for privacy, the trees lining the drive thinned out, giving him a view of the property. A three-story house faced in rough, tan granite—what a real estate agent would probably describe as "rustic"—sat in the center of a decidedly un-manicured lawn, more of a meadow. Some magazine articles had sneered at the house, calling it a McMansion, but it didn't look shiny or plastic or ostentatious to Shawn. It was big, yes, but the stone was mellow and the big house looked like it fit in with the landscape, the granite barely darker than the summer-yellowed grasses of the hill that rose behind it.

A lower fence, green-painted wood, encircled a good chunk of the rough lawn to one side, plus a couple of single story, wooden buildings. More dogs ran around the smaller enclosure—at least a dozen, Shawn guessed.

The guard drove by in Shawn's car, at a slow crawl to give the dogs plenty of time to get out of the way. Shawn watched him park next to two other cars to one side of the house, in front of a patch of bushes.

Shawn was sweating pretty heavily by the time he made it to the house. The Corcorans were waiting for him, their faces familiar from dozens of magazine covers.

"Mr. McCay," Al Corcoran called with a smile. "Didn't mean for you to start working quite so soon."

"No one told the dog," said Shawn, grinning back and trying hard not to sound winded. "Or whoever tied him to your gate."

"That happens a lot," said Dina Corcoran, with a sigh. "People know we love dogs, so they figure we'll take care of their strays. Someone left a pit bull—a real sweetheart, wonderfully behaved—last Wednesday, and a box of puppies two weeks ago."

Shawn paused for breath, then asked, "Where do you want me to take him? He needs a flea bath before he goes into the house, or near other dogs, and something to eat before that."

"We have isolation rooms," said Dina. She came down off the porch and led Shawn down a gravel path toward the fenced area with all the dogs. "When we built the dog run, we figured we'd probably end up with more than we hoped for, so we planned ahead."

They walked around two sides of the wooden fence, the half-dozen dogs from the gate following along, and most of the dogs inside the fenced enclosure following from their side. One of the buildings straddled the fence, and they entered—Dina, then Shawn with the dog, then Al, moving carefully to keep the dogs out.

Inside, the building had a concrete floor with a drain in the middle. The entryway was large and bright, with windows on three sides. Low shelves and cupboards ran under the windows, with taller ones on the wall opposite the front door, on either side of a door that led deeper into the building.

"I'll get him some food," said Al.

Dina nodded, then said to Shawn, "Through here, we'll get him set up in a room." She led him through the door to a hallway with four doors, two on either side. She opened one and walked in.

Shawn followed her into a room the size of a small bedroom. It had cheap, tough carpet in a dark tan, and a battered sofa sat on the wall to the left of the door. A large size dog bed with a thick pillow sat in a corner to the right. A coffee table dominated the middle of the floor. A TV hung low on the wall opposite the sofa, and a low bookcase full of well-used paperbacks sat under the window.

"Many of your dogs read?" Shawn asked.

Dina laughed. "Not that I've noticed. But if a dog is going to tear up the furniture, or grab things off shelves, we want to find out here, not in the main house. And some dogs do better with the TV on—noise, voices, just as background."

"Makes sense," said Shawn. He squatted down and set the Retriever on his feet. "There you go, buddy, easy. This is your space for a while. Wanna check it out?" He untied the rope from the dog's collar, then stood up to let him explore.

"You're going to need a flea bath yourself, I think," said Dina.

"I've been showering with flea shampoo for years," said Shawn with a shrug, watching the dog sniff around, slow and cautious.

"That's a thought," said Dina. "I'll have to keep it in mind. Do you recommend a particular brand?"

Before he could figure out if she was teasing, Al sidled through the door with a big bowl of canned dog food. That caught the dog's attention, and he jumped up on his hind legs to start gobbling food before Al even had a chance to put the bowl on the floor.

"Hungry, poor guy," said Al. "At least that's easy to fix."

They watched the dog eating for a bit, then Dina said, "The bathroom is right next door. It's stocked with flea shampoo, regular soap, towels and a hair dryer. When he's done, you can give him his flea bath, clean up yourself, then come up to the house. Put him in the room across the hall after he's had his bath, in case any fleas jumped off in here."

"That works," said Shawn. "Sorry for the delay."

"Not your fault," said Al. "Good to see you willing to jump right in, actually. I think this'll work out fine, but we'll check all the boxes anyway, just for drill. Come on up to the house when you're done, no rush."

He and his wife smiled and left Shawn with the dog, who was polishing his bowl to a high shine.

"Just us, huh, Buddy?"

It took about half an hour to get Buddy his flea bath. The bathroom had a tub/shower, and Shawn just stripped down and got in with the dog. The water was warm and Buddy didn't seem to mind getting wet. Getting soaped up made him give Shawn big, sad, puppy eyes, but he didn't struggle too much.

He didn't like the hair dryer, though.

Shawn didn't have anything to change into, so he sprayed his clothes and shoes down with flea spray and put them back on. The sharp, chemical smell wasn't pleasant, but he was used to it.

He settled Buddy into his new room, which was pretty much the same as the first one, complete with TV and book case. Shawn turned on the TV for him—might as well, right?—and spotted some toys in a plastic box next to the sofa. Good, Buddy'd have some things to play with and chew on if he got bored.

It was pushing an hour by the time Shawn trotted up the steps to the porch of the main house. He thought about ringing the bell, but the Corcorans had said to come right in, so he did.

The entry hall was tiled in grey granite, scuffed up and lived-in, with a round wooden table in the center. A bunch of raggedy roses bloomed yellow in a plain clay vase. Paintings of more flowers, purple and yellow and orange, kinds Shawn couldn't name, hung on the walls. To the right, a door stood open and the security guy sat in front of a desk with a computer on it and three monitors mounted on the wall in front of him.

"They're in the family room," said Security Guy. "Straight down the hall, then left."

"Thanks," said Shawn. He gave the guy a wave, then headed down the hall.

It was a long hallway, and halfway down he saw another open door. The large room inside had a desk with another computer, with a couple of filing cabinets and a tall bookcase nearby. On the other end of the room were two black leather sofas, a leather love seat and two upholstered chairs, all grouped around a burlwood table with half a dozen electrical outlets grouped in the center. Thick grey carpet padded the floor, and the walls were painted a light beige and dotted with photos. It was clearly an office with a meeting space. Shawn glanced up and down the hall, then stepped inside.

The walls were covered with photos. He recognized some of the people in them, aside from the Corcorans—famous business people, techies and entrepreneurs, a few actors, a few musicians, and even a couple of presidents.

One picture, next to a window where the light made him squint to make it out, was a group photo of eight teenagers, all dressed up in tuxedos and prom dresses. He recognized Al and Dina, and—

"Senior Ball, from 1989," said Al, from the doorway.

Shawn stood up and blushed. "Sorry, I just…I really like photos. Especially old— I mean, not *old* old, but you know, pictures of people from back before."

Al gave him a sideways smirk. "You only regret getting older if you wasted the time," he said. He stepped up next to Shawn and started pointing to people in the picture. "Margie Hamilton, Bob Cassidy, Mindy Tran, Eddie Daugherty. They all work with us at Playbotics. We were the head geeks on campus."

Shawn waited a moment, then nodded to the last, unnamed couple. "That's Dino Casselli, isn't it? I don't know his girlfriend."

"Yeah, that's Dino. Arch-rival, ex-best-friends, blah-blah. Everyone knows that crap. He was with Amy Kowalski then. She was killed in a car wreck a few months later."

"I'm sorry," said Shawn.

Al shrugged. "I never knew her very well. Still a damn shame. She'd broken up with Dino by then, and her new boyfriend was an asshole who was plastered out of his mind when he ran into a phone pole. They both died." He glared at the picture for a second, then turned away.

Shawn followed him out the door and down the hall to the family room, where Dina was sitting on a sofa with a tablet. A brindle and white pit bull was flopped on the cushion next to her, with its head on her thigh. A Husky mix and a Dachshund lay at her feet, and a dog with a lot of Shepherd in him got up and trotted over to nose Al's hand before sniffing at Shawn.

Shawn let the dog get a good sniff before scritching him behind the ears.

"Well," Dina said, "you're obviously good with dogs. You can't really tell from a resume."

Shawn took a seat on a loveseat Al waved him toward before sitting on the sofa opposite his wife, with the Pit in between them. The other dogs redistributed themselves, and Shawn ended up with the Husky mix half standing, half lying on its forelegs on the cushion next to him. He petted the dog while watching Al and Dina.

"I've always loved dogs," said Shawn. "I've run into a couple of 'trainers' who I guess got all the right blather out of a book, but couldn't actually work with dogs when it came down to it. I don't know why anyone would bother—it's not like you get rich at this job."

"No," said Dina with a half smile. "We are prepared to pay a good wage, though."

"Well, good," said Shawn with an uncomfortable smile of his own. He always hated this part. "And, umm, I'll be living here as well?"

"Yes," said Dina. "Room and board are provided. You'll have

regular working hours, but if something sets the dogs off at two in the morning, it'll be up to you to figure out what's up and get them calmed down. Or if someone dumps another litter of puppies and they need to be fed every three hours, that sort of thing."

Shawn nodded. "That's fine. You've got a great facility, what I saw of it. The dogs seem happy, and they have plenty of space."

"There's about two acres inside the dog fence," said Al. "We have room to expand if we need to, but I hope we never need to."

"We have plans to start a no-kill shelter on some land in Alameda," said Dina. "We're working on permits and such. The idea is to move most of the dogs there, and keep here only the ones we've gotten personally attached to. We can't do right by all of them, however much we want to. A purpose built facility with a larger staff than we'd want here would be better for everyone, including the dogs."

"Would you want me to move over to the shelter when it's ready to open?" asked Shawn.

"Not necessarily," said Al. "It'll be at least a year, probably closer to two, before it's ready to open. If this works out, then when the time comes you can decide if you want to move or not. We'll probably always have at least ten or so dogs here, so there's plenty of work for a full-time person. Brian and Ellie have been feeding and playing with the dogs when they have time—Brian's our day security guard, you met him earlier, and Ellie's the house-keeper. But we didn't hire them to take care of the dogs, and it's an unfair burden."

"We never intended to have quite this many," Dina said with a pained smile. "We thought five or six at first, but then a year or so ago, people started leaving dogs at the gate. It's horrible, but what can you do?"

Shawn hesitated for a moment, then said, "I've always wondered...you're known for loving dogs, real dogs, so, considering how many unwanted dogs there are in the world, how many are euthanized every year, I've been wondering why you're developing robot dogs?"

Al and Dina sighed in unison without even looking at one another.

"I'm sorry," said Dina. "It's just that it seems so obvious to us. Nothing will ever replace a real dog, of course." She smiled down at the Pit and scratched the big, ugly head resting on her thigh. "But not everyone can take care of a dog properly. Someone who lives in a small apartment, whose work or health won't let them give the dog proper exercise. If they can't afford to hire a dog walker, then what?"

"And assistance dogs," said Al. "For some people, caring for a dog is another burden in an already difficult life, but the dog provides help that makes their life easier in other ways. A robot assistance dog could provide the help without the burden."

"My cousin's blind—not completely, but mostly," said Shawn. "She has an assistance dog. She has no problem taking care of Wesley."

"I'm sure she doesn't," said Al. "Most blind people don't, as I understand. But there are others who do."

"We're not trying to eliminate the need for real working dogs, or companion dogs either," Dina said. "But a lot of people would love to have a dog, whether as a companion or an assistance dog, but can't for whatever reason. A robot dog might fill that need."

"I guess that makes sense," said Shawn. "That's why there's a race to get the first workable robot dog on the market?"

"There've been robot dogs for a while," said Dina. "Aibo, Tekno, Chip, Zoomer, the Jenx dog—when Al and I were kids there were toy dogs with batteries that could walk and bark. It's not a matter of being first, it's a matter of being best—developing a robot dog that can do more than walk and bark and fetch a ball."

Shawn nodded and said, "That makes sense." They hadn't said anything that hadn't been written up online or in magazines; it was probably straight out of a press release.

The Corcorans asked him about his experience as a trainer, and they talked about work details for a while—actual hours, days off, special needs of some of the dogs, and the adoption events they wanted to put on every month or two, so long as new dogs kept showing up at their gate. Shawn agreed that the puppies would be easy to adopt out, because healthy puppies usually were, especially with the celebrity push of the Corcorans' name behind the effort.

"I really hate all that 'celebrity' crap," said Dina with a scowl. "But if it'll help, then fine."

"So," said Al, "are we doing this?" He gave Shawn a big smile, and Shawn smiled back.

"I think so," he said. "You have a great place, and I'd love to work here."

"Great!" said Al. "I'll have my guy draw up a contract. You didn't bring your bags, right?" Shawn shook his head. "Fine, that's what I figured. So you'll sleep at your own place tonight, and when you come back tomorrow you can sign all the crap HR wants signed, and we'll be good to go."

They all stood up and shook hands, the dogs dancing around their legs, sensing that the people were happy about something and wanting to get in on it.

After a few minutes, Al said, "I have a meeting to get ready for. Shawn, good to have you." He gave his wife a kiss, then headed out, the Shepherd mix and the Dachshund following at his heels.

Shawn went down on one knee and let the Pit sniff him, then gave it some scritchies. "Is this the Pit that was left at the gate? He's a big, strong boy, healthy build."

"Yes," said Dina. "He wasn't a stray, and doesn't seem to have been fought, thank goodness. I think someone got him as a puppy, and then when he grew up they became afraid of him. It's ridiculous, really. Pit bulls are perfectly gentle dogs if you treat them well and don't train them to fight. Sweetie's a big baby, aren't you, Sweetie?" She bent down to pet the dog and got her face washed.

Shawn laughed. "Sweetie?"

"I know," said Dina with a grin. "I couldn't help it. I've always loved Pits, and he *is* a sweetie. He started following me around right away, and I love him to pieces."

"Do you think the robot dogs will ever be like that?" Shawn

asked. "Really affectionate, able to bond with people, and people able to love them? I mean, more than a kid with a teddy bear?"

"I think it depends on the person," said Dina. "I loved my teddy very much when I was little."

"Sure, I had a stuffed snake until I was thirteen, and once he got lost and I kinda freaked. But still, it's different with something living. It'd take a heck of an advanced AI to make a dog *feel* real, wouldn't it?"

Dina's smile tightened for a moment. "Baby steps," she said. "We have a ways to go before we have AI at that level. We're making good progress, though." She straightened up and said, "I'll show you to your room. Staff dinner is in the kitchen at seven. Breakfast at six, lunch at eleven-thirty."

Shawn shut up and followed her upstairs, Sweetie and the Husky mix trailing after them.

His room was nice, a decent size, with a queen bed, a dresser and a desk and chair. It had a window that looked over the dog run, and the tree-dotted meadow beyond it. Dina excused herself and left, Sweetie trotting along behind her.

Since Shawn didn't have anything to unpack, he played with the Husky, who'd stuck around in Shawn's room. A tag on her collar said "Squirrely."

"Well, that's not nice," said Shawn with a grin. "I think you're a perfectly calm dog, and I'll bet you're smart, 'cause most Huskies are. Maybe you chase squirrels?"

Squirrely wagged her tail and panted through a big smile.

"Okay, I guess that fits, then. Gotta watch those squirrels!"

Squirrely woofed and went into a play bow. Shawn laughed and ducked down in response, making razzle-hands, pretending to grab at her. She woofed and dashed around the small amount of open floor space in the room.

"Okay, how about if we go outside," said Shawn. "I need to check out the territory some more, introduce myself to the rest of the dogs, and playing in here isn't going to be much fun."

He headed downstairs and out to the fenced area, which only a couple of tech billionaires would call a "dog run." He tried tossing a stick he found on the lawn, but Squirrely just watched the stick fly off, then turned and stared at him. It seemed she only chased squirrels.

It was a short hike across the grass to the gate he spotted in the fence. He wasn't sure if the house dogs were supposed to mix with the run dogs, so he left Squirrely outside. He got mobbed by fourteen bouncy dogs—he finally had a chance to count them—all mutts of one sort or another. He spent the next couple of hours playing with them, throwing balls and sticks and ropes, shifting his attention from dog to dog, trying to get a feel for their personalities. They seemed reasonably well socialized, at least outside.

He checked out the second, larger building inside the run, and found a larger supply of food, both dry and canned, grooming equipment, flea treatment, some basic medicines, and a wall of crates in various sizes. A rack held collars and leashes. The back half of the building was all dog runs, concrete with drains and wire mesh doors, each with a padded bed, a blanket, and a water bowl.

Pretty good setup for people who only planned on maybe six dogs, he thought. Of course, someone who plans for six dogs is probably going to end up with more, especially with this much acreage. Figuring that out in time to make building plans is just smart.

The Corcorans were definitely smart. Which made Shawn's job a lot easier.

His information said that the meeting Al had mentioned was set for four. It was twenty till.

Shawn closed up the kennel building and wandered back across the grass, petting dogs and tossing balls all the way to the gate. He let himself out, careful not to let any of the dogs escape, then headed up to the house.

He waved at Brian the security guy on his way through the entry, then walked down the hall, his steps silent on the stone floor. He paused and squatted to retie his shoe, and listened.

A thread of conversation floated down the hall, two female

voices. One sounded like Dina. The other was probably the house-keeper. He paused, listened, but the voices didn't move.

Good.

He stood up and slipped into the office.

He slipped a hand into his pocket and pulled a nickel out from among all the other coins. It was the only nickel he had, and it wasn't actually a nickel.

There weren't any convenient piles of change to add the nickel to, so he dropped it onto the carpet under the burl table. It looked just like any other dropped coin.

Still fifteen minutes till the meeting. Shawn stood still and listened. The women's voices had vanished, and he didn't hear any footsteps.

The sound of a car door slamming signaled that the meeting would be starting soon. Perfect.

Shawn left the office and walked, slow and casual, down the hall toward the entryway. He heard footsteps on the stairs from the second floor—heavy footsteps, which meant Al.

Al opened his own door, unlike most rich people on TV, and a gaggle of people in their forties moved inside, calling greetings to Al, to Brian, to the dogs. Four of the guests were people Shawn recognized from the group photo on the office wall.

As expected, this was going to be a business meeting.

He circled around the far side of the table in the entry hall, just a good employee who didn't want to get in the way of his boss's guests. A few people who weren't petting the dogs looked up at his approach, giving him curious looks. He smiled politely and kept going.

"Wait, I know you," said one of the women. Mindy Tran—Dr. Tran, a computer scientist.

"Me?" said Shawn. "I don't think so. Or, do you walk your dog in Westland Park?"

"No, I don't have a dog," she said. "I've seen you before, though. I have an excellent memory for faces."

Everyone was looking at him. Shawn let a shade of upset pass across his face, just for a moment. "Maybe at a mall? Where do you shop?" He took another step toward the front door.

Dina came in, Sweetie by her side. "Hey, all—" She stopped and looked around. "What's up?"

Dr. Tran snapped her fingers and pointed at Shawn. "You were at the Miami AI Conference! You're one of Dino Casselli's security people!"

"Security? I'm a dog trainer, ma'am." Another step toward the door, but Brian had appeared, as though he'd teleported.

"No, I remember," said Dr. Tran. "You were wearing a blue blazer and had one of those things in your ear. You were following Casselli around."

Al wasn't smiling anymore. "Brian, sweep the office."

Shawn protested, but no one was listening. Brian found the nickel bug, of course, and that did it. They couldn't prove he'd left it, but they hadn't actually hired him yet, so they didn't need to fire him —just kick him off the property.

Brian the security guy hustled him out to his car, a tight grip on Shawn's arm and a grim look on his face. Dina approached with Buddy on a new-looking leather leash. "Here," she said. "I assume he's yours? A way to play on our sympathies by taking care of the poor, neglected dog? You should be ashamed, letting him get into that condition just for your caper!" She thrust the leash into his hand and stalked away.

"But he's not my dog...?" Shawn protested. Brian ignored him, just stood and glared until Shawn shrugged and unlocked his car. He put Buddy in the back seat and hoped he stayed there. Bonus if he didn't get car sick.

He pulled out and backed down the drive. The gate opened for him automatically, and closed behind him.

Buddy panted hard, which was a bad sign, but he sat up on the back seat, looking out the windows. At least he wasn't panicking, or dashing around the car. Shawn could work with that.

He drove the twenty minutes back into town, then pulled over into a parking lot by a grocery store and got his laptop out of the trunk. He sat in the back seat, next to Buddy, and logged into the feed from Sweetie.

Just as they'd planned, the pit bull—Dina Corcoran's favorite breed of dog—was sitting next to her in the office. The video from the dog's eyes was a bit choppy, but not bad. The audio was great.

The Corcorans and their friends/employees were talking about their AI developments. Their robot dog project was just a milestone —they were actually going for the big cheese, although they were barely a couple of steps down the path.

Mr. Casselli had thought so, but wanted confirmation. When he announced his own robot dog next month, he'd also tell the world that his arch-rivals, the Corcorans, had "adopted" one of his new robot dogs weeks earlier, and hadn't been able to tell it wasn't real.

You couldn't buy the kind of publicity *that* would stir up.

And Shawn's awkward attempt at industrial espionage would convince them they were ahead of the game, that Mr. Casselli was desperate to know what they were up to, but unable to get a line into their inner circle.

At least, not a two-footed one.

Shawn gave Buddy a scritch—at least he'd gotten a pretty good dog out of the deal—and shut his laptop. Mr. Casselli would be watching the same feed, and recording everything. Shawn's work was done, and he was due a bonus.

"Come on, Buddy. Let's go home and meet Boomer and Kodi. You'll like them, and you'll all be friends."

Buddy woofed and gave him a lick on the cheek.

The world always looked better through the eyes of a dog.

CAT AND MICE

JAMIE MCNABB

In my world, you can't have a dog story without providing a cat story as well. Although, in truth, this is a mouse story, since the cat is the villain in this piece.

Yes, the cat and mice in the title are actual animals. In an Animal Farm kind of way. They're very literate creatures with names that—if you pay attention—will add a depth to this story that makes it worth several reads.

"Cat and Mice" marks Jaime's seventh appearance in Fiction River. His most recent appearance was in Editor's Choice. His stories vary by genre and subject matter. My favorites include the wry voice you find here, with a lot of depth and insight, packed into a fable that isn't as outré as you might think.

Georgie Mouse was dead. Of all the things that could have been said about good old Georgie, the one sure thing was that he was incontrovertibly dead.

Eaten.

There was in fact not much left of him: a piece of his tail, his head, and a few bones. These sad remains lay scattered around on the kitchen linoleum.

"Lionel is quite thorough in his way," Chester Housemouseleader said to the mice who had gathered around.

Lionel was the housecat. He was large, orange, fast, and always hungry. He dozed, but he never slept soundly. At the moment, he was outside.

Around the gathered mice, the house seemed to be holding its breath. The refrigerator hummed, the mantel clock in the living room ticked, and the bathroom faucet dripped, but all with seemingly mournful notes.

"Just look at his sweet little face," Leni Mouseweaver said. "Why, if I were to weave that face into one of my tapestries, you'd say that it was the very image of a mouse at peace."

"He must have accepted his fate, right at the end," Deepak Mousesage said. "Very wise of him, very wise indeed."

"Yes, it is comforting in a way," Chester said. "Georgie may have suffered, but at least he knew he wasn't going to be wasted."

"Oh, yes," Homer Mousebard said. "He shall live on in the sagas."

"I don't give a rat's rear end about the sagas," Greta Seniormouseleader said. "Georgie was the fourth of us to get eaten in as many days."

"Yes, yes. Quite right, quite right," Chester said. "We're mice, *not* a feeding program for that cat."

"Hear him! Hear him!" several of the mice cheered.

"So? What are you going to do about Lionel?" Greta demanded.

Leave it to Greta. She was worth at least ten of anybody else.

And thus the debate began.

Felix Mousepionage smiled and listened to the talk and kept his own counsel. He didn't doubt that he could help, but until they were ready to listen, there was no point in offering a solution.

What Chester Housemouseleader and the others decided to do was to take the problem to their ultimate authority, Dolf Mouseleader.

They found him in the upstairs bathroom. He'd filled the tub with water and was zooming back and forth aboard a toy speedboat, creating a veritable storm of splashes and waves. He was laughing with undisguised glee.

"Hahaha! Whee! Whee!" Noticing them, he cried, "This is more fun than a trip to Paris!"

When Chester and the others finally had Dolf's undivided attention, they told him about Lionel, and Chester asked, "What, my Mouseleader, is to be done?"

"You sound like a filthy rabble of commune mice. Right off the farms. Whine, whine, whine."

"I apologize, my Mouseleader, but, uh, we were, hmm, hoping to benefit from your experience and insight."

"No, you weren't," Dolf yelled. "You are hoping to make this debacle my fault."

"No, my Mouseleader. I assure you that the situation is very grave and that we are in desperate need of your unparalleled leadership."

Dolf dried his ears with a towel. "Very well." He tossed the towel onto the heap at the base of the clothes hamper. "But really, Chester, must I solve every problem for you? I'm your leader, not your dictator. I'm not stopping you from taking decisive action, am I?"

"No, my Mouseleader, you are not. Nevertheless..."

"All right, all right," Dolf said. He thought for a moment, grooming his whiskers. "Tell me, are you willing to kill Lionel?"

"What? Kill the cat?"

"Yes. It's either kill the cat or feed the cat. There's no third alternative. You must be either the hammer or the anvil. Speaking for myself, I choose to be the hammer."

"Yes indeed, my Mouseleader, but we're mice, not murderers."

Dolf grinned. "It wouldn't be murder. It would be preemptive self-defense."

"That's true," Deepak Mousesage said, speaking for the first time. "Preemptive self-defense."

"Still, it's killing."

"What difference does that make? We mice kill all the time, don't we? To eat, to protect our young, to gain room to live in."

"Yes indeed, my Mouseleader."

"So, now that cat has given you an unparalleled opportunity to demonstrate the superiority of our species and to prove your dedication to the house, Housemouseleader. Kill the cat."

"Yes indeed, my Mouseleader!" Chester said, clicking his hind paws together. "It shall be done."

But it was not done.

They tried poisoning Lionel's cat treats, but he turned up his nose and ignored them.

They tried rigging the back of the couch, where Lionel loved to doze, with the 110 house current in the hope of electrocuting him, but Lionel batted the wires away.

They tried shooting him with a hunting rifle, but when they fired it, the bullet went wild and the recoil shattered Billy Mousearmorer's paw and smashed Danny Mousesoldier's skull.

That's when Donovan Mousecommando volunteered to slit Lionel's throat. He'd do it while the orange menace was sleeping. It was a harebrained plan, but Donovan pledged it would work.

After several rounds of debate, Chester finally agreed.

Donovan Mousecommando decided to set off at three o'clock on a sunny afternoon. Lionel was sleeping on the back of the couch and the house was quiet, but outside a lawnmower was making enough racket to mask Donovan's approach. The conditions were perfect.

"Good luck and good hunting, Donovan," Chester said. "I wish I were going with you."

"Thank you, sir. See you soon."

Donovan saluted and took his departure.

All through the balance of the day, the mice kept watch and listened intently, but they saw and heard nothing to indicate that Lionel had met his well-deserved end.

"Donovan is biding his time," Leni said.

"Success is the reward of patience," Deepak said.

"He's too good an operator to fail," Chester said.

That night, the house stilled and a grim, worried silence descended.

In the morning Lionel went to his litterbox and then went to his bowl and ate his breakfast.

Donovan was never seen or heard from again—no head, no tail, no paws, no blood smear, no final squeak. Nothing.

The mice hung a commemorative star on the wall of the nest.

Throughout all of these stirring events, Felix Mousepionage had a hard time keeping his mouth shut. However, keep it shut he did, despite the loose-bowelled stench of fear that had begun to pervade the nest. The odor was so strong that it seeped out through the walls and the floors. It filtered down from the ceilings. Nowhere was free of it.

The days dragged by.

The nest's food supplies dwindled, but no one dared to venture out of the nest to forage.

"We're under siege," Barbara Mousehistorian said. "We may as well be living in a medieval castle. It isn't August, is it?"

"No," Chester Housemouseleader said. "Maybe that's why the hunting rifle didn't work. It isn't August."

"The guns didn't work that time, either," Barbara said, "not in the way anyone wanted them to."

"Isn't that always the way of it?" Deepak Mousesage commented.

"Lionel is hoping for us to grow so desperate that we'll venture into the kitchen," Chester said. "Then he'll pounce."

"Good plan on his part," Greta Seniormouseleader said. "We'll be starving soon."

"We could forage in the garden," Chester suggested.

"What a wonderful idea," Leni Mouseweaver said. Her eyes were shining and her whiskers were twitching with excitement. "I haven't been outside in ages."

Greta glared at her. "If you go outside, you'll end up inside— inside a raccoon or a hawk or a crow."

"That's not necessarily true," Leni said, "and there are wonderful things in the garden."

"What a saga it would make," Homer Mousebard said. "*The Quest for Food.* A heroic band of lovable misfits sets out on a perilous search for—"

"Talk sense, the both of you," Greta said sharply. "Food comes from the kitchen—"

Unless we happen to be what's on the menu, Felix said to himself.

"—and if we can't get our paws on some of it and damn soon, we're going to starve to death."

"That's true," Chester said. "Maybe I should talk to Dolf Mouseleader again."

"No," Deepak said. "I wouldn't want to bother him with such minor matters as a temporary diminution in our food supplies."

Everyone, including Felix, nodded. In his line of work, it was important to blend in.

"Well, Chester," Greta said. "It's up to you. You're the housemouseleader. Lead! What are we going to do?"

Leave it to Greta.

What Chester Housemouseleader decided to do was to send Zoltan Mousesoldier to spy on Lionel. It was, Chester admitted, not a solution *per se*, but a proof-of-concept operation. If a mouse could spy on the cat and get the intelligence product back to the nest, then the mice could go about foraging in the kitchen in relative safety.

Before sending him off, Chester shook Zoltan's paw. "It's a magnificent thing that you're doing for the mice in this house."

"For all mice everywhere," Deepak Mousesage chimed in.

"As I was saying," Chester said. "A magnificent thing. Vital work."

Zoltan looked as though he had eaten something that didn't agree with him. He tried to smile but couldn't bring it off.

"Do you remember how to operate the signal lamp?" Chester asked.

Zoltan nodded. "Yes, sir."

"Good," Chester said. "Now, I want you to remember that no mouse ever won a struggle against a cat by dying for his nest. He won it by making the poor, dumb cat die for *his* place on the back of the couch. So be careful and come back alive."

Zoltan saluted smartly and marched out of the nest and into the glare of the kitchen. The kitchen was a bright, sunshine-yellow room, albeit one that smelled of bleach and floor wax.

Ammonia, too, especially after Georgie's unfortunate demise.

"Oh, what a hero!" Leni said. "I'll weave a tapestry to commemorate his bravery."

"And I shall compose an epic poem in his honor," Homer said.

"And when he returns, I shall award him a medal," Chester said.

"If he returns," Greta said.

Leave it to Greta.

And thus the wait began.

Felix smiled and silently returned to his nest. He'd always liked Zoltan. Not the sharpest chisel in the toolbox, but a good kid. Felix was going to miss him.

Felix Mousepionage lived in his own nest, not in a section of the communal one. The house itself was a 3100-square-foot split-level with an addition off the back. Its large perimeter foundation enclosed seemingly endless crawlspaces, and because the various builders had cut a few corners, there were ways from the crawlspaces up into the walls and, especially, up into the spaces beneath the built-in cabinetry.

And so it was that Felix's nest occupied the large, comfortable space beneath the vanity in the downstairs bathroom, the guest bathroom. The space had a two inch overhead and plenty of square-footage, and because it was in the guest bathroom and because guests were infrequent, quiet reigned.

Felix nibbled on a piece of carrot and then went back to work on his current batch of sketches. They were schematics, cross-referenced to an assortment of electronics-supply catalogues.

It was hard to find exactly the right parts for what he had in mind, but item by item he identified them.

Zoltan's messages soon began to come in. Lionel was downstairs.

Lionel was in the garage. Lionel was in the kitchen. Lionel was sleeping on the couch.

Chester and Greta recorded the times and the movements, and soon a pattern began to build up.

"Do we have enough to resume foraging?" Chester asked.

"He's only been at it for a few hours," Greta said. "We have a few data points, yes, but not enough to establish a pattern. Lionel isn't stupid. He may be changing his locations randomly."

"What are you saying?"

"That we need more data and more time to analyze it."

"Analysis," Chester said. "That's always the tricky part, isn't it?"

Indeed, it is, Felix thought. Almost as tricky as deciding what to do with the product of that analysis. To act, or not to act, that is the question.

Alvin Seniormouseplatoonleader said, "We'd best leave him out until morning." Alvin spat on the floor. "That way he'll come back with a pretty clear picture of what Ol' Orange Face is up to, his kitty-cat ways and such like."

"An excellent idea," Chester said. "Issue the necessary orders."

The sun went down, the house quieted, and Zoltan's messages became less and less frequent. The last informed the mice that Lionel was sleeping on the bed in the master bedroom.

Chester, Greta, and Alvin went to bed.

Felix made himself a pot of hot, sweet tea, and returned to his schematics.

They found Zoltan in the morning.

He was hanging by a rope from a scaffold that had been erected just outside the main door to the nest. His eyes looked as though they were about to pop out of their sockets and his tongue was lolling out of his mouth. He did not appear to have found any sort of purpose or peace in his death, let alone any measure of acceptance of it.

A sign hung around his neck:

Death to Spies!

Dolf Mouseleader made a point of being on hand when Alvin and a few of the others brought Zoltan's body into the nest.

"He shall live in our hearts forever," Homer said.

"His sacrifice shall be our lasting inspiration," Leni said.

"He was a good mouse. The best," Alvin said, and spat on the floor for emphasis.

"Death and life are two sides of the same illusion," Deepak Mousesage said. "We are all united in the inexorable flow of the great transcendental immediacy."

"He marches with us in spirit," Horst Mouseassaultleader said.

"He weren't et," Tommy Mousesoldier said.

This, Felix thought, was perhaps the truest thing anyone had said so far.

Chester Housemouseleader awarded Zoltan the Remarkable Service Emblem with Paw. The award was posthumous, of course, but Zoltan's next of kin seemed comforted, buoyed up, by it.

With these preliminaries out of the way, Dolf Mouseleader climbed up onto a matchbox in front of the crowd.

Cheers of "Hail Victory! Hail Victory!" filled the nest. They echoed from the walls, the floor, the ceiling. The mice had gone wild with their desire for victory over the cat, for revenge. Noses crinkled, tails lashed, and paws pounded on the floor. Cries of "Never again! Never again!" joined the chorus.

Dolf called for quiet. He smiled and made quieting gestures with his front paws.

When the crowd had settled, he said, "I won't keep you long. Zoltan was a fine soldier. He was a true servant of the house and of its mice. Although we are saddened by his untimely passing, we must remember that he knew and accepted the risks of his chosen profession. Indeed, the highest calling that any of us can attain to is to give our lives in the service of the mice. We must resolve that he shall not have died in vain." Dolf looked back and forth at the enrapt faces shining up at him. "Death to the cat! Form ranks! Hail victory!"

Their eyes flashed like lightning, and their cheers rolled through the nest like thunder.

It went on and on, but eventually the mice shouted themselves hoarse and quieted down. Dolf departed amidst more calls for victory and death to the enemies of the mice. The crowd disbursed.

A few stayed behind.

They were mostly quiet, basking in their grief and their lust for revenge.

Chester said, "Zoltan made a valiant attempt."

"Yes, but it didn't work," Greta said.

Leave it to Greta.

Felix studied their faces: Chester's face, Greta's face, Homer's face, even Deepak's face. In twenty-four hours, after they'd sobered up, they would be ready to listen.

Chester's portion of the nest did not smell of the incipient hunger stalking the mice, nor was it furnished with torn pieces of newspaper and shopping circulars. No, no, there would be no traces of printer's ink on Chester's fur. Instead, he lived among strips of leather, cotton and wool cloth, and the freshest wood shavings.

Felix set up his materials in the midst of this luxury and waited, refusing to answer any of Chester's questions.

"In due time," Felix explained.

"When?"

"When the others are here."

Greta was the first to arrive. She sniffed the air, smiled her approval, and found a comfortable place. Homer, Leni, and Alvin followed in short order.

"All right, Felix, we're all here," Chester said. "What do you want to tell us?"

"We have the means to take advantage of this, uh, feline opportunity," Felix said. It was also important to sound optimistic. "We may even have a way to enhance our exports."

Chester's eyebrows shot up, his ears cocked forward, and his nose went into a spasm of twitching.

Felix's plan was simple to explain. Using materials from the workshop in the garage, they would build three devices: a radio transmitter and two radio receivers with directional antennas.

Felix had to explain what a directional antenna was, but no matter. They were hanging on his every word.

By the time he'd finished his presentation, they were nodding their heads and giggling.

"Where do the exports come in?" Homer Mousebard asked. Exports meant transporting products to other, distant houses. It meant the chance of adventure, of going on odysseys, on treks, of going where no mouse had gone before.

"We manufacture and sell the transmitters and receivers, and we consult on their use," Felix said. "The possibilities are endless."

"Ah, I see," Deepak Mousesage said. "It will be as though an invisible paw were guiding the affairs of mice."

"What do you mean?" Chester asked.

"I mean that it will be as though an invisible paw were moving our products from here to there."

"And moving their money from there to here," Greta said, an unusually dreamy expression on her otherwise stern face.

Chester asked, "But once they've bought the units, then—"

"We sell them new-and-improved units," Felix said. "After all, how can our customers be truly safe if they're using last year's unit? Good in their day, but totally obsolete *now*."

"It would be irresponsible not to keep up," Chester said, and licked his lips.

Whoever said that mice lacked a killer instinct had never seen the gleam in Chester's eyes.

———

They built the units, and they set up the receivers and the plotting table in the nest. They sneaked a sleeping pill from the medicine cabinet into Lionel's food, mixing it in thoroughly. The orange glutton gobbled it right down without a moment's pause. Evidently, he could only detect actual poisons. At any rate, he was in a deep sleep within minutes. From there, it was the work of a moment to strap and glue the transmitter to the monster's left hind leg.

The receivers came up.

The first angles were established.

And the first plot was made.

Yes! Success! The plot showed Lionel to be in the blue armchair, and, sure enough, he *was* in the blue armchair, sleeping off the sleeping pill.

Their fortunes were made.

Hurray!

The mice wasted no time in sending scouts and foragers into the kitchen.

Food! Bags of it. Boxes of it. Cupboards filled with it. Breakfast cereal. Oatmeal. Flour. Carrots. Apples. Bread. Cheese. Beef jerky. Peanut butter. Endless varieties and amounts of lovely, delicious food.

Theirs for the taking.

Now they would *never* go hungry again.

It was a mouse paradise.

———

The days flew by. They were happy, secure days, days in which no one was found ripped apart and eaten.

Felix Mousepionage, however, was not happy, nor did he feel secure. It could have been his suspicious nature, but he thought not.

While the other mice stuffed themselves, while they grew to behave as though the kitchen belonged to them, Felix hung out in the plotting room. He studied Lionel's movements: the couch, the chair, the kitchen, the rug in front of the fireplace, the rooms upstairs, the garage, the garden, the litter box, the backyard, the coat closet.

Felix read the plot logs, too, and he conducted his own reconnaissance.

Felix didn't bother with the kitchen. He scouted the chairs, the back of the couch, the garage, the rugs, the rest of the house.

Above everything else, he tried to match the physical evidence he was collecting with Lionel's movements as plotted.

Food eaten at such and such a time. Had the cat been near his food then? Fresh cat hairs on the back of the couch. Had the cat been there recently? Cat prints on the upstairs landing. Had the cat gone through there? New droppings in the litter box. Had the cat been there to have used it?

In most cases, the answer was yes.

But in some cases, the answer was no.

An inexplicable tuft of hair on the stairs.

Tracks in the bathroom that shouldn't have been there.

And strange gaps. Strange behaviors.

"What behaviors?" Chester Housemouseleader asked.

"He's spending a lot of time in the garage," Felix answered.

"Didn't he always?"

"No, he didn't. It's new. Since we tagged him."

"Anything else?"

"Several items have gone missing. The wheels from the toy dump truck, a sawblade, a crowbar, other things." For the first time in his life, Felix was at a loss for words. "It's somewhat disquieting."

"Your conclusion?"

"I don't have enough data to draw any firm conclusions, but the data I do have are rather worrying."

Chester chewed thoughtfully on a piece of jerky. "But no hard data, you say?"

"Not yet," Felix admitted.

"Well, I suspect it's nothing."

"And if it isn't?" Greta asked. She burped. Cheese-stuffed celery did it to her every time.

Still, leave it to Greta.

On October 29, a Tuesday, Felix went out into the garage. He ought to have checked the plot first, but he hadn't. It might be just as well to catch an accidental glimpse of the orange fiend.

The garage was neat, tidy, and as bright as two small windows could make it on a cloudy fall day. The air was thick with the aromas of improperly sealed paint cans, laundry detergent, fabric softener, dust, concrete, motor oil, and the gasoline fumes rising from the lawnmower.

Lionel had chosen to go elsewhere.

Felix wasn't sure whether this was a good thing or not.

He confirmed that the missing items remained missing, and he discovered that several additional items had joined them: a screwdriver, a pair of pliers, a length of pipe, and a soldering iron.

It made no sense.

Unless...

A sudden but entirely explicable panic overwhelmed Felix, and he raced back to the plotting room.

Panting as much from consternation as from the run, he asked, "Where...where's Lionel?" Felix went to the plotting table and stared down at the plot.

The plotter stopped nibbling on a chocolate-covered coffee bean. "Garage," he said. He gestured with the coffee bean. "Have you tried these? They're wonderful. He's been in there for most of the morning."

"I've just come from the garage. He's not there."

"You don't say," the plotter said, and lifted his nibbled-on coffee bean toward his mouth.

The treat didn't make it.

Felix batted it away.

The plotter's eyes widened, and he began to tremble from the tip of his tail to the top of his head.

"He's not *there*," Felix said. "When was your last fix?"

"Uh...Uh..." The plotter flipped through the log. "Uh...Here it is. Twenty-two minutes ago. Yep. Twenty-two minutes. Twenty-three by now, I suppose."

"Twenty-three minutes!" Felix shouted. He pointed at the table. "That plot is supposed to be kept current at all times. At all times. Just what part of 'at all times' don't you understand?"

"Look, I'm sorry, but I only plot the bearings. I can't plot bearings they don't give me."

"Did it ever occur to you to ask for new bearings? Or to inform your superiors of missing reports?"

"I, well, we—"

How far did the rot go? "Who gave you those coffee beans?"

The plotter looked down at the floor. "One of the radio-receiver operators."

It was worse than Felix had feared. The whole tracking crew was too busy stuffing their faces to do their jobs properly.

"You blithering idiot!" Felix growled.

"Come on, be reasonable, that cat hasn't moved for the better part of an hour. He's sleeping."

"In the garage!? In the GARAGE!? Even you can't be that stupid. Lionel *never* sleeps in the garage. Never! What kind of a moron are you?"

Felix grabbed the headset away from the plotter.

The sound of munching came from the other end.

"The bearings on Lionel," Felix said. "What are they?"

Munch, munch, munch. Swallow.

"We reported a set not five minutes ago," responded a female voice.

"Your last report was at least twenty-four minutes ago. Now give me those bearings."

"You don't have to get huffy."

"Give them to me this instant or I'll feed you to that damn cat myself!"

The bearings came through.

Felix plotted them.

"See?" the plotter said. "I told you he was in the garage. You must have missed him."

"Like hell I did," Felix said, and slammed his paw down on the alarm button.

But he was too late.

As though struck by a sledgehammer, the plotting-room wall burst inward in a hail of drywall fragments, wood splinters, and dust. The glare from the kitchen spilled in through the gap like an avalanche of garish light. The motes swirled violently in the air.

And everywhere there was the stench of a hungry cat.

OUR MAN IN BASINGSTOKE

SABRINA CHASE

*I love many things about Sabrina Chase's story, "Our Man in Basingstoke,"
but one of the things I love the most is the voice. It's pitch perfect and utterly
delightful. The delightful element makes it the ideal follow-up to Jaime
McNabb's story. I think of them as a pair, even though Sabrina's story is, in
some ways, the kind of spy story I had hoped to get when I initially thought
of this volume.*

Well...kinda. As you'll see.

"Our Man in Basingstoke" marks Sabrina's first appearance in Fiction
River, *but it won't be her last. She has stories upcoming. If you want to find
more of her work, pick up* Pulphouse Magazine Issue Zero, *which
WMG also publishes. Or find any one of her ten books, including two science
fiction series* (Sequoyah *and* Argonauts of Space), *a fantasy series*
(Guardian's Compact), *and a "bureaucrat-punk" short story collection that,
she says, was absolutely* not *inspired by events witnessed while working at
the Naval Research Laboratory in Washington, DC.*

*Her inspiration for this story? Well, besides a lifelong love of pulp fiction,
she "encountered a diagram of an explosive-stuffed dead rat" while reading a
history of World War II and the story took off from there.*

The prisoner showed no sign of fear when brought into Sir
Almsley's office. On the contrary—he appeared to consider
the experience a high treat, despite muddy trousers and bramble-
scratches on his round, beaming face. He appeared to be no more
than nine years old, and was looking about with great interest and
absolutely no embarrassment despite Sergeant Ross's firm grip on his
collar.

"It's the second time 'e's tried to get in," Ross stated. "Willins
sent him off from the front gate yesterday." While Ross maintained a
stony demeanor, the fact that he was barely moving his jaw when he
spoke informed those who knew him well that his volcanic temper
was under considerable strain. "I found 'im by the stables just now."

Sir Almsley sighed and removed his pince-nez, placing it on the scattered piles of papers on his desk before rubbing his aching head. "Did he use the front gate today as well?" Private Willins was...not entirely reliable as a guard, but he and Ross had decided he would cause the least harm there. A decision they might have to revisit.

"I found a hole under the fence in the forest," the boy said proudly. "I think it was a badger's." His wandering gaze snagged on an antique bronze statuette of Ganesha. "I say...is that a mystic idol from a hidden jungle kingdom guarded by fanatic dervishes in black masks covered with jewels?"

It took Sir Almsley a moment to collect his stunned thoughts. "Er, no. I bought it in a bazaar in Bombay." He stifled an impulse to apologize for this apparent lapse in good taste. "Do you have any excuse for your trespassing, young man? We are engaged in important war work here and do not have time for interruptions."

The boy nodded vigorously. "That's why I've come. To volunteer! And to see the secret underground base."

Sir Almsley's headache escalated to sharp, stabbing pain behind his eyes. He had quite enough to worry about without scrubby schoolboys being added to the mix.

"There are absolutely no secret underground bases anywhere on the grounds," he snapped. It was something of a sore point that the War Office had given him a difficult task and hardly anything to do it with. He hadn't even been allotted extra petrol rations—or, more importantly, competent guards.

"I know you have to say that to people, in case they are German spies," the boy said, unabashed. "I saw that in *The Spies of the Red Hand*. Ripping film, even if it did have some mushy romance stuff in it. But you can *see* I'm not German, can't you? My father is with the 47th Berkshires. You could ring them up and ask! My name is Peter Tilling. They sent me up from London on account of the air raids." A frown darkened his sunny expression. "I could've helped if they let me stay. Mum did, even though all she seems to do with the Air Raid wardens is stand around wearing an armband and serve coffee. *I* can do that, and I'm not quite ten!"

Although he knew he would regret it, Sir Almsley felt compelled to ask. "Why did you think there was an underground base here?"

"Before the war my father worked for a mining company. He let me push the detonator once for a tunnel! I heard an explosion a few days ago and there aren't mines here, just cows. So of *course* it had to be for a secret base! Do you have mechanized mole machines? You know, the ones that travel underground." Peter dug out a large and rather grubby notebook from under his shirt. "See, I had ideas to make 'em even better. I thought of a way to make a periscope for one. That way they can stay underground and not be seen. Like a submarine, you know. Then you can win the war and my father can come home."

Sir Almsley's fascinated gaze fell on the page young Peter had presented for his edification. A quite detailed drawing of some kind of armored cigar-shaped vehicle with treads and a corkscrew nose was shown, and a device with nested pipes and a long auger that appeared to create the hole for the periscope. He replaced his pince-nez to examine it more closely.

"I say, that is quite clever." He looked up at Ross, bemused. "*Do* we have these...underground mole machines?" Modern life moved far too fast for him. It seemed incredible, but he had thought the aeroplane a hoax at first and now his youngest son was *flying* one of the damned things.

"Never heard of 'em." Sergeant Ross's tone implied if they did exist, he didn't approve of that fact.

"It was in an illustrated number of *Stupendous Stories*," Peter informed them. "I got *lots* of ideas from that, and *Thrilling Zeppelin Tales*. *Boys Own Adventure* has ripping stories too, but I can't think how finding lost civilizations in Brazil can help fight the war." His bright eyes looked eagerly at Ross and Sir Almsley, as if they might have noticed something he'd missed.

Ross scratched his head. "'ere, lad. If they sent you up from London who took you in? Shouldn't you be helping them, then? Won't they be worried if they can't find you?"

Peter rolled his eyes and sighed heavily. "It's a *farm*. They don't have anything to read, or even a wireless! Well, when I got there I tried to train the cows to attack on command. That would be useful, wouldn't it? Bet that would surprise any German invaders! But the farmer just got angry and locked me in my room. So I climbed down a tree and decided to find something else to do." Peter did not appear to hold a grudge over his treatment. "All the posters say 'England Needs You.' I know I'm not old enough to join up, but there has to be *something* I can do to help."

There was just a touch of wistfulness in the boy's voice that caused a sympathetic twinge in Sir Almsley. Hadn't he done much the same thing? Between his age and the lingering ill-health from Indian fevers that had cut short his youthful military career, he had little to offer personally in the service of King and country. His two sons were, of course, serving with courage and it weighed heavily on him that he could do nothing to assist them as they went in harm's way.

Then he had heard through an old friend in government how someone had made their house and grounds available for some hush-hush project—Bletchley Park, as he recalled. No one had any idea exactly what they did there, but many clever fellows from Oxford were going there and seemed to be quite busy. The house had been far too quiet with the absence of his sons, and his wife had been dead many years. No one would be troubled if the government moved in, and he could observe and perhaps talk to the clever fellows and find a way to be of further assistance.

The reality was far otherwise. The government had accepted his offer of the use of Dunglenn and grounds, and a chap from the War Office contacted him about what he had termed "covert operations." Sir Almsley had been under the vague impression that this was somehow connected to hunting, which he remembered enjoying in his youth. But then to his shock he was informed that this was their new programme to develop...what was their phrase for it? "Espionage doctrine, techniques, and equipment."

Sir Almsley was of a generation that firmly believed gentlemen did not read each other's mail, and most certainly did not engage in what could only be described as skullduggery. While he appreciated times had changed and the Hun certainly did not have such nice notions, he was at a loss on what he could do to assist.

He'd also thought that the government would bring their own people in to run the thing, and he would merely observe from the periphery. Instead they had put him in charge, and instead of clever fellows from Oxford he had been given a store of dynamite and old ammunition in calibres no longer used by the military, and a group of soldiers that Sergeant Ross had apostrophized as a human scrap metal drive. He suspected a few had even engaged in poaching and other illicit activities.

Now he was expected to report on what he and his miniscule team had accomplished, which wasn't much. Certainly, they had learned how to detonate dynamite but no clever tricks had occurred to anyone in the process. He anticipated his upcoming visit to Head-quarters with utter gloom. He had hoped to plead for more resources, but given how little the Dunglenn project had produced the danger was the War Office would write the whole thing off as a failure.

Until then, however, he had a duty. He remembered enough of his military training to know an officer's duty included supporting the morale of his men by example. He paged through Peter's note-book, pausing to study a few of the diagrams and capture loose pages that escaped the covers.

"Your enthusiasm is admirable," Sir Almsley said. "England needs us all to do our utmost for victory, does it not? I am afraid I have no position suited to your talents...but perhaps you would be willing to leave your notebook with me? I promise I will give it full consideration."

Peter nodded vigorously, eyes glowing with delight.

Then Sir Almsley was inspired to a very mild deception. For the lad's own good, and Sir Almsley's peace of mind. "But I must ask you not to come here again—unless we contact you, of course." That had been a narrow escape. "There are spies everywhere now, and what if they followed you and uncovered...our secrets?" *How I dearly wish we had any worth stealing.*

"Oh!" Peter blinked. "Gosh. No, that would ruin everything! I'm staying at Hereston Farm, near the village of Basingstoke. Well, they say it is a village but it doesn't have much. I don't expect they have any spies, either."

"Nevertheless, we must take every precaution," Sir Almsley said firmly. "Sergeant Ross, will you escort young Mr. Tilling to the, er, badger hole? So he may return without being observed." He hoped his meaningful gaze was correctly interpreted as instructing him to block that means of entry in future.

With a cheery wave, Peter left under official escort and Sir Almsley returned to the hopeless muddle on his desk. But only minutes later there came a knock and the information that the car waited to take him to the station.

His trip to London, and he still had not prepared his report! In a panic, Sir Almsley stuffed as many of the papers as he could fit in a large leather satchel. Perhaps he could work on the train—and in any event, it would serve to show he'd not been slacking.

With his poor health, travel always fatigued him, and so did the frenetic activity of London despite the gloom of the blackout restrictions and wartime rationing. Far too many buildings had been reduced to piles of rubble, making travel difficult, and people on the street looked tired and drawn. Everyone carried a small case with a gas mask. But even through his fatigue he noticed the people at the War Office seemed abstracted, paying only cursory attention to what he was saying. He'd hoped that perhaps he could make a case for more resources, or at least a few men with all their limbs and no prison records, but his time with the department heads was cut short by some urgent issue and he was handed over to a polite but bored young man with pale eyes who introduced himself as George Smythe.

"It's odds on we'll get a pasting tonight," Smythe said, looking at the clock in the meeting room. "Bomber's moon, don't you know. You should think about leaving before dark, sir."

"But my files...I haven't shown you any of them."

A faint glimmer in the pale eyes. "You may leave them with me if you like, sir, and I will hand them on. With respect, I think you would find the air raid shelters rather uncomfortable—and of course, the bombing makes it hard to sleep."

Sir Almsley accepted defeat, and handed over his files with a heavy heart. It was marginally preferable to be informed via letter that there was nothing of use, versus being told so in person.

He heard nothing for several days after his return to Dunglenn. After ten days he resolutely sent a telegram to inquire, which did not elicit a response.

The next day, however, a nervous lieutenant appeared at his door, with a startling letter from the War Office.

"Stolen?" Sir Almsley stared at the lieutenant, who mopped his brow.

"Yes sir. We only noticed once we got your telegram. You see, Smythe never mentioned he had your files so we'd thought you'd taken them back with you, and with the confusion of the bombing... well, once we started asking around Smythe vanished. We...we think he was a spy, sir."

Sir Almsley's first reaction was, strangely, satisfaction. The stolen files were certainly not crucial to the war effort, and had exposed a dangerous spy in the heart of the War Office before real damage was done.

"Bad show, that," he said finally. The lieutenant was still nervous.

"There's more, sir. We, well, of course we have our own spies. Without saying how we know this, we've learned the Germans seem quite worked up about something in those files. They mentioned Dunglenn specifically, sir. They've been observed driving iron rods into the ground around some of their more sensitive installations, huge numbers of them. Iron they can scarcely spare. And they've been sending messages back and forth about what we think is called a...*Erdepanzer*, or earth tank. We were hoping you could tell us more."

Sir Almsley removed his pince-nez, distantly amazed that his hands did not shake. He shifted the papers on his desk until he found it, a ratty notebook. The page with the mole machine was indeed missing—and thinking back, he recalled how some of the pages had come loose, and how he'd been in such a hurry he'd simply gathered the papers on his desk to take with him.

A daring plan suddenly emerged from the depths of his mind, awe-inspiring in its audacity. With a single piece of paper, young Peter Tilling had sown chaos and confusion in the German war machine, making them waste rare and valuable resources that could no longer be used to make tanks and weapons.

And he could never confess that a nine-year-old boy had done it. Not if he intended to do it again.

"Not to worry," he said, and leaned back. "This little incident is an excellent proof of one of the cunning ideas this project devised. A very clever fellow came up with that—a trifle eccentric, perhaps—but I saw the potential. That was a deliberate ploy. There are no *Erdepanzers*, but we made them think there were, eh? And all to our advantage in the end. Jerry is running around defending against something that doesn't exist. Quite a cost-effective stratagem, what?"

Sir Almsley was quite gratified by the lieutenant's gaping expression. "Sir! You did this...on purpose?"

Not yet inured to the demands of spycraft, he could only nod to give the wrong impression rather than voice an outright lie. "And there are more where that came from." He tossed over the notebook. "The War Office will doubtless know where they can be used to best effect. Where you think you might have a spy or two, eh?"

"That's bloody brilliant, sir! Er, pardon my language." The lieutenant stood. "I'd best get back immediately. What a relief! We thought we'd cocked it up proper. Shall I take this?" He held up Peter's notebook.

Sir Almsley nodded gravely. "Guard it well."

"This come wi' the mail, sir." The soldier was completely unidentifiable, in black clothes and with grease smeared over his face. He held a brown paper parcel, and placed it on the table in the sunny side parlor.

"Ah, our research materials have arrived. Thank you. Any luck? It's nearly noon." Sir Almsley, amused, observed the man's jaw tighten.

"He's a slippery one, and no mistake. We'll earn that brandy yet, sir!" The soldier gave a determined nod and left.

The package contained the latest issues of several booklets with lurid covers promising adventure and excitement. Sir Almsley observed the time wanted but five minutes to twelve, and then saw the sash of one window lift slightly, followed shortly by Peter wriggling through the opening. He had several twigs and a small feather stuck in his hair, and a wide grin on his face.

"They've gotten loads better, Sir Almsley! I nearly didn't make it in time!"

Sir Almsley smiled. "You've been an excellent trainer. I've gotten word from Sergeant Ross, by-the-bye. He tells me his new unit has made excellent use of what he learned from you about sneaking to great purpose." And since the commandos were doing amazing things in the war, this earned his project even more credit. He was told that the Dunglenn training program had become very much in demand in certain departments of the army. "I daresay they will earn their prize of brandy in a few days."

Young Peter's skill in getting into places he shouldn't had been given new purpose in the training. A discreet visit to the farm, with a cover story of "needing a boy to help the groundskeeper," had covered matters on that end with no one the wiser and the farmer relieved. Ross had come up with the idea of the competition as an incentive to the men. Every day, Peter set out from the farm at the same time with the goal of getting inside the house before noon without detection. Once the soldiers caught him, Sir Almsley awarded them a bottle from his private stock.

"We have new material to research," he said, indicating the pulp magazines. "I thought we could do a working lunch. I've requested jam sandwiches to be served, and an excellent vintage of ginger-beer."

Peter sighed with satisfaction. "Absolutely ripping. Oh look, this one's got 'Metal Men from Mars'! Did they like the one with the model aeroplanes steered by wireless?"

"I believe they are giving it further study." While Peter was definitely the brains of the project, Sir Almsley served as the filter of realism for his wilder notions. A remotely piloted craft was too fantastic for even the Germans to fall for. In a similar vein, the trivial idea Peter had thought merely a good practical joke was presently causing no end of destruction in the paranoid Third Reich. Who would have thought a simple diagram of a dead rat stuffed with dynamite would cause so much panic? But there was never a shortage of real dead rats in a war zone and thanks to Peter's sketch the Germans thought every one could be a bomb and took steps accordingly. In Sir Almsley's considered opinion, Peter's practical joke had been every bit as effective as a bombing run.

"I did enjoy the plan for the secret zeppelin base in the Himalayas, however—brought back memories of my time in India. I fear the cost of construction will be prohibitive until the war is over, but I do hope they build it eventually. I should like to visit again."

"They should do a secret base on the Moon!" Peter grabbed one of the sandwiches and devoured it. "Bet the Metal Men of Mars wouldn't expect that!"

"Indeed." Sir Almsley smiled at his co-conspirator. The numbing silence of his home was a thing of the past, and they had both found a way to help the war effort despite their limitations. Perhaps the two of them could one day make war a thing of the past as well. "Now, what else do we have to work with here?"

NIGHT FLIGHT

JONATHAN KORT

Our World War II stories needed to hang out together. They deal with different aspects of the war, and their tone is very different as well. But they share a few things in common, as you'll see.

"Night Flight" is Jonathan's second appearance in Fiction River. *His first story appeared in* Editor Saves *and is quite different from this one. He writes children's books for early readers, including* Twinkles and the Moon Rabbit *and* Twinkles and the Fox. *"Night Flight" isn't for early readers. It's for adults. But it still shows Jonathan's love for children.*

His grandfather inspired this story. Jonathan writes, "My grandfather was Jewish, and although he never got to fight in the war due to health reasons I heard the stories about how many times he tried to enlist (8) many times throughout my childhood."

There are a wide variety of ways to fight a foe, as Jonathan so ably illustrates here.

"Halt! Papers please." The Nazi stood there beside the sandbags at the checkpoint, his wool coat turned up at the collar to keep away the night chill. His companions loitered farther back beside their rifles at the makeshift wall where they were smoking, hands cupped around the glowing embers that lit their faces with a ghoulish glow.

My heart quickened in my chest as I reached inside my jacket to pull out the *carte d'identité* from where it rested in my breast pocket. No matter how many times we performed this dance, it never failed to excite me. Was this to be the time that they would smell the Jew standing before them, or would the false papers with my French name again protect me?

I handed over my papers with a steady hand and looked over at my companion, who also had her papers out and ready. It was good to be accompanied by Jeannine, who, with her stylish hat, modest dress, and perpetual smile was the type of woman the Nazis enjoyed talking with a moment before letting go. Which is exactly how it appeared to be going this time. As the soldier was looking over our papers, Jeannine made a lighthearted comment about how if he looked too long she'd think he was memorizing her address to drop by later with his friends. This flustered him, and he quickly lowered the papers from where he had been holding them up close to his face and returned them, before waving us through the checkpoint.

We stowed our papers, and I held my arm out for Jeannine. She grabbed it lightly and after blowing the other soldiers a quick kiss and waving gaily at their startled grins, she led the way across the imaginary line that separated the square in Collonges-sous-Salève from the surrounding countryside.

"Do you really have to flirt with them so much?" I grumbled under my breath as we started along the road toward home.

"Marcel, you of all people should know it helps," she said with a smile as she patted my arm affectionately.

I sighed. It was hard to argue with her when she knew she was right. We had been making this same trip for weeks, ever since she had begun sleeping with the local regiment leader. I didn't like it, but since our false papers listed us as siblings, I escorted her on the road between the camp and our house that was nestled beneath Le Salève. This was still only about once or twice a week, but it was more contact with the Nazis than I wanted to have.

I preferred to spend most of my days clambering up and down Le Salève behind the house. I liked finding new paths through the forest and helping one of the local shepherds keep his sheep from falling off the cliffs in return for the occasional bit of mutton or cheese. There was something about the mountain that called to me. Once I was up there in the crisp air, I felt free. I would stare down at the white city of Genève on the edge of lac Léman with its Jet d'Eau looking like a perfect quill pen stuck into the shore and I could pretend that there wasn't a war going on that sought to eradicate me and my people.

But eventually, I had to return to the valley, and the problems of living in Occupied France. Even if I had wanted to leave my country and escape to the safety of Switzerland, I couldn't. They had closed the border to anyone over the age of sixteen, choosing only to save the children.

"Slow down a minute," Jeannine said, tugging on my arm. "You know I can't go up these hills as fast as you can."

"You could if you'd get outside and walk around more," I said as I slowed down so that she could catch her breath. "You spend too much time in your room with that sewing machine of yours."

"Well, somebody needs to bring in some money around here," she said quickly. "You seem to think we can all live on cheese and meat."

I tried to think of a scathing reply that would remind her what I thought of someone who willingly consorted with Nazis, but couldn't. We fell silent as we turned up the hill and began to climb. There was no point in bickering when the road got this steep, even if we'd had the wind to do so. It had taken me an entire month after moving here to get used to the hills and lack of air here in the mountains. But now, after living here for six months, I was finally able to walk from the border to the top of the mountain without gasping.

As we got close to the house that we stayed in with our "uncle," I noticed that he had left laundry out on the line even though it was getting dark out as a signal. From the way he had hung the pants upside down next to the handkerchief, I could tell that another group had arrived.

This was the other reason that I spent all of my time out on the mountain. Robert, the man that they had sent Jeannine and me to live with, was part of the Underground that was responsible for smuggling Jewish children to safety. When we had first arrived I had asked permission to help him but was told that I couldn't until I knew the surrounding countryside like the back of my hand. It was dangerous work to lead refugees around in the dark, where one wrong turn could send the group into a patrol that would kill everyone without a second thought.

I ran up the steps and opened the door for Jeannine. Perhaps tonight would be the night that Robert would let me help with the border crossing. I followed her into the warm house and after leaving my boots and jacket by the door, went into the sitting room where Robert was reading beside the stove. He was a short man, only coming up to my chin, but he was strong and kind, with a twinkle in his eye and a ready joke for any occasion.

Robert looked up from his book as I entered the room and carefully placed a marker between the pages and set it on the table beside his chair. Jeannine was on her way down the hall to her room when Robert cleared his throat and called for her to come into the sitting room. I stood there awkwardly waiting for her to come, wondering what he had to say to both of us.

"I'm afraid that I'm going to need both of your help tonight," Robert began. "Jaques fell on the rocks this morning and broke his leg, and we were shorthanded enough that I was going to ask Marcel here to help already." He looked at Jeannine. "I know you aren't as familiar with the area as we'd like, but this time we could use every person who can help."

"Where will we be taking them?" Jeannine asked.

"This is a rather large group," said Robert. "We will be crossing to the west, between here and Saint-Julien. There is another guide on the Swiss side that will take them from there."

Jeannine looked down at her hands and bit her lip for a moment before replying. "That's not going to work. They're expecting you on that route." She reached into her blouse and retrieved a piece of paper. "Here is a copy of the orders that Franz received today that says they'll be doing extra patrols in the west for the next few days. They have been noticing a pattern in where you were crossing at the border. I was going to leave this for you to find, but we don't have time for that."

Robert took the paper and read it quickly.

"I'll leave you two to get ready," he said as he stood up. "I need to go and radio our contacts on the other side, We'll need to figure out a new route fast."

He started out of the room but turned to give Jeannine a grateful look.

"We'll talk later about what you're doing," he said as he held up the paper meaningfully.

Then he left the room and we could hear him noisily pulling on his coat and boots before the door slammed and he was off into the twilight.

I looked over at Jeannine, suddenly seeing her in a new light. I now felt bad for all the times I had complained about walking her to the checkpoint to see her boyfriend. I had so many questions now about why she was spying on the Nazis and who she worked for.

"Marcel," she said seriously as if she could read my mind. "Go get ready. Robert will be back for us soon."

She got up and left the room then, leaving me to sit for a moment before I too got up to go get ready. It was going to be a long night and I was finally going to be making a difference.

I had just finished going to the bathroom and finding an extra shirt and sweater when there was a knock at my door and I heard Jeannine say that Robert was back and waiting for us to go. I hurriedly dressed and followed down the hall after her.

When we got downstairs, Robert handed us a couple of dark jackets and motioned for us to put them on.

"You don't want to be wearing your overcoats out there tonight," he said. "We wouldn't want them to snag on any brush and make too much noise."

After we had put the jackets on, Robert motioned for us to follow him out the back of the house.

"Keep the talking to a minimum," he said, pausing at the door. "There will be plenty of time for questions when we're done."

I nodded, and we went out the back into the night.

It was a clear night, the half-moon above us provided just enough light to see with as we made our way down the road in single file. As we approached the end of our lane, Robert motioned us to follow him into the woods. We cut through the trees and headed up toward Le Saléve. Once we were sufficiently off the road, Robert pulled out a lantern that he carefully lit. It had shutters on it so that he could control how much light shone out. He adjusted it so that it provided enough light that we wouldn't walk into the boulders and trees that littered the landscape. We continued on until we came to the base of the cliff.

There we turned left and followed a goat trail off into a nearby copse of trees. I was confused as I had followed this track before and there was nothing but cliffs and trees. But once we had travelled in a little way, Robert paused and waved us close to him. He pointed to a nearby thicket of bushes and signaled us to follow him as he carefully pushed his way through. I followed along after Jeannine and once I was through, was surprised to see an opening to a cave.

No one had mentioned to me that there were caves beneath Le Saléve. I had been warned about the steep trails that were close to the edge of the cliffs and that people fell off and died every so often but not about this. Once we were inside the cave, I shivered as the temperature dropped. It felt moist inside. Robert opened up the lantern to reveal a natural tunnel in the limestone that went back into the mountain. He motioned for us to stay and disappeared down the tunnel with the light.

When he turned the corner ahead, Jeannine and I were left in utter darkness. I had been outside on moonless nights in thick clouds before and thought I knew what the dark was, but it was nothing compared to the pitch blackness of the cave. It made my skin crawl. I stood there listening to the sounds of water dripping and rocks falling in the dark and began to feel as though there was something watching me. I nearly jumped out of my skin when Jeannine reached out and grabbed my hand. There was no way to know how long we stood there, but we were both relieved when we could hear the sounds of footsteps from ahead of us and the lantern appeared.

I blinked and rubbed my eyes as Robert came into view looking like a mother hen with a group of children clustered around him like chicks in the light of the lantern. There were more than I expected. I did a quick count and came up with twenty-three children that looked to be between the ages of eight and fifteen. They were all uniformly filthy from the reddish mud in the cave, and all of them had the same tired look on their faces that said that they had seen too much and slept too little.

As Robert drew close he stopped and spoke in a low voice.

"Listen to me, everyone. We're going to be going on a walk in the woods now. It's mostly downhill but I need everyone to be as quiet as possible. Marcel and Jeannine here will be coming with us to help. But this only works if all of us pay attention to where we are going and don't attract attention. Once we get to the border we'll have about twenty minutes between patrols, so you'll have to move quickly when we tell you to. After you're on the other side there won't be anyone to meet you until you get closer to Troinex but we'll be able to see the lights from the border, so you only have to head toward the lights as fast as you can."

The kids all nodded and looked up at us hopefully as Robert continued.

"I'll go out first to see if anyone is about. When you hear me whistle, I want the kids to come out in groups of five or so until we're all out. Jeannine, I want you to help keep everyone together. Marcel, I want you to follow behind to help keep the stragglers moving." He looked around again before nodding and carefully making his way out of the cave.

After a few moments we heard him whistle and the kids began grouping up and carefully leaving the cave. As I watched them go, I felt restless and tense. Sure, Robert had done this many times before, but it only took one failure to get everyone killed. When it was my turn to follow along after everyone else, I vowed that the failure wouldn't come from me.

I left the cave and we made our way carefully across the country-side. We could have moved faster, since it was all downhill but we still needed to be careful about kicking loose rocks and sending them off noisily down the hill. Everyone did their part though and we made it down into the valley without any incident.

It took us longer than I thought to make our way across the kilometer that separated us from the border. Every time we approached a road or crossed another walking path we had to take the time to make sure that no one else was around before carefully crossing in small groups. It must have been around midnight by the time we were nearing the end of our trek and some of the younger children were beginning to stumble. Several of the older children and I offered to carry them to keep them quiet, and in this way we were able to approach the border without being seen or heard by anyone.

When we got close Robert motioned for everyone to stop and wait while he went ahead. I stood there waiting with my hair held tightly by the little boy sitting on my shoulders. Nearby one of the little boys began to cry, the sound of his sobbing echoing out through the trees.

"Hush!" I said quietly. "You must be quiet."

He didn't stop crying. If anything, I only made things worse.

Robert looked back at us with wide eyes, waiting by the coils of razor wire.

Jeannine went over to the little boy and held him, stroking the back of his head.

"You wouldn't want to wake up the animals that are sleeping here would you?" she asked him quietly. And like magic he calmed down.

We sat there in the blessed silence and waited to hear the alarms of the border patrols. But there was only the sound of the wind through the trees.

Robert removed a log that was lying on the wire to cover up a cut and carefully dragged it far enough for the children to pass through. He began to wave the kids through the fence in small groups. I bent down and let the boy I was carrying off of my back so that he could go with the others and then watched as the last of them disappeared across the field and into the night.

After they had all gone I helped Robert drag the wires back together and carefully conceal the break. Then Robert, Jeannine, and

I made our way back toward home. As we walked along together I took a deep breath and savored the clean smell of the forest at dawn. The smell of fresh bread wafted on the breeze from the boulangerie in the square and finally here in the valley I was as at peace with myself as I was on the mountain.

END OF THE LINE

DAVID H. HENDRICKSON

David H. Hendrickson had to rewrite his bio for "End of the Line" three times, because he had a heck of a great month. First, his story "Death in the Serengeti" from Fiction River: Pulse Pounders Adrenaline *got picked up for* The Best American Mystery Stories. *And then, not long after, the same story won the Derringer Award, honoring excellence in the best short mystery field.*

The rest of his bio remained the same...at least that we know of. He has published seven sports-related novels, which is a natural, considering his long career in sports journalism. His novel Offside, *has been adopted for high school student required reading.*

You'll see more of Dave's work in Fiction River *as well. He has sold to many of the upcoming issues. He had two stories in* Fiction River: Editor Saves. *You'll also find his short fiction in five of our other previous issues.*

About this story, he writes: "I meet my mother for dinner every week at the senior living facility where she now lives. (It serves as the model for the one in this story.) We're often seated with two other residents, some of whom are struggling, as is my mother, with memory issues. Not surprisingly, I find myself writing with increasing frequency about aging."

Dave's amazing ability has taken a story about aging and added a great deal of suspense. Enjoy "End of the Line."

A ll Ferguson had been getting was shit assignments. It had been that way for years. Shit, followed by crap, then finally crapola. And when that was done, Gallagher assigned him shit all over again to restart the cycle. Ferguson could barely remember his last prime assignment, one that had actually made him work at it a little, and not just go through the motions.

He didn't complain. Who was he going to complain to? And who, after listening, would be able to do anything about it? When it came to The Unit, Gallagher answered to no one, and it had been that way for over thirty years, so no one was foolish enough to complain to him. So each time Gallagher dropped a new load of shit on him, Ferguson kept his mouth shut and grabbed a shovel.

This assignment, however, was a new low. Lower than shit, crap, and crapola. Not just beneath him, but beneath him all the way down to the center of the Earth.

An insult to his intelligence, to his abilities, to his decades in The Unit.

Only one way he'd have to work at all on this one.

Sal Saviano's handshake practically broke half the bones in Ferguson's hand. The old man had just turned eighty-one and had lived in the posh retirement home known as Golden Vistas for almost a decade, but he still had his fastball. Still the same distinguished, lawyer-like, thick white hair, the same cinnamon-scented cologne, and the same barrel-shaped chest and thick, powerful forearms that made any handshake with him just another form of hand wrestling. Impeccably dressed, as always, he wore a tailored beige sports jacket over a crisp blue shirt that made Ferguson's unbuttoned winter coat and beneath it, the shiny, black sports jacket and white shirt look shabby by comparison.

Plastic surgery had smoothed out most of Saviano's facial wrinkles, making him look even younger than Ferguson, who was twenty years his junior. And though Saviano needed a walker, he'd blasted out of his apartment without even inviting Ferguson inside, and now was racing double-time with that black-and-maroon walker of his down the hallway, two steps ahead of Ferguson, as if he'd planted a bomb back in his own apartment and they'd better clear the area before it went off.

"You look fabulous, Sal," Ferguson said, quickening his stride to keep up as they streaked past one apartment door after another, each adjacent wall decorated in some unique way: flowers, framed art, and especially, pictures of grandkids and great-grandkids. "I'll bet you're popular with the ladies, just like in the old days. Comforting the widows every afternoon?"

"How you think I broke my hip?" Saviano said, and they both guffawed. The broken hip had necessitated the walker, according to the reports, but otherwise didn't seem to have slowed the old man down.

They stepped onto the elevator, and Saviano pressed the button for the second floor, which, in addition to more apartments, housed the nicest of the five restaurants in the facility, at least according to the reports. This was Ferguson's first visit.

"Are you sure you don't want to go out to eat?" Ferguson asked. "Legal Seafoods. Magianno's. Ruth's Chris for a thick, juicy steak. You name it. Get some fresh air. Get out of this place for a few hours."

"It's thirteen degrees out there," Saviano said, as the elevator door opened. "Down to three or four with the wind chill. I have no interest in freezing my nuts off. If you do, be my guest and I'll meet you back at the apartment in a couple hours."

Ferguson declined.

"Besides, it's near the end of the month, and I haven't used all the meals on my plan. Use 'em or lose 'em. So it's free. And the food's good."

Saviano had always been frugal, Ferguson recalled. Probably why he could afford this most luxurious of retirement homes. He'd also been the best at what they did. A legend. And there had been, no doubt, opportunities on the side.

They stepped off the elevator and Saviano raced off with his walker, once again leaving Ferguson in his wake to hustle and catch up. Saviano passed other residents going the same way like a new, red Ferrari zooming past rusted-out Hyundais, nodding and smiling and waving as he did but never slowing down. Residents walking in the other direction all flashed him warm smiles and the occasional greeting. By the time they reached the restaurant several hundred yards from the elevator, Ferguson's awe for the old man had only increased.

This whole assignment was a waste of time.

Saviano put his name in with the *maître d*, a pretty, dark-haired young woman barely out of high school, and took a buzzer in return. They retired to a side waiting room filled on one side with twenty or so rectangular tables, mostly empty except for men and women playing bridge in one corner and two men played chess in the other. On the other side, a dozen dark brown leather lounge chairs formed a half circle around a blazing fireplace. Saviano ordered them both a glass of Cabernet from a tuxedoed Latin young man, and they settled into a pair of the middle lounge chairs, three chairs away from the nearest resident.

Following Saviano's lead, Ferguson sniffed the wine, then sipped it. It was *good*, far better than the cheap stuff he could afford.

"You've done well," Ferguson said, gesturing to their surroundings as a log in the fireplace snapped.

Saviano smiled. "I'm comfortable. Take down enough tin-pot dictators, and opportunities present themselves. I'm sure that hasn't changed. The spoils of war, my boy. The spoils of war."

Ferguson looked about and behind them, trying to look casual even though every muscle in his body had tightened. When he saw that no one had been close enough to hear—and not even he was paranoid enough to believe their enemies bugged old age homes—he turned back to Saviano, and leaned as close as he could.

"Are you nuts?" Ferguson said. "Someone could have heard you."

Saviano swatted a dismissive hand through the air. "Relax. This is a place for retired CEOs and CFOs. Former doctors, dentists, and lawyers. They're harmless. Although I must say, one of the CEOs is a real bastard!" He chuckled at his own joke. "Not an enemy agent in the bunch. Enemy agents don't live this long." Saviano boomed with even more laughter, and slapped a hand on his knee.

If not for his training, Ferguson would have shifted uneasily in his seat, his hands grown clammy, and his mouth gone dry. Instead, he looked at Saviano impassively as if nothing at all had happened.

"Sal, you need to—"

The pretty *maître d* who had taken Saviano's name approached, smiling pleasantly. "Mr. Saviano, your table is ready."

Carrying his Cabernet for him, she led them to the dining area and a square table at the far end near the windows, where outside darkness had already fallen. The table was set for four with a white tablecloth and two lighted red candles. Before wheeling away Saviano's walker, she gave them their menus and said, "Your two guests are joining you now."

Ferguson frowned. "I thought it would just be the two of us."

"Nonsense," Saviano said with a dismissive flick of the wrist, sitting down to Ferguson's right. "They do this to improve social interaction and everyone here is delightful."

Their two guests were both women, both using walkers which the *maître d* also wheeled away. The younger looking of the two was a redhead named Lydia, who had moved in two years earlier. She sat opposite Saviano. The other woman, sitting opposite Ferguson, was a white-haired, excessively thin, frail-looking woman named Theresa. She'd been there five years, but didn't look to Ferguson as though she'd last much longer.

Their waitress, a high school girl named Julie with brown hair tied back in a ponytail, took their drink orders and in almost no time at all returned with the drinks and fresh, warm bread that smelled of oats, and asked if they were ready to order. They were. Along with the associated salads and soups, Lydia ordered the shrimp scampi over angel hair pasta, Theresa the baked stuffed haddock, Saviano the salmon Florentine, and Ferguson the filet mignon, medium rare.

Almost instantly the waitress arrived with Waldorf salads for all but Theresa, who had opted for the Caesar salad, along with bowls of New England clam chowder for all of them but Theresa.

Ferguson dug into the chowder, thick, and rich, and creamy. It tasted delicious, almost as good as Legal's.

Amidst bites of their salads. the two women shared their favorite activities. Though she'd only been there a short time, Lydia had joined the Bridge Club, the Backgammon Club, and the Classical Music Lovers Society. Theresa had cut back to just the Quilting Club and played lots of mahjong. When it got to Saviano's turn, he leaned close and grinned conspiratorially.

"You fine young ladies, I'm going to tell you a wonderful secret," he announced. "Ferguson here is a...*spy!*"

Ferguson choked and half a mouthful of hot clam chowder backed up into his nose.

"Really?" Lydia exclaimed. "How exciting!"

"Like James Bond," Theresa said, sitting across from Ferguson. "Only not as handsome." She blinked and apparently realizing what she'd just said, put the tips of her fingers over her mouth and turned red. "I am *so* sorry!"

"That's quite all right," Ferguson said with a shrug. "Not even my mother would say I'm as handsome as James Bond." And as Theresa tittered, her hand still over her mouth, he added in a conspiratorial whisper, "But I'm not really a spy."

Ferguson tried to get Saviano's eye, but the old man was having none of it.

"The two of us got shot one time during a top secret operation together in Honduras," Saviano said.

The words sent an icy chill up and down Ferguson's spine. They were all too close to the truth. It had been El Salvador, and they'd both gotten shot, he in the shoulder and Saviano in the rear end.

Ferguson grabbed Saviano's thick forearm and squeezed, but not before the old man added, "I took it in the right buttocks."

"Oh my," Lydia and Theresa said in unison.

Ferguson squeezed harder, as if that could choke off the words, but Saviano's forearms were like chiseled granite. The old man kept grinning and winked. "If you play your cards right, ladies, I just might show it to you."

Lydia blushed and giggled.

"Show what?" Theresa asked.

"His ass!" Lydia answered in a stage whisper, which got them both blushing and giggling like teenagers.

"Could I speak to you privately?" Ferguson said, gritting his teeth and maxing out his pressure on Saviano's arm. He pulled up on the old man's arm, as if to drag him away from the table before realizing

Saviano's walker was gone. Not that he, Ferguson, could drag Saviano anywhere he didn't want to go in the first place.

Ferguson released his grip, and settled back in his chair. If he couldn't drag the old man away from the table or muzzle him somehow, what could he do? He'd have to try something else. There was only so much of this talk that could be laughed off and dismissed. Any more, and he'd have to take drastic measures right here, in full view of everyone, and deal with the consequences later.

The solution came to Ferguson when Lydia asked him, "And where did you get hit?"

Ferguson smiled warmly. "I didn't really get hit by a bullet. And I'm not really a spy. It's a fun fantasy, but I'm actually quite boring. I sell life insurance."

"Really? Theresa said, and took a bite of her salad. "How fascinating."

Before Ferguson could marvel at how anyone could consider life insurance fascinating, Saviano jumped in.

"He got hit in the right shoulder. A couple inches the other way..." Saviano shook his head at the wonder of it. "...and Ferguson here would have been a dead man."

"Oh my," the two ladies said again in unison.

"Where did you say this happened?" Lydia asked.

"Brazil," Saviano said emphatically before Ferguson could stop him.

Ferguson stared at Saviano, who didn't seem to notice any more than the two ladies that he'd switched from one erroneous country to another.

Julie, their waitress, approached with a wide, silver, circular tray loaded down with their entrees. She set it down on a stand ten feet behind Saviano, and brought the first plate over.

"Who had the salmon Florentine?" she asked.

Ferguson waited for Saviano to claim his dish, but the old man sat there unmoving, eyes darting about as did the two women, their faces masks of fear, the fear of a student who has shown up for an exam without having studied.

"I'm sorry," Julie said. "I left my order book back in the kitchen. Let me go get it."

Ferguson gestured toward Saviano. "Sal had the salmon."

"Yes! The salmon!" Saviano said in a near gasp of gratitude. "That's right. I had the salmon."

Ferguson added, "Lydia had the shrimp scampi, Theresa ordered the haddock, and I had the filet."

"Yes!" the women exclaimed. Lydia added, "That's right. I'm sure of it. This young man has saved the day."

Ferguson wasn't so sure that sixty-one ranked as young but he supposed that in this audience it did.

"So many of us are having memory issues," Lydia said. "It's a terrible thing. Oh to be young like you."

He began once again to think of a way to cover the tracks Saviano's motor mouth had left behind when the old man solved the problem.

"Did you know, ladies, that Ferguson here is...a spy?" Saviano asked.

Lydia and Theresa nodded and busied themselves with their food. They had the look of women who had watched this mental deterioration happen to so many others, knowing that someday, the bell of dementia, and maybe even Alzheimer's, might toll for them. So they would not disrespect this man here and point out his failing since they knew it could just as easily be them. Instead, they would act as though they were hearing all this for the first time, even if feigning that same level of surprise was beyond them, because they knew that for Saviano, as far as he knew, he was telling it for the first time.

"We both got shot once," Saviano said, "in Guatemala."

Ferguson wondered if they stayed here long enough, would Saviano complete an entire tour of Latin America, specifying a different country each time, going through all of them except the real one, El Salvador? Probably not. That would be twenty countries.

Well, there wasn't much worry now that these ladies would believe this far-fetched story of spies and getting shot, breaching security. They would dismiss Saviano's words as those of yet another sad dementia case.

"You want to know where I got shot?" Saviano asked. "In the *ass*!" He winked. "And if you play your cards right, ladies, I just might show it to you."

Lydia and Theresa smiled awkwardly, then busily cut their food, as if it had become the most interesting thing in the world.

By the time all of them polished off their entrees and desserts of baked apple pie a la mode, Saviano had repeatedly told of his spying escapades with Ferguson, navigating from the Honduras and Brazil the first time, Guatemala the second, followed by Panama, Bolivia, and Peru.

Ferguson didn't have a worry in the world that either of the ladies believed it.

When the two men got back up to Saviano's apartment on the seventh floor, the old man opened a bottle of Cabernet, and they sat at his small kitchen table, a new one by the looks of it, and using Tiffany crystal wine goblets, toasted to old times and good friends.

"So how is that old bastard, Gallagher?" Saviano asked.

"Still an old bastard," Ferguson said.

He felt badly about what he was going to have to do, but knew it had to be done.

"I would have thought they'd put him out to pasture by now," Saviano said.

"It's a wonder they're keeping any of us old-timers around," Ferguson said. "The new generation is all about technology. Not about brain power and outsmarting the bad guys. It all comes down to an electronic chip that can do this, and another electronic chip that can do that. Not like the old days."

Ferguson wanted to keep talking, to make the end for Saviano as pleasant and as easy as possible. He had to go. There was no question about it at all. Blabbing about one old mission after another left them no choice.

He had to go.

And so Ferguson had palmed the capsule and slipped it into the old man's wine when he wasn't looking. It would be doing the trick any time now. Easy and painless.

Ferguson had thought this was nothing but a shit mission, checking on Saviano like all the guys who had checked on him before, making sure he could still be trusted. It'd be a rubber stamp, he'd thought. Just another shit mission that any flunky could do. Have dinner with the old man. Make sure he still had his marbles.

Well, the old man's body was still good, that barrel chest and Popeye forearms and good looks, but Saviano's mind was going, going, gone.

So the shit mission had turned into an I-gotta-do-a-shitty-thing mission.

Part of the job.

No choice.

But this was a shitty thing.

Just another minute or two. Ferguson sipped his wine.

"I noticed you left out the real country where we got shot," Ferguson said, to pass the time.

"El Salvador," Saviano said, nodding.

"I thought...I thought it was just a subconscious thing what with you..." Ferguson shrugged.

"Me telling the same story five times?" Saviano asked, raising a knowing eyebrow.

"You knew?"

Ferguson tried to get to his feet, but his arms and legs didn't want to work.

"And me forgetting that I ordered salmon Florentine?" Saviano said, shaking his head. "The ladies, Lydia and Theresa, do have memory issues and they're getting worse, especially Theresa. Not bad enough to think my spy story was new each time, but they're starting to have a tough time. I'm sure it'll happen to me sooner or later, too. But not yet."

Ferguson felt an intense need to urinate. A warmth filled his gut and abdomen. He wondered if he'd already let loose.

"What's going on?" he asked, noting his words were slurred.

"You're not the first one who has come to check on me," Saviano said. "You won't be the last."

"But—"

"You thought you were testing me to see if I was still safe, but the test was a double-edged sword. You were being tested, too."

Ferguson felt the warmth inside his chest about to explode. "But it was supposed to be *you*. You, if you were...if you were a threat."

"I keep going as long as I can outsmart the likes of you," Saviano said. "When I retired, that was my deal with Gallagher, that sonuvabitch. It was really a stroke a genius, if I don't say so myself. He could send me the likes of you, the end-of-the-line cases he thought should be terminated, and if they got the best of me—without employing brutish techniques, of course, since no one is a match for a bullet, a knife, or a garrote—then that would let him know they weren't quite at the end of the line.

"So for Gallagher, this is a win-win. I either thin his herd for him, rid him of all of you over-the-hill types who don't have your fastball anymore, or if you finish me off, then I was a danger he's gotten rid of, and he's gotten proof you still have what it takes. You walk away, knowing it'll look like I've died of natural causes. He calls off the disposal team that's scheduled to arrive with a replacement for my perpetually faulty refrigerator, or with a new piece of furniture, or perhaps—" Saviano licked his lips "—four or five cases of my favorite Cabernet. The team wheels in *something* in a large boxed crate, and leaves with a significantly heavier boxed crate. In your case, about two hundred pounds heavier."

Ferguson wanted to argue that he still had his fastball. That he wasn't ready to get stuffed into a refrigerator or whatever boxed crate was waiting for him.

But his mouth wouldn't work. His mind wasn't doing so well either. It felt like a cloudy, spinning mess.

"Think of it, my friend," Saviano said in a soft, hypnotic voice. "How long has it been since Gallagher gave you a really prime assignment? How long since he trusted you with anything good?"

Forever! Ferguson wanted to shout the word, wanted to scream it. His lips tried to form the letter F but could not.

"Turns out, he was right," Saviano said. "You got sloppy tonight, very sloppy, thinking I was just an old fool." He smiled wanly. "I am not an old fool."

No, he wasn't, Ferguson had to admit, his heart sinking even as the fire in his chest raged and the numbness spread down his legs. *I'm the old fool. He conned me good, and he didn't even have to work at it.*

I haven't just lost my fastball, I've lost my curve and changeup, too.

"But I also am not a cruel man. Better that I send you off into the night than one of our enemies," Saviano said gently.

Ferguson's eyes felt impossibly heavy. All about the room everything was growing dark and cold.

"And so my friend," Saviano said, "on behalf of our government and that bastard Gallagher, I thank you for your service. Good night, and farewell."

And in the instant before his lights went out for the final time, Ferguson nodded.

THE FLORENTINE EXCHANGE

DAYLE A. DERMATIS

Dave's story brings spies together in the same room, and so does Dayle's. "The Florentine Exchange" was nearly the volume's opening story, because it seems traditional, although it does subvert traditional spy story gender norms. But, surprisingly to me, I didn't get many other stories like it, so I decided that as the lead-off, this story would lead readers to think they'd find more stories like it...and there are no stories like this one.

Dayle is a Fiction River *regular. She's published so many stories in our pages that she's lost count. We haven't. Thirteen so far, most recently in* Wishes. *She has edited a volume of* Fiction River, Doorways to Enchantment, *which will appear in 2019.*

Her non Fiction River *stories, more than a hundred of them in multiple genres, have appeared in a variety of venues, including* Alfred Hitchcock's Mystery Magazine *and* The Best New England Crime Stories. *Her most recent novel is* Ghosted, *which features Nikki Ashburne, a character who made her first appearance in* Fiction River.

There are no ghosts here. Just some highly suspenseful twists and turns and some fascinating spies.

L ibby normally didn't mind the narrow, five-story staircase that spiraled up to their apartment at the top of the 15th-century former monastery, because the lack of elevator was a small price to pay for living in Florence, Italy—and living her dream job in covert operations.

She minded the lack of air conditioning, however, especially on days like this: hot, stuffy, breezeless, with only a few high clouds that did nothing to break the sun's spell. The wooden stair treads dipped and angled, worn by centuries of footfalls; if she didn't step carefully, she'd trip. The only minor plus was that the building smelled of tomato sauce and oregano and onions—a vast improvement from the odor of exhaust trapped in the narrow streets outside.

By the time she'd lugged the heavy bag of clean laundry up the stairs, she was sticky with humidity and ready to peel off her damp clothes and throw them right into the bag. The problem with going to a launderette was you couldn't be naked while you washed your clothes.

She unlocked the door and shoved it with her shoulder—the wood always swelled and the upper right corner stuck—and stumbled inside.

The studio apartment was long and narrow, with unadorned white walls, tall enough that there was room for a loft at one end. You could stand beneath the loft, but only sit upright, not stand, when you were up there. The loft had the only window, so they'd dragged the mattresses up there to sleep, grateful for the cooler night air.

She assumed Antonia had already left for her assignment, but then she heard the toilet flush. The bathroom had been added at a later time, a boxy corner room with a ceiling as high as the loft floor, creating a flat surface above, where they'd shoved suitcases and other things they didn't use regularly. From the loft, you had a view of the dust in the corners.

When Antonia emerged, Libby took in the details in one glance, just as she'd been trained: The fact that Antonia was wearing cut-off grey sweatpants and a red tank top when she should have been dressed for the cocktail reception at which she was assigned to do a data exchange. The fact that Antonia was barefoot, hopping on her right foot. The fact that an Ace bandage figure-eighted around her left ankle and foot.

Antonia—tiny, ashy-blond, and surprisingly unassuming when she was bare-faced and uncoiffed—grimaced. She hopped the few feet to the broken-springed loveseat and collapsed into it sideways, propping her leg up on the far arm.

"What happened?" Libby asked, dropping the laundry on the wooden straight chair that served as a dining chair, desk chair, and the only other seating in the apartment.

"My own stupidity," Antonia said. "You'll have to go to the embassy event instead. It's a simple exchange. You're ready for it." She glanced at her watch. "How soon can you leave?"

Soon enough, because that was the job. Libby had learned how to shower, dress, do makeup and hair in record time. She didn't wash her hair, just rinsed the sweat off her body under the shower nozzle that stuck out of the bathroom wall, no curtain or surround, one of those weird Italian things she'd grown used to, along with no wash-cloths and the disturbingly frequent public toilets without seats.

She was here largely as backup for Antonia, a more seasoned agent, and to learn from her. This would be her first solo assignment.

The flurry in her stomach wasn't nerves. Like Antonia had said, it was a simple exchange. She already knew who her contact was; Antonia had gone over that with her as a training exercise. LIbby was finally getting to *do* something that was real, not a test, not a simulation.

She twisted her hair up into an artfully messy knot, the dampness making it easier to style, actually. Long and dyed dark brown, so she didn't stand out. Italian men noticed blonds, fawned over redheads. They commented on her height, five-foot-ten in bare feet (and nobody went barefoot in Italy), but there was little she could do about that except not wear the sky-high heels so fashionable nowa-days. Easier to run, maneuver, fight if it came to that, in lower heels anyway.

Before Antonia zipped her into her cocktail dress, a sleek dark red number with a plunging neckline, Libby knelt in the bathroom, pulled out the plastic tub of cleaning supplies under the sink, pried up the false bottom in the cabinet, and opened the small, flat safe beneath.

She grabbed the ID she'd need—the one naming her as the daughter of a diplomat, just the type of person who'd be attending one of these parties—and the tiny thumb drive she'd be passing on to her contact. The drive was smaller than her thumbnail, no more than the part that inserted into a computer and the cover to protect it.

A quick glance in the mirror. Hair good, makeup good. A sedate strand of pearls around her neck, with complementary pearl-and-gold earrings and pin.

Then it was quickly back down the wooden spiral staircase, all five stories, the click of her heels echoing.

Late afternoon sun slanted down the narrow street, turning the sandstone walls to gold and the terra cotta roofs to burnished flame. As the blissfully air-conditioned taxi pulled into a wider street, she could see the sky cast in shades of butter and salmon, a sight that thrilled her every evening.

She settled back against the seat and opened her purse. It had room for a slim wallet and her passport, lipstick and powder and emergency tampon, and her phone...as well as a secret compartment for her gun. She dipped into the main section to grab the thumb drive, intending to transfer it to the private compartment, but came up with a few coins and *two* thumb drives.

Two identical thumb drives.

She'd washed a few of Antonia's clothes at the launderette along with her own, and when she'd checked the pockets of one pair of slacks, she'd dumped the loose change into her purse. Apparently there had been a tiny thumb drive as well, jumbled with the coins.

She examined both drives. Same brand, size; both black. No way to tell them apart unless she looked at the contents of each.

And that wasn't something she could do in the cab.

Antonia waited a full five minutes after Libby's departure, patiently counting the seconds and minutes, just to make sure Libby didn't run back because she'd forgotten something. Antonia didn't expect that. Libby was at the very least conscientious, and at most borderline obsessive; she rarely forgot anything.

She was just young, naïve, and easily manipulated.

Antonia lounged on the sagging loveseat, still and sure, and when the five minutes were up, she sat up and stripped the Ace bandage from her perfectly fine ankle.

Libby would exchange the fake thumb drive with her contact,

and Antonia would pass on the real one to someone who was willing to pay a hell of a lot more money than Antonia's meager salary.

She hadn't been expecting glitz and glamour, sure, but she also hadn't expected to be dumped in a shitty box of an apartment that felt like a sauna or to be expected to act as an errand girl.

She was done. Beyond done.

She headed to the bathroom, stripping out of her shorts and tank top on the way, leaving them where they fell, and dug down to the safe beneath the sink. She grabbed her various passports—she'd dispose of the government-issued ones later, keep only the one she'd had made—and the stacks of cash from all over the world, more than enough to get her out of the country.

A few steps across the room and she was at her wardrobe, a prefab, rickety thing tucked under the loft. She'd cultivated a habit of being messy, of scattering things around, to keep Libby from noticing things out of place. Habits were deadly in this business. So instead of putting the clothes she planned to wear somewhere obvious, such as laid out or hung at the front of the wardrobe, she'd tossed them in the bottom of the wardrobe with a few other random items, an ever-changing mishmash.

But the pale pink, three-quarter-sleeve shirt and the oatmeal-colored wide-legged linen pants were gone. The bras, the scarf, the jumble of shoes was still there, but no outfit.

Antonia stared, stunned, for a moment before whirling to scan the rest of the room. When her gaze hit the mesh laundry bag Libby had dropped on the chair by the door, she muttered a few choice curse words under her breath.

When Libby had said she was going to do laundry and did Antonia want her to throw any of her things in, Antonia had called out from the bathroom, where she'd been showering, to grab whatever was lying around—figuring Libby would pick up the items on the bed, draped over the chair, kicked in the corner. She'd never thought Libby would look in the wardrobe for dirty laundry.

But Libby was precise, thorough.

Antonia had underestimated Libby, and that was her own damn fault.

She upended the laundry bag onto Libby's bed, dumping the carefully folded clothes into a jumbled heap, and pawed through. Found her slacks.

The pockets were empty.

Antonia threw the slacks across the room.

Then she stood stock still, took in a low, slow, deep breath, and composed herself.

She had to think, make a plan. Stay focused.

Libby had both drives. The question was, did she realize it? Probably. Did she know what was on each drive? She wouldn't know which one to exchange otherwise.

Libby followed rules. Her job was to deliver the correct drive. She'd do everything possible to complete that job.

So, Antonia had to get to Libby before Libby exchanged the drive Antonia needed.

Antonia went back to the wardrobe and yanked out a new outfit.

In Italian, Libby asked the driver for a new destination: the Santa Maria Novella station, Florence's train hub. She paid him in cash, with a nice but unmemorable tip, and went inside.

The last of the sunlight streamed through the panes of glass that made up the roof and a sloping wall that reached the top of the ticket counters, dappling the heads of the travelers. A busy time of day, which was good—everyone was focused on their destination, on catching their train or getting outside to continue on their way, and not focused on each other. Beneath the hum of conversation, Libby's heels clicked on the floor of long stripes of veined marble, alternating off-white and dusty rose.

Past the people smelling of perfume and aftershave and body odor, past the ticket booths and machines, past the shops selling sandwiches and coffee and last-minute travel wares and gifts, to the storage room with its walls of lockers, a place for day tourists to store their travel gear.

From one of the lockers, Libby pulled a shopping bag, red with an understated gold logo, from a high-end, expensive boutique. The kind that ladies of leisure all over the city carried on a day of browsing; the kind nobody would look twice at. Her emergency stash.

She locked the locker, pocketed the key. She'd toss it somewhere after she wiped it down, just to be safe.

Back outside, where the sun hovered on the horizon, casting long shadows, she hailed another blessedly air-conditioned taxi to take her to the cocktail party.

She sat in the back behind the passenger seat; the driver would have to turn his head to see her, not just glance in his mirror. Holding her items below his sightline, she pulled a small device, which looked like an external phone battery, from the shopping bag and inserted one end into her phone. In the other, she slipped one of the thumb drives.

Although her phone didn't have all the functionality of a computer, it did have some extra capabilities—thanks to her employer—that would allow her to get a general sense of what was on the two drives.

It was easy to tell the difference, at least. The false drive initially looked as though it contained the correct information, but the files were too small.

Then again, the operative slated to receive the drive wouldn't have the chance to look at it until well after the exchange had been made, and by then it would have been too late.

Libby touched her teeth to her lower lip; not actively chewing on it, though, which would have marred her lipstick.

Did Antonia have a separate job, one she hadn't been allowed to tell Libby about? It was possible, but unlikely. Libby had been sent here to shadow Antonia, to learn from her. As far as she'd been led to believe, they had the same clearance. There was no reason for Libby not to know Antonia's schedule.

Libby shook her head, and put each drive in a separate place in her purse, making sure she knew which one was which. She tucked the device reader back into the shopping bag, beneath the folds of tissue paper that covered some new items from the high-end store, just as the taxi pulled up at her destination.

Whatever weirdness was going on with Antonia, the bottom line was that Libby had a job to do.

She'd worry about the rest of it later.

Antonia slipped into the black skirt that skimmed just below her knees and the plain white button-down shirt, pairing the outfit with low-heeled black pumps. Added a wig: a short black bob. About as unassuming an outfit she could put together, rendering herself as invisible as she could manage.

She was sweating. Moving too quickly in this stifling, monk's cell excuse for an apartment. Speed was of the essence, but not so much that she'd make a mistake. She took another long, slow breath in, out, calming herself.

She considered calling their boss, claiming Libby had gone rogue or some other excuse that would get Libby's fake passport blocked so she couldn't enter the party. But there was no telling how long that would take, and it would put the spotlight on Antonia, too.

She couldn't risk that.

She had to do this herself.

She grabbed one of her few extravagances: a breathtakingly expensive tote bag, buttery-soft black Italian leather with gold buckles. She stashed in it the passports and money, and a few other essentials she'd need over the next few days.

She'd planned to just leave, but now she had to get the thumb drive back first.

When the apartment door stuck, she didn't bother to yank it all the way shut, much less lock it, before she headed down the worn wooden staircase. Let someone steal everything. It wasn't her problem anymore. She wouldn't be coming back.

And depending on how things went down, Libby might not, either.

———

The cocktail party was being held at Casa Martelli, a fifteenth-century house that had been turned into a museum, still preserved in its original state to show how a wealthy Medici-era family would have lived. Libby had been on the guided tour already; she'd taken advantage of being stationed in Florence by hitting all the sites.

She handed her ID to the black-suited security guard at the door. He scanned it, glanced at the information that came up on his tablet.

"Welcome, Signora Parker," he said in accented English as he handed her passport back.

"Grazie," she responded. "Is there a place I can safely put this?" She held up the shopping bag.

He directed her to a small room set up as a coat check, where a bored attendant—nobody had coats to check on this still-warm evening—took her bag, gave her a numbered ticket, and set the bag next to a short line of leather briefcases, no doubt from diplomats stopping at the party on their way home from work.

She glanced at the slim gold watch on her wrist. She was actually a few minutes early. She had time to order a glass of Pellegrino fizzy water from the bar and fill a tiny plate with a few delicacies: prosciutto-wrapped melon; carefully stacked slices of red tomatoes, fresh white mozzarella and green basil leaves; glistening black caviar on toast points topped with a tiny dollop of cream.

One of the rules was, eat when you can safely do so. You never know where your next meal will be coming from, or what it might contain.

Libby made her way through the room of gold wallpaper, the blue-painted room covered in paintings and a very prominent crucifix, and finally to the one of the rooms with its walls covered with frescoes.

The Winter Garden Room had supposedly been painted to make

up for the fact that the house had no outdoor garden space. It was breathtaking. Vines trailed up columns and across the vaulted ceiling. Vine-covered arches opened onto scenes of the city, or of fountains with the setting sun glowing in the distance.

Libby eased her way among partygoers to reach a wall near one corner. Between two painted, vine-spiraled columns and beneath an actual real window, two painted cats played at the edge of a fountain.

She finished her hors d'oeuvres, passed the plate to a red-vested waiter, and sipped her Pellegrino.

A moment later, a man stepped up next to her.

As expected, he wore a pink pocket square with slate-grey dots in his grey suit jacket.

She made a miniscule gesture with her glass. "I believe cats to be spirits come to earth."

"A cat, I am sure, could walk on a cloud without coming through," he said, finishing the Jules Verne quote and thus confirming himself as her contact.

He was a tall black man, handsome despite the acne scars pitting his cheeks. Or perhaps because of; they gave his face character.

They both spoke Italian, but his had the slightest of French accents beneath.

"You're not who I expected," he said. His expression didn't change, but she heard the thread of suspicion in his voice.

Shit. Antonia should have let her handler know Libby would be making the exchange, allowing the information to pass through the appropriate channels.

Maybe there hadn't been time.

Then again, the second flash drive put Antonia under suspicion in a major way.

Libby had to decide what to do, and fast.

Antonia had the taxi driver drop her off a block and a half away from Casa Martelli. She would have done that in any instance, to disguise her true destination and to give her time to see if she'd been followed. But Casa Martelli was sandwiched in between shops, the entire block of buildings snugging up against each other as if expecting a siege. The only way to the back door was through narrow alleys twisting between those buildings, accessible one street over.

The air cooled a few degrees in the high-walled alleys where the slanted rays of the sun didn't reach. Pigeons cooed in the recesses in the bricks high above as the street noise faded the deeper she went.

Antonia knocked at the back door of Casa Martelli. She had to wait several minutes before someone answered, a harried-looking man who opened the door with an exasperated "What?" in Italian.

Well, dammit. She'd gotten the white button-down and black skirt right, but the wait staff uniforms for this function apparently also included red vests.

If you were dressed similarly enough, were pretty (or handsome) without being overly so, and had a tray of drinks or delectable-looking morsels, nobody noticed you weren't in the exact uniform of the rest of the wait staff.

Now, she could either stay with her initial plan of sweet-talking her way in, claiming to be a member of the staff who had gotten lost (and forgotten her vest), or she could go with Plan B.

She'd stick out like a sore thumb without the vest. Plan B it was.

She spoke softly, indicating her throat as if to imply she had laryngitis, and used a mix of broken Italian and English.

The waiter leaned close to hear her.

She jammed the syringe into his neck.

His eyes widened and he gave a short bark of surprise, but thankfully nobody heard. The drug didn't knock him out immediately, but made him both woozy and pliable as it entered his bloodstream. Antonia was able to support him, stumbling, around the corner of the alley, where he finally collapsed. Good. Another member of the wait staff stepping outside for a cigarette wouldn't see him.

He wouldn't come to until she was well gone, and he'd have a spot of amnesia covering a few hours before his attack.

It took a few moments to roll him this way and that so she could strip the vest off him. It was far too big for her, but she grabbed a few safety pins from her tote and nipped in the seams, which helped.

She pulled a plastic trash bag from her tote and stuffed the tote into it, setting the bag in the small pile of trash already by the back door. She'd do what she needed to do and be back before anyone cleared away the garbage.

Then she slipped inside, grabbed a tray of bacon-wrapped figs, and popped one in her mouth. The bacon had been soaked in maple syrup, and the taste was incredible.

Tray in hand, she entered the cocktail party.

Libby tapped the gold-and-pearl pin at her shoulder, activating the sound cancelling that would pick the ambient music—a string quartet in the next room—rather than their conversation.

"I think my partner has been compromised," she said to her contact. "She sent me here in her place. Check the information on the drive carefully. She tried to replace it, but I found what I believe is the original, which I'm giving to you."

"Why don't you give me both?" he asked.

Fair question. "I need proof about what she's done."

He nodded slowly, and reached into his pocket, presumably to retrieve the drive he'd exchange for hers.

She'd turned from the frescoed wall once he'd arrived, keeping a casual eye on the room. She saw Antonia, dressed as wait staff in an ill-fitting red vest, a black wig not disguise enough. She froze.

"She's here," she murmured. "I have to go. We'll reschedule the drop. I'm sorry."

He was already scanning the crowd, but Libby was gone, ducking left and then right through the partygoers, losing herself in the small crowd. It wasn't easy at her height, but most people had imbibed at least one drink, and she'd learned how to hunch, to make herself less obvious.

Her heart pounded in her throat. Antonia must have discovered the missing thumb drive faster than Libby had expected.

If Antonia wanted that drive, she'd stop at nothing to get it. Libby was sure of that. Antonia might be a casual slob, might take her duties lightly, but she had an undercurrent of steeliness that she'd tried to hide from Libby.

Unbeknownst to Antonia, she'd failed at that.

Libby threw her ticket at the coat check attendant and forced herself not to grab her own bag, but let the attendant hand it to her. She had to not be too obvious, too memorable. That meant people would pay attention. Remember her.

She ducked into the ladies room, locked the door, and yanked things out of her shopping bag.

A few moments later, she exited the back door—the wait staff were too busy to notice her, even as unassuming as she was.

Her shapeless black dress was padded so she looked heavier, and she hunched her shoulders. She'd changed her shoes to black, soft-soled lace-ups, one of which had a pebble in it to throw her gait off, make her limp slightly. Half of her hair was shoved under a big straw hat that obscured her face; the other half straggled down, giving the impression that her hair was thinner than it was.

The rest of her belongings, including the high-end shopping bag, were stuffed in a generic woven-string market bag.

All of it told the casual eye: I'm old. I'm nobody. I'm an average, unassuming Italian matriarch headed home to make dinner.

It was only a ten-minute walk to the Arno River, but she took a good forty minutes, wandering down alleys and side streets, alert to any sign of a tail.

Libby was good—Antonia would give her that much. It didn't surprise Antonia; Libby surely would have taken her training seriously, focused on doing everything right.

Unfortunately for Libby, Antonia had put a tracking software on her phone ages ago. If Libby ever found it, Antonia would have said it was a test to see how fast Libby found it. She hadn't thus far.

So as soon as Antonia figured out where Libby was going, she abandoned trying to track her through the streets and doubled back.

She knew how to get there first.

Libby was stepping onto Ponte Vecchio, one of the most famous bridges in the world.

Dating back to the Middle Ages, the stone bridge over the Arno River was lined with shops along each side. Originally butcher shops, they now housed primarily jewelry shops catering to the tourists.

Tourists who were still crowding the bridge on this balmy summer evening, taking advantage of the later shopping hours. Now that the sun had set, the air had cooled, soft on Antonia's face.

Libby would have to fight her way through that throng...but there was another way across the Ponte Vecchio.

In the sixteenth century, Cosimo de Medici had ordered built an enclosed corridor along the top of the shops to ease his passage between his palace and the town hall. About ten years ago, the Vasari Corridor had been opened for public tours. Then, last year, it had been closed again for maintenance.

Antonia knew where the entrance was on this side of the river.

Either Libby intended to lose herself in the crowd—in which case Antonia would be waiting for her on the other side—or Libby knew of another entrance to the corridor—in which case Antonia would meet her inside.

And if Libby doubled back, the tracking software would let Antonia know. She could be at either end before Libby.

Then she could get the damn thumb drive back, hopefully the drive from their contact as well, and be on her way to her money and freedom.

She wasn't going to let by-the-rules Libby ruin everything for her.

Libby cut her way through the crowd, occasionally murmuring,

"Scusami. Scusami, grazie." People paid her little mind, barely glanced at her. Her hip hurt, thanks to the pebble that made her limp. She was dearly looking forward to fixing that problem.

It was no doubt the least of her problems.

But she was close to her goal, and she hadn't spotted a tail. She hunched a little shorter, continuing to make her height less conspicuous and give the impression of age. Her soft-soled shoes made no sound on the stone bridge, not that footsteps would be audible above the sounds of chattering tourists.

About a quarter of the way down, she ducked into a shop between the glass cases that bordered the door. She nodded at the shop clerk, and asked, in Italian, for Mondavian gold.

Something that didn't exist.

The man nodded in recognition and drew her to the back of the shop as if to show her what she sought. Once the shop was empty, she slipped through the door into the back storage area.

Then it was a simple matter of sliding a shelving unit sideways, unlocking the door behind it, sliding the shelf back after she'd entered the tiny room, and squeezing into a corner so she could swing the door back shut and lock it again.

She'd paid the shopkeepers handsomely for this, after poring over schematics of the Ponte Vecchio and the Vasari Corridor—private schematics she'd also paid handsomely for the privilege of viewing.

The room she was now in was little more than a wide square chimney with ancient iron hand- and footholds affixed into the stone, leading up. The only light was from a tiny bit that bled around the door from the shop's storage room, but Libby had done this once with a flashlight in her teeth, and didn't need more practice than that.

She climbed the ladder, counting the rungs to know when she'd reached the top. Then, she unlocked the door there and entered a storage closet, and from there stepped into the Vasari Corridor.

The floor was brick-red tiles in a herringbone pattern; the walls were pale cream. No paintings hung on the walls now, as they did when the passageway was open for tours. The evenly spaced windows high on the outer wall didn't provide light now at night, but a series of pale emergency lights along the wall near the floor, each about a foot long with a molded opaque white cover, gave a little illumination.

Just enough to see the hulking outlines of the scaffolding, the piles of materials, the locked toolboxes.

Antonia had impressed upon her the importance of stashing a go-bag somewhere in the city, in case she had to leave quickly but couldn't get back to the apartment. The train station lockers made sense, because that made it easy to leave by public transportation. Antonia probably had a bag stashed there, too.

Libby seriously doubted Antonia knew she had this one.

She popped open the front casing on one of the small modern light fixtures near the floor and used the folds of her skirt to protect her fingers as she removed the hot bulb. Then she carefully unscrewed the fixture, and reached behind to find the small canvas bag she'd left there.

Passport, money, a burner phone. The bare essentials for an escape, in case she was compromised and in danger, and the American Embassy wasn't an option.

She shoved it into her string bag, then removed her shoe and shook out the offending pebble. She didn't bother to replace the light. So what if someone came across it tomorrow? She'd be long gone.

She leaned against the wall. She'd wait a bit, just to make sure no one had followed her onto the Ponte Vecchio below.

Then she heard a noise down the corridor. A metallic hum, as if someone had brushed against scaffolding, then stopped the vibration with their hand on the piping.

Not breathing, Libby slowly, silently reached for her gun, and hid it in the folds of her skirt.

Antonia—or someone—had found her after all.

Antonia crept forward, barefoot, her shoes in her tote. The bare, enclosed corridor would amplify footsteps. She'd barely brushed against the scaffolding, and caught it a moment after it hummed, but she still cursed herself, cursed her eyes that hadn't fully adjusted to the dim emergency lights.

Couldn't be helped now.

She was rushing too much. Picking the lock without being seen had taken longer than she'd expected. The noises she'd heard up ahead must be Libby.

She was so over this. Over Florence, over Libby, over the job.

That was no reason to get sloppy, though.

So she changed her tactic and walked up to Libby as if she owned the damn place.

"What are you doing hiding in here, Libby?" she asked. "This isn't part of the drop."

Libby was on her feet, standing next to the net shopping bag she'd been carrying. Her hand was half-hidden in the folds of her skirt. Probably concealing her gun.

She wouldn't shoot unless she had to, though. Libby's training was solid, and she followed rules. Antonia could use that to her advantage, if it came to it.

"I ended up with two thumb drives," Libby said. "That was weird, so I knew something was up. I thought it would be safer to lie low and monitor the situation."

Antonia mentally rolled her eyes. "You panicked. And your disguise wasn't nearly good enough: I picked you out right away."

"So why'd it take you so long to get to me?" Libby asked.

"*I* was monitoring *you*," Antonia said. "This was a test."

Libby shook her head. "If this was a test, then call HQ and have them confirm it."

Well, it had been worth a try.

"Just give me the thumb drive, Libby."

"I don't have it," Libby said. "I made the exchange."

"Then give me the drive you received."

"I don't have it on me."

"Then take me to it," Antonia said. "Just give me one of the drives—one of the real drives—and I'll be out of your hair."

"You haven't been following me around Florence just to get the drive and let me go," Libby said.

"Okay, then," Antonia said amiably, because she'd long guessed it was going to come to this. "Then I'll shoot you and take the drive."

She saw Libby's hand move in the folds of her skirt.

Two painfully loud reports, almost simultaneous, slammed through the corridor.

Libby's ears rang, aching from the gunshot. But she was alive, somehow. She'd brought her gun out, but Antonia had been faster....

Now, as Antonia spun and crumpled to the ground, crimson blossoming on the front of her white button-down blouse, Libby stared in shock at the tall black man who'd come up behind Antonia. Her contact from the cocktail party.

"How did you...?" She automatically spoke in Italian.

He shrugged as he stepped forward, sliding his gun under his jacket. "When I saw your partner leave after you, I followed her. She didn't expect a tail, so she never noticed. Sloppy."

Libby's cheek stung. She touched it, and in the dim light saw plaster dust and a smear of blood. Antonia's shot had just missed Libby's head, ricocheting off the plaster wall. Some of the plaster must have grazed her.

"But why?" Libby asked the man, her mind spinning through possible scenarios. Her heart was slowing to normal, thanks to her training.

"You said she might be compromised, and I was concerned for your safety. I don't leave fellow agents behind."

Libby knelt beside Antonia's body. Antonia's gun had fallen next to her hand, half under her lifeless form. She leaned closer, peering at her. "That's odd," she said.

"What?" the other agent asked, squatting down on the other side of the body.

Libby shot him in the head with Antonia's gun.

"I'm sorry," she said, only half-meaning it. His damn gallantry had ruined everything. He'd expect her to come with him, sort things out together, be her backup when she gave her report—and she didn't have time for any of that. Her cover was blown here, and he was the only witness. She had to get away before anyone else in the American agency came looking for her or Antonia.

Libby eased the gun, which she'd held in the fabric of her skirt to avoid leaving prints, into Antonia's hand. Let them sort out who'd killed who, the hows and the whys of it.

As for Antonia... Libby sniffed as she checked the woman's pockets for anything useful—or incriminating. Antonia wasn't much better than a child playing at spycraft. She'd fallen so easily for Libby's ruses: the pretense of following rules, the neatness, the good humor.

Of course, they all had. She'd found it amusing to go through all the training a second time in a new country, passing herself off as an American, never quite doing things perfectly so she didn't stand out, didn't look suspicious. Learning a few secrets along the way.

Her assignment had been to stay deeply imbedded in the American system, but this incident changed things.

It was time to go home.

Elizaveta Papanova was going home, out of the sticky humidity and back to the crisp, chill air of her beloved Russia....

At least until her next assignment.

THE MESSAGE

C.A. ROWLAND

We go from two female spies in modern Italy to two female spies in 1860s Virginia. C.A. Rowland combines well-known historical figures and famous spies with a fascinating look at life in the Civil War South.

C.A. has a deep interest in history. She writes: "When I first moved to Virginia, I lived in a subdivision called Mosby Woods. That sparked my interest in Mosby, who was a Confederate colonel during the Civil War and why he was important. When I first approached the idea of a spies story, I was intrigued with unlikely spies and possible women spies during the Civil War. That search led me to a number of women, including Antonia Ford who crossed paths with Mosby..."

"The Message" marks C.A's first appearance in Fiction River, *but not her last.*

S issie stood in the corner in the gathering shadows, her faded blue and white checked dress, a hand-me-down from another servant who'd been handed down the same dress from Miss Antonia, melding with the whitewashed walls. Silent and still as she'd been taught, her dark brown hands clasped together. Close by in case Miss Antonia needed her. She edged toward the window as she listened to the scratching against the paper. Miss Antonia had been sitting at the rectangular dressing table that served as her desk for nigh on two hours now. Sissie wondered what was so important.

Bam. Bam. Fists pounded on the front door of the red brick colonial serving as a temporary home for Master James and his daughter. Sissie started at the noise. She knew the family and some servants had moved to Fairfax after fleeing their plantation fifty miles away. Master James had Confederate friends who were allowing them the use of the house while the friends stayed with their children. Sissie wondered why Master James had chosen Fairfax since it didn't seem safe with all the Union soldiers around but she figured Master James must have his reasons.

An arrival with the last rays of the yellow orange sun could not be good news. Sissie glanced out the second story window, catching sight of the horse-drawn buggy before she turned back to check her mistress. Miss Antonia's face had paled against her brown hair, parted in the middle and gathered in a bun at the back of her neck. Since being confined to the house by the Union forces that frequented her home, Miss Antonia had only worn black dresses with white collars. A small resistance but one Sissie knew was important to her.

"Quickly, open the chest," Miss Antonia said as she stood.

"Yes ma'am," Sissie said as she stepped to the end of the bed, lifting the heavy cedar chest lid and releasing the stagnant smell. She helped lay the quill and ink bottle inside, and cover them with bed clothes. Sissie added Miss Antonia's fabric sewing kit holding her needles, together with the thread she used to alter clothes for the servants. Sissie had been with Miss Antonia for three years and there were not many hiding places she didn't know. She moved quickly.

Even with the warming spring, Sissie's bare feet welcomed the warmth of the wool rug on the floor, her skirt swishing as she moved. Virginia winters brought ice and snow. With the scarcity of wood, the red brick fireplace was used only when the temperature was unbearable. Still, the smell of burnt wood hung in the air throughout the house. Sissie could almost taste the bread she knew was cooking below.

The kitchen was on the first floor, with another brick fireplace for cooking, on the opposite side of the house. On days such as this, the downstairs fireplace warmed the lower floor and added a bit of heat to the side of the house with Miss Antonia's room.

The canopy bed dominated the room, covered with a cotton coverlet. Candles sat everywhere since Miss Antonia read late in the day. Talking was her second love since they'd arrived in Fairfax. Telling Sissie how wonderful things would be when the war was over. Food aplenty. Men and women free to visit and go to parties. Of course, Miss Antonia was talking about white folks. Not Sissie or her kind.

Miss Antonia had nearly talked Sissie's ear off the first weeks, before Miss Antonia had made a few acquaintances. Then she sent Sissie to this shop and that one, sometimes just to look to see what they had. So different from the plantation house where Miss Antonia's orders were quick and to the point—"Bake bread today. Gather a bucket of pecans. Bring in a load of firewood." Everything had had a purpose and Miss Antonia had little time for trifling matters. There, Miss Antonia had been free to come and go, as long as the men her father traded with were treated with hospitality, unlike here where movements were restricted and it felt like eyes were everywhere, watching.

The world just seemed to be like a bucket turned over with everything running amuck and mixed up all kinds of different ways. Only last week Sissie had overheard that the plantation house had been burned to the ground several weeks ago in a battle. Sissie liked knowing what was expected of her and when. In this town, every day brought something or someone new to the door that could turn the household upside down.

Today was rainy and the air was thick with moisture. No doubt the men who were at the door would track in mud from the street. Miss Antonia gathered up the paper she'd been writing, blew on it to set the ink, then layered it between her underclothes and petticoat, and the outer black dress. No man had yet been willing to search her or require that she stand. Several had asked but she'd stood her ground until they left. Sissie wondered if there was a man alive capable of that feat. Maybe Miss Antonia's daddy, but no one else.

Miss Antonia gestured for Sissie to take up her station in the corner, as she asked, "What did you see?"

"Nothing, ma'am."

"Don't lie. I saw you look outside. Tell me. Were they on horseback?"

"No, ma'am. A buggy. And a driver. Two soldiers on the front steps. I didn't see nothing else."

Miss Antonia stared at Sissie, as if weighing her answer, then sat in the forest green Queen Anne's chair beside the table.

Waiting.

More waiting.

Sissie never knew if there would be a knock on the door but Miss Antonia sat at the ready. Tonight, the knock came late which likely meant that it was a dinner guest.

"Miss Antonia?"

Sissie heard the voice of Clara, the head house maid. She'd served the James family for all of her forty-five years. No taller than five feet and built solid, she stood eye to eye with Miss Antonia, running the house on Mrs. James's strict schedule. Even now, five years after Miss Antonia's mother's death.

"Come in Clara."

Sissie thought she could almost see Miss Antonia breathe a sigh of relief.

"Ma'am?"

"What is it? Am I being summoned?" Miss Antonia asked.

"No, ma'am. Supper will be in five minutes. Master James asked that I fetch you." Clara said.

"And the visitors?"

"Colonel Wyndham here to talk some with your daddy. Two of his men. They're staying for supper," Clara said.

"You know we don't allow that familiarity, Clara. Tell Mr. James I'll be down shortly," Miss Antonia said as she turned her head to Sissie.

Clara huffed and left, closing the door behind her.

"I need to hide this paper with some underclothes. And fix my dress. Is it wrinkled?"

Sissie helped her straighten her clothes, checking the room to make sure they hadn't missed anything someone would question before they started down the stairs, Miss Antonia in the lead with Sissie following.

Hours later, Sissie took the steps behind Miss Antonia up the stairs. Sissie helped her change clothes and get into bed.

"Will there be anything else, Miss Antonia?"

"No, Sissie. That will be all. I'll need to be up early in the morning. I have an invitation to send to a friend that I'll need you to take."

Sissie nodded, left the room and headed to her bed in the attic. The room was tiny, with one small bed set so far under the rafters you'd hit your head if you sat upright. For Clara and her to share. The house had been made solid so there weren't too many drafts. Still, the room was freezing in the winter and hot as blazes in the summer. Tonight, Clara brought up bread for Sissie's meal since she'd stood in the corner of the dining room, followed by time in the drawing room. She ate quickly and crawled in bed, grateful for the warmth of another beside her.

But Sissie stayed awake for a while, mulling over the evening. Colonel Wyndham had been a tall thin man, whose Union uniform hung on him. Sissie watched his eyes grow wide at the meat on the table, something Master James only served for important guests. Sissie wondered at who he was to Master James since it didn't seem like there was any trade of goods to be done.

Master James met with Union soldiers every few days. With Virginia being Confederate, or at least mostly so, Sissie wasn't sure what to make of all that. Or how Master James could do that. She wondered what he and Miss Antonia were really doing with all these people since they no longer had any goods to trade. Was Master James betraying someone? Or helping someone? And what about all the servants? Who would take care of Sissie and the others if the Union won?

The dinner conversation had covered many subjects, although Sissie couldn't hear but a few words every now and then. But she heard General Stoughton mentioned, a Union general of a group of infantry men, and she noticed the slight change in Miss Antonia. She had continued to pick at the cheese on her plate but Sissie knew she was listening closely. She laughed a bit more at his words and Sissie had seen she was working to keep the Colonel at ease and talking about the happenings around town as if they were the most important thing in her life, all the while charming him into talking about his work.

Before she drifted off to sleep, Sissie wondered what Miss Antonia had really been doing at dinner and who would be visiting her for tea. And why.

Well before the sun rose, Clara shoved Sissie out of bed. Sissie hurried to dress in the second of her two dresses, a brown and white plaid, and tiptoed downstairs. She brought in firewood and helped Clara build the fire in the fireplace. Eliza, the cook, slept in the kitchen and as the fire started rose to bake bread. Sissie sat on the hand-hewn bench on one side of the wooden table that served for meal preparation, laundry sorting and the servants' table for meals. The shelves were emptier now. Baskets holding potatoes were only half full. With the spring, crops could be put in if the war didn't keep them all from the fields. And bags of flour were stacked in one corner instead of two. A bit of stale bread and coffee served as Sissie's breakfast. The smell of burning wood filled her nose. As she made a second trip for more firewood, George walked in.

"About time," Clara said to the six-foot broad-shouldered man who handled all the heavy chores for the household. Sissie envied his work. He did a lot of heavy lifting, but he also took care of Master James's needs, which meant he was out and about in the town of Fairfax. More than Sissie got to be.

"Where've you been? We done laid the fire already," Clara said.

"I guess I overslept. Master James sat up late last night. Surprised ya'll are up already," George said as he winked at Sissie.

"Don't you go eyeing this girl. She ain't for you," Clara said. She continued to cluck as she ushered Sissie out of the kitchen and upstairs to wait on Miss Antonia.

As Sissie opened the curtains to let in the early morning sun, Miss Antonia stirred. "Sissie, I need you to take a missive to Rose Greenhow. You've been there before. Two streets over. Do you remember?"

"I do, ma'am."

"Help me dress. I want to send it early. I expect Rose will be here for tea. Be sure to tell Clara that as well."

"Yes ma'am," Sissie said as she helped Miss Antonia into her black dress with white collar.

Miss Antonia pulled away as soon as the buttons were done. "I need the quill and ink," she said as she pulled open the small drawer on the right side of her dressing table. She took out her stationery. A few minutes later, she finished writing and laid the paper on her table to dry.

"You are to deliver this to Miss Rose directly. Don't hand it off to a servant. Tell them I insisted. Can you do that?"

"Yes ma'am," Sissie said.

Miss Antonia lifted the paper and blew on it. Ran a finger along the bottom line and smiled as she checked to make sure the ink was dry. She folded it in two.

"Run along. And make sure you tell Clara about tea. Then come straight back. Understand?" Miss Antonia asked.

Sissie nodded.

"And if anyone stops you—like a soldier and asks what you're doing out on the street, you just tell them you're taking a note for me. And if they ask to see it, you show it to them. It's just an invitation to tea for my friend."

Sissie headed downstairs, note in hand. She stopped in the kitchen to tell Clara about tea, who raised one eyebrow and then clucked about more work. Looking around, Sissie headed out the back door. She wasn't sure what was happening but she knew Miss Antonia never invited anyone to tea the same day.

Sissie delivered the missive without anyone stopping her. She waited while Miss Rose prepared a response which Sissie carried back to the James house. Handing it to Miss Antonia, she watched her read it and smile.

"Miss Rose is coming to tea. I think I'll wear my navy dress for the occasion, seeing as it's a friend who'll be here. I'm going to read for a while. Why don't you see what Clara needs?"

Sissie spent the morning in the warm kitchen, helping the cook make bread and washing some clothes. Sissie ran back upstairs just before noon to check on Miss Antonia and whether she wanted a tray for her meal.

"I think I'll just have tea when Rose arrives. She should be here within the hour," Miss Antonia said. "Help me change."

Sissie heard a knock on the front door just as she finished redoing Miss Antonia's bun. "That will be all for now. Once Rose is here, go down to the kitchen and bring up tea. And open the door."

Sissie nodded, pulled the door back to expose the hallway, and moved back to her usual corner.

Rose swept into the room, pushing past Clara who had brought her upstairs, her olive-green dress swishing through the narrow doorway. A tall woman, she had deep auburn hair done up in a bun on her head, with tendril curls on each side of her face. Her mouth curled up into a welcoming smile.

Miss Antonia rose and greeted her friend. "It's so good to see you. Come sit by the desk," Miss Antonia said as she motioned for Sissie to leave and close the door.

"You haven't been out much," Miss Rose said as she sat in the chair matching Miss Antonia's.

"No, but I'm sure you have. What have you been doing with yourself?"

In the kitchen, Clara had the tray ready. Sissie picked it up and returned upstairs. She laid it on the bed and brought the china cups to the dressing table. Then brought the pot over to pour tea. She made a third trip to add a plate of biscuits and some dried fruit.

As she moved, Sissie listened to the gossip before the conversation turned to the dinner the night before. Miss Antonia motioned for her to close the door.

"I heard Colonel Wyndham had dinner with your father last night," Miss Rose said.

"Actually, he had dinner with me as well," Miss Antonia said.

"And how did you find him?"

"He is a stickler for military rules. Seemed to have no sense of humor at all, although he likely thinks he does."

"Why is he here? Do you know?" Miss Rose asked.

"That's why I wanted to talk to you. He's expecting General Stoughton. Across the street at the Fairfax Court House."

"Really? Did he happen to say when?"

"Three days hence. I think he was checking out who lives on this street."

"I suspect John Singleton Mosby might be interested in that bit of information," Miss Rose said.

Sissie sucked in a shallow breath as she realized why Miss Antonia had kept the Colonel talking at dinner. She was gathering information. Sissie had heard of Mosby. A partisan ranger who commanded a Virginia Cavalry unit known as Mosby's Rangers for the Confederacy. His lightning-quick raids and ability to blend in with the local farmers and townsmen had earned him the nickname of the Gray Ghost.

"I think so too. But I am confined to my house. Without the ability to travel. And my missives are subject to search," Miss Antonia said. "You, on the other hand, do not have such restraints."

"No, but since we are having tea, this could be traced to us both," Miss Rose said.

"Only if we are not careful. I intend to have tea with several others in the next two days. While someone may suspect something, they will not have proof. You should do the same."

"I'm not sure I can get word to Mr. Mosby. Perhaps it would be better to send a servant? And should you have one in here as we talk?"

"No. Mr. Mosby would never believe them. I think you have to do this yourself. And Sissie doesn't understand any of this."

Sissie bristled at the words and held her breath. She wasn't sure what Mr. Mosby would do but something big was happening. She watched Miss Rose consider what Miss Antonia had said.

"I'll do my best. But this could be dangerous for us both. If they discover we passed on the information. And not just us. For you and your family as well as mine," Miss Rose said.

"I know. But we need this war to be over. We have to take the chance," Miss Antonia said.

"All right, let's decide on who we will each have come to tea."

Sissie settled against the wall while the women discussed the names. And then the two drew up notes for the ladies they were inviting. It would be a busy few days for Sissie and she'd need to warn Clara that Miss Antonia was entertaining again.

When the notes were finished, Miss Rose gathered her things. "It was so good to see you again. We should do this more often."

"I wish we could. I miss our talks and will be glad when this war is over. For now, we should keep our distance. At least until we see what happens," Miss Antonia said as she walked Miss Rose down the stairs to the front door.

Sissie gathered up the leavings from the tea and headed downstairs.

In the kitchen, Clara's head raised up and she asked, "Have you seen George? We need firewood."

"No, I haven't," Sissie said.

"I need you to bring in some small pieces until he shows up. Then you can go back to Miss Antonia and her guest."

"Yes, but Miss Antonia's guest left. I think she plans on having guests for the next few days as well," Sissie said as she headed out the back to the woodpile.

As she gathered up a few logs, George rounded the woodpile. "Where've you been? Clara needs wood for the fire," Sissie said.

"Just around. Here and there for Master James." He paused.

"What'd Miss Antonia talk to Miss Rose about? Anything I need to know?"

Sissie stomach turned and she looked around to see if anyone was nearby. "You know they'll whip me if I tell you what they's said."

George laughed. "There's no one around. Why you think I let the wood go low? I knew Clara'd send you out here. I sent everyone away that might be close by."

Sissie's shoulders relaxed. "Miss Antonia thinks I don't understand any of this. I don't know anything."

George stared at her. "She said that while Miss Rose was there?"

Sissie nodded.

"Miss Antonia is a smart woman. Think she might be keeping you safe. Like I do. Keep you out of things you don't need to know or that others shouldn't think you know."

Sissie considered it. Would it hurt to tell him? She'd already told him other bits of information in the past she was sure he'd passed on somehow so what was one more time. "General Stoughton, the Union general. He'll be here in three days."

"How many men with him?"

Sissie shook her head with a hint of a smile. "That's all I know."

"You know more than that. I can see it in your face," George said.

"Someone's gonna tell John Mosby about it."

George backed up. "So, they're gonna try to take the General, are they?"

"Maybe. I don't know. Miss Rose will try to get word to Mr. Mosby. Does that help?" Sissie asked already knowing the answer.

"You know it does. We got three runaways hiding outside of town. We were gonna move them in a day or so... depending on the weather and who was in town. I'll pass it along. You did good," George said with a smile. "But we need..."

"Sissie, where you be?" Clara called.

"I'm on my way back," Sissie called.

"Find out all you can on this," George said as he headed in with the wood, before calling out, "Aw, Clara, Sissie's just helping me load up with enough wood for the rest of the day."

Sissie carried messages to three women the next day. She worried about George, who George might give the information to and whether anyone would find out she had told him. Or that she had learned it from Miss Antonia.

Sissie was stopped twice by Colonel Wyndham's men, who were headquartered in the Fairfax Court House, down the street and around the corner from Master James' house. The brigade was hunting John Mosby and had already had several battles in the past weeks. Each time the soldiers blocked her way, she struggled to keep her hands from shaking as she told them what Miss Antonia said and showed them the notes. Each time, they let her go.

The third time, Colonel Wyndham stopped her. "Miss Antonia seems to be entertaining a lot these days."

"Yes sir."

"Is there a reason?"

"Don't know, sir. I just deliver the messages."

"Tell her, I'm watching her. And her friends. Can you remember that?"

Sissie bristled at his words but nodded, keeping her eyes on the ground.

"Go along then."

Sissie hurried to deliver the note and receive the response. She went straight to Miss Antonia when she returned.

"He said that? Are you sure?"

"Yes ma'am. He seemed to want you to know he is watching."

"Good gracious. I wish I could warn Rose," Miss Antonia said. "She should not meet with Mr. Mosby. Or maybe the Colonel wants me to show my hand. I will think on it."

Miss Antonia walked over to her chair and sat. "Find Clara. She'll give you something to do."

Sissie headed downstairs. Clara sent her to help with laundry. Sissie never understood how there could be so many clothes and sheets that needed washing. But while still a bit chilly, the air would dry things quickly. She gathered up a basket and took it outdoors.

At the line, she began hanging the larger pieces. As she raised one shirt to push it over the line, George's face appeared.

"Did you find out anything else?" he asked.

"No, and you can't be hanging around here. You'll get me in trouble." Sissie said.

"Where you been going?"

"Miss Antonia invited friends to tea."

"Saw you stopped by soldiers. What they want?" George asked.

"To know what I was doing and where I'd been."

"What else?"

Sissie sighed. It was no use keeping anything from George. He'd suck it out of you like a mosquito. "I think they think Miss Antonia's telling someone about the General's visit."

George stared at her. "Do you think they're trying to trick you?"

"Don't know. But I think you should wait to move anyone along the underground until whatever's gonna happen does. They can wait a few days. And I'll find out whatever I can and tell you."

"The General's coming. I heard it from two other boys. Best you tell me if you hear anything else. But with the raid on the General, no one will be looking for no runaways."

"I don't like it. Better to wait."

"No. Too long in one place. Folks get caught. I am good at getting them out."

Sissie shook her head. "Now, leave me alone. I need to hang these sheets."

The night before General Stoughton was to arrive, Sissie tossed and turned so much that Clara threatened to send her downstairs to sleep with the cook. George took too many risks. And those that were hiding had no way to know what they might be walking into.

Sissie could tell Miss Antonia was nervous and hadn't slept well either. Miss Antonia kept moving things from one place to the other, then back again. Asking Sissie to run downstairs for a glass of water. Then back for a book. Then to find out what Miss Antonia's daddy was doing.

At supper, Miss Antonia barely said a word. Afterward, she told Sissie to make up a bed on the floor of Miss Antonia's bedroom. She didn't want to be alone.

Miss Antonia had Sissie stand by the window to watch the building across the street. As night fell, Sissie helped Miss Antonia get ready for bed.

"If I fall asleep, wake me if something happens. And you can sleep on the floor when you get too tired to watch."

Sissie wasn't sure how long it was before she started to see shadows moving. She'd been nodding off, trying to stay awake.

"Miss Antonia," she whispered. "I think something's happening."

Before she received an answer, the night burst forth in sound.

Shots fired.

Sissie heard shouts and screams.

"Can you see what's happening? Who's winning?" Miss Antonia asked as she joined Sissie at the window.

"No. I can't. Just a bit of movement and shots."

"Keep the curtain mostly closed. We don't want anyone to see us or shoot here," Miss Antonia said.

The two stared out the window, until, just as quickly as it had started, silence took over.

"Get one of my day dresses. No light. Daddy will be downstairs. I want to find out what he saw."

Sissie struggled in the dark to find Miss Antonia's dress. Then to help her dress. Sissie grabbed the shawl Miss Antonia wore in her room during the day and wrapped it around her shoulders.

Sissie moved behind Miss Antonia as she opened her door. With no moon, the hallway was dark and they shuffled forward, finding the banister for the stairs. They crept downstairs and into the dining room.

A curtain closed and Sissie could see Master James' shape by the window.

"What are you doing here, Antonia?" he asked.

"Were those shots? It woke me," she said.

"Bunch of damn fools. I think Mosby learned Stoughton was in town. Not sure if Mosby got him but sounds like it is over. Wyndham had no business telling people when the General would arrive. I just hope he told more people than you and I... if that's what's happened," Mr. James said. "Otherwise, they'll be looking at our house closely. Which is very bad for our family. I hope you are not part of this. You did promise me no more intrigue or passing of secrets."

"Now Daddy, I am sure whatever happened has nothing to do with us," Miss Antonia said.

Mr. James sighed. "I know you love Virginia and want the Union out of here just as much as I do. We must be careful in what we do to support our friends that are fighting. Promise me you won't take any unnecessary risks. We don't have a home to return to now and we need to wait out the war here before we can go back and rebuild. In the meantime, I must keep up my relationships with those who have traded with us—no matter which side they are on in this war."

"I won't take risks if you won't," Miss Antonia said with a soft laugh.

"Get back up to bed. Is that Sissie with you? Both of you, upstairs. Say nothing. There's nothing to learn tonight."

Sissie woke, stiff from sleeping on the floor, to the sounds of pounding.

"Quick, I need to dress," Miss Antonia said as she pulled her covers off. "I can't be found undressed. And I must hide a few papers."

Sissie jumped up and found her black dress. She buttoned the back as fast as her fingers could go. Then began Miss Antonia's hair. Before she could finish, they heard heavy footsteps on the stairs.

Miss Antonia pulled away and tucked the papers inside her dress. She sat at her table and motioned Sissie to brush her hair.

A heaving pounding sounded on the door. "Open up, Miss Antonia James."

"It's open," Miss Antonia said.

The door swung open and Sissie almost fainted at the sight of a young soldier in a Union uniform standing with his rifle in hand. Sissie could see he couldn't be more than sixteen, with brown hair and hardly a stubble.

"What can I do for you?" Miss Antonia asked as she turned to face him.

"I'll have to search you, ma'am. My orders."

"And why, pray tell, would that be necessary?" Miss Antonia said.

"General Stoughton was captured last night. We have reason to believe that you were involved."

"Nonsense. I haven't left this room in months. I could not have done what you are accusing me of," Miss Antonia said as she smoothed her dress.

"I have my orders. And your slave too. She's been seen on the streets," the soldier said as he straightened his shoulders.

"Sissie runs my errands. She delivered invitations to my friends for tea. I believe she was stopped and my notes read. Isn't that right, Sissie?" Miss Antonia said as she turned to Sissie.

"Yes ma'am," Sissie said, staring at the floor while she clenched her hands together in the folds of her skirt.

"See. You have no business here. Move along. I'll not be touched by a man on such a scurrilous charge," Miss Antonia said.

"Ma'am, I have my orders. A slave in your household was shot last night. Helping runaway slaves no doubt. I have to insist," the soldier said.

"I don't know what you're talking about. My daddy would know about all our servants. And it can't be Sissie, she's not dead and she's been with me all night. And I handle any doctoring of our servants.

If someone was shot, I'd know it. I insist you leave at once," Miss Antonia said, her face a mask of determination.

Sissie watched the soldier stare at Miss Antonia before he hung his head and turned around, taking the stairs one step at a time. Clara waited at the bottom to escort him out.

Miss Antonia gestured for Sissie to watch him leave. As the front door closed, Sissie shut the bedroom door.

Miss Antonia opened the drawer on the right side of her dressing table and lifted it out. Underneath, she pulled out a wooden piece and removed two papers, before replacing the wood. She slid the drawer back in place.

"Take this," Miss Antonia said. "Does your dress have the extra pocket in it?

Sissie started and was tongue-tied.

"Yes. I know about that. I helped sew them in. We don't have any time to waste," Miss Antonia said as she headed to the door. "If George was shot or seen, he'll need papers to move north."

Sissie fled down the stairs to the kitchen. Clara looked up, fear on her face. George was stretched out on the bench.

"I can't stop the bleeding. I'm sorry ma'am. I couldn't turn him away," Clara said.

"You did right, Clara. Sissie, find my medicine bag. Where's my father?"

"Out on business. Since early this morning," Clara said.

Sissie scurried off, returning with the black bag.

Miss Antonia lifted George's shirt. "He's shot in the side. Looks like it went clear through. We have to stop the bleeding. Clara, help me get this shirt up."

Clara moved forward as Sissie stood watching in horror.

"Sissie, I need a piece of wood, red hot on the end. Bring one to me."

Miss Antonia pressed the hot wood against the wound on his stomach as George groaned, his eyes wide as the pain brought him back to consciousness. She and Clara rolled him on his side and she pressed it again on his back. This time, George passed out.

"Clara, wash off the blood. I think it's stopped, at least for now. Sissie, bring me a clean shirt. We have to burn the old one with the blood on it."

Clara and Sissie did as they were told.

George came too and groaned in pain.

Miss Antonia left and brought back some whiskey. "Drink this. It'll help with the pain."

George drank deeply and relaxed a bit on the bench.

"What now, Miss Antonia?" Sissie asked.

"I have to leave," George said as he grimaced. "They'll be coming after me."

"They already are," Miss Antonia said. "They'll most likely be back tomorrow. By then you need to be on your way. Clara, feed him something to strengthen him. Sissie, you'll give him the pass I gave you once he's able to walk. I've already filled in George's name."

George and Sissie nodded.

"Sissie, you'll need to find out from George who he is working with for the runaways. And in answer to the question on your face, I have been helping many travel north during this awful war using blank passes my father or I have secured. We must not allow the line to be disrupted. The others involved most likely know George has been shot and they need to know he's leaving. They need to take him along as they would any others. And they need to replace him. Whoever that is can contact you. I don't want to know any of this so I can answer that I honestly don't know. Without that knowledge, I can't endanger the whole underground railroad. I'll do what I've always done—once we get George moving."

"Thank you, Miss Antonia." George said. "I'll not be here in the morning, even if I have to crawl away."

Sissie couldn't speak. She'd had no idea Miss Antonia knew all that had been going on under this roof and in the countryside, although she realized she should have since Miss Antonia had always known everything going on at the plantation. Here she'd been afraid to give George the tiny information she'd overheard, when others and Miss Antonia had risked their lives to help people. Everyone in the house seemed to know all this, except her. She dropped her shoulders, thinking she'd have to watch Miss Antonia and Master James for clues of what they were doing.

And took a breath.

"Yes, ma'am," Sissie said, standing a bit taller. She could do more. Help others get north. Play a part in keeping them safe as they traveled. Sissie reached over and put her hand in George's. "I'll help you. And the others to come."

NOT WHAT YOU'D EXPECT

LEAH CUTTER

We've been deep inside the point of view of spies (and spying critters) throughout this volume. But what about ordinary folk who stumble across a spy in their daily lives?

Leah Cutter's story "Not What You'd Expect" has its beginning in real life...and if I tell you much more, I'll spoil the story.

Leah is also a Fiction River regular. Her work has appeared in the Fiction River volumes Unnatural Worlds, Hex in the City, Past Crime, Pulse Pounders (the Kobo Special Edition), Haunted, Editor's Choice and Pulse Pounders: Countdown. Her short fiction has also appeared in Alfred Hitchcock's Mystery Magazine, Talebones, and The Uncollected Anthology. She has also edited a future volume, Stolen, which will appear in 2019. She has published a number of novels, including the Shadow Wars series, and she is the publisher of Knotted Road Press.

Imagine going out for coffee and learning something...surprising.

I knew a spy, once.

Patty may, or may not, have fit your stereotypical ideal of a spy. She was in her late twenties, blonde, buxom, and brilliant. I found out later that she had a PhD in aeronautical engineering, along with an MBA. While her official title at one of the big airplane manufacturers in Seattle was Business Analyst, she actually worked as a corporate spy.

We met at yoga class. Thirty people packed the tiny studio three times a week. The air was always humid in there, soft and warm. Condensation covered the windows, hiding the busy street outside. Spider plants hung from the ceiling, sprouting like mad. Yoga mats filled the floor, with mere inches between them. The students tended toward younger, upper-middle-class women, wearing expensive yoga shirts and pants, but a few of us older hippies had snuck in, with our cheap tights and cut-up T-shirts.

The instructor always invited the best students to fill the first two of the four rows of students. Her reasoning was that if the people in the back couldn't see the instructor, they could still watch yogini modeling the proper poses.

I started that class in the far back corner, away from the door and the windows. I'd long since passed my fortieth birthday and fifty loomed alarmingly ahead of me. I wasn't in horrid shape, but I was beginning to feel my age.

Patty started taking classes about the same time I did, and was also relegated to the back. She wore the proper yoga uniform: sports bra, flowered yoga shirt, skin-tight yoga pants, all in coordinated blues and greens. Since we were about the same height (short) we paired up together to do partner work.

She had great breath control, and walked me through how to stop panting like a racehorse.

I'm not sure what she said that intrigued me enough to ask her to go out for tea after class.

It might just have been because she was so beautiful and I'm only human. (Though I was 95% certain that Patty didn't like girls. At least, not that way, not like me.)

Despite the chilly October winds blowing down the street, I held my jacket in one hand, letting the evening air cool me down after the overheated room. I had my yoga mat rolled up and tucked under my arm, certain it would also be stinking and soaking wet like the rest of me. Patty, of course, had the proper carrier for her yoga mat and strapped it to her back like a good yoga warrior.

As we walked, cars rushed by on the busy street, hurrying to their warm houses. The air carried the smell of rain and wet leaves. We talked of how we'd arrived in Seattle (me, through random choice, her, supposedly because her sister had moved out here and Patty had followed. Later, I wondered about that story, if she'd actually arrived here because of the aeronautical industry. Patty said a lot of things that I questioned afterward.).

The tea shop itself was a blend of modern minimalism and hippy sensibilities: only the best organic ingredients went into the tea blends sitting in numbered canisters behind the counter; the shiny white case at the front of the store held primarily vegan and "healthy" treats; while the floor was plain gray concrete and artistic bunches of bare white branches decorated the walls.

It was hot and humid in the tea shop, which was part of the reason why I hadn't worn my jacket: I knew I'd get warm again quickly. The shop always smelled of cinnamon and vanilla, with the tangy undertone of good black tea. Patty and I agreed to split a cranberry-orange scone as our treat for working so hard in class.

I volunteered to sit on the cold metal chair at our table, with my back to the room. Patty seemed to appreciate being able to sit on the cushioned bench, but also to be able to watch everyone. I wouldn't say that she was paranoid, exactly. Maybe just overly cautious, her eyes flicking up and observing every person as they walked in, cataloging them before she looked back at me.

I told Patty of my day job, working as a project manager for a well-known Seattle software company. I complained bitterly of the long hours and stress, which was also, in part, why I'd started taking yoga and meditating.

Then I asked her what she did.

"I'm a spy," she announced rather proudly.

I just nodded sagely, taking another sip of my orgasmic peppermint-and-vanilla rooibos tea. I mean, "spy" wasn't the most outrageous job title I'd ever heard of. A good friend of mine taught fighting at the CIA. He specialized in underwater hand-to-hand combat. He was the one who'd taught me not just how to defend myself, but how to fight *dirty* if it came to that, with explicit instructions, demonstrations, and practice on how to break a man's knee.

"I work in the aeronautics industry," Patty said after she sipped more of her own tea. "Mainly I do business analysis. I scrutinize every piece of literature the competition produces. Particularly their quarterly business reports."

"Okay," I said, nodding as if that sounded great, all the while thinking: *just shoot me now*. I couldn't imagine how dull it must be to have to go over those reports with a fine-toothed comb. I had to produce quarterly numbers for those damned reports for my own projects.

"But sometimes, I get to go to industry events," Patty said. She leaned a little closer over the table, as if telling me a secret. "Play the dumb blonde. Lead conversations this way and that."

I couldn't help but roll my eyes at the "dumb blonde" part. You only had to spend about two minutes in Patty's presence to realize how brilliant she was.

But men would only see what they wanted to. Particularly if someone like Patty was playing a part and showing off her fantastic breasts.

"I think that's fascinating," I told her honestly. And it made sense to me that her company would send someone like her to an event, a person who knew all the jargon, had read all the collateral, and could read between the lines of the conversations going on around her. The men would probably assume that she couldn't follow what they were talking about anyway.

Hell, the software company I worked for might do the exact same thing. They weren't the company known for "do no evil."

Patty gave me a big grin. "I knew you'd understand my position," she said. She leaned in a little closer.

I did as well. The intimacy, being that close to a beautiful woman, smelling her sweet musk, made me flush. Not that I'd cooled down that much from the yoga class.

And I'm certain that Patty saw my attraction and courted it. She wanted to use it to her advantage.

I was old enough to know what she was doing, but also flattered that she had decided I was worthy enough to be played.

"There's an event," Patty said, almost whispering. "Celebrating the industry innovators. It takes place a week from Friday. I need a date. Want to come?"

"Of course," I answered immediately. "Tell me how to dress, how to best support you."

Patty leaned back. While her eyes had shifted to something

cooler and more calculating, she still said warmly, "Thank you so much! I knew you'd help me out."

I nodded, sitting back myself.

I didn't expect payment. Hell, I figured I'd never see her again after the event.

But I was planning on having one hell of an adventure in the meantime.

———

Patty and I chatted on the phone several times over the next week, as well as met after yoga class, going over our roles and goals.

For the event, I wore what I called my award dress. It was black, sleeveless, and went to the ground, hugging my curves nicely. The front of it was sheer from just above my knees down to the hem. I wore my mother's amethyst necklace and matching earrings, worth a small fortune.

Of course, even with all that elegance, I still wore sensible shoes. Flat black sandals that probably weren't appropriate for the Seattle October weather. However, I didn't want to hide my beautifully painted, scarlet toenails. I'd used the same color on my fingernails, and found a lipstick color that matched as well. I wasn't about to hide my gray hair—besides, it was turning a gorgeous silver. I'd earned every single damned wrinkle in my face, so I didn't try to hide those, either. I still took extra care with my makeup, making my skin look soft and luminous.

Patty picked me up at my place. She texted me when she arrived, waiting in the taxi at the curb. I wore my long faux-fur coat, vintage and gorgeous. I knew that even in the dim evening light I presented quite a sight walking down the short staircase from my building to the street.

The driver stood by the back door of the black town car. He wore a black suit with a white shirt, and wasn't much taller than me. Cute black curls flared out under his black cap. He opened the door with a flash of white teeth against his dark skin. "Good evening, Ma'am," he said.

"Thank you," I told him graciously as I slid into the car.

Patty sat in the back, her smile radiant. She also wore a black dress, though shorter than mine and gathered along her left side, giving her an asymmetric hem. She'd blown out her blonde hair that night, making it softly flow around her face like a shiny mane. Her makeup was impeccable with luscious red lips that I knew I wouldn't be kissing, but that wasn't about to stop me from thinking about it.

"Remember, you're playing a part," Patty said quietly as the car smoothly left the curb and joined traffic.

"I know," I said, keeping my voice down as well. Though there was a glass between the backseat and the driver, I knew we didn't want to be heard. "I'm just an older friend who's come into town for a vacation. I never worked outside the house, and I certainly don't know anything about those newfangled computers."

Patty grinned at me. "You look too young to use *newfangled* you know."

"Thank you," I said. Then I added, "You look stunning. I don't think any of the men will be able to keep their eyes off you. Or to stop themselves from talking to you, or answering your questions."

Her cover story was that she wrote up articles for one of the local neighborhood blogs in her spare time, and had thought dressing up for a night would be fun.

Patty nodded, acknowledging the truth of what I said, confident in her beauty. "Make sure you get the men to talk about their automatic control systems. Get them to explain it to you. We'll debrief after the event."

"I'll keep track of all the details," I promised her. "And will let you know if there's anything that they say that raises my interest, that I think is reaching for something new, not the standard applications."

"Thank you," Patty said. "I think this is going to be brilliant fun. I should have thought about bringing a computer specialist with me before."

Though her words brought a spike of pleasure to me, I told myself again to not get ahead of myself.

This was a one-night stand. Not forever or for keeps.

The event was being held out at the Museum of Flight. I'd always found the museum impressive, with the huge planes hanging from the glass roof.

I also had really good memories of my first visit, when I'd come with my dad. He'd been the crew-chief of a DC-3 during WWII, and when I was a kid, had built model airplanes out of balsa wood. He'd been familiar with almost all the vehicles we saw in the WWII wing, gave me the history as well as some of the engine flaws.

That night, tables and a banquet spread had been set up in the southern wing of the museum. It was a smaller gathering than I'd expected: maybe seventy people. However, there were only about half a dozen other women there. They all seemed to be attached, wives of the men who'd been invited.

Though it was an open bar, I stuck to a single glass of red wine that I nursed through the "meet and greet" portion of the evening. It wasn't that I was a light weight, but I wanted to stay sharp all night, and any type of alcohol made me sleepy eventually.

Of course, the men all talked to themselves. Didn't want to risk girl cooties or something. I softened my stance, trying to act more like a hetero-woman, instead of an out-and-proud lesbian. I wore a nametag like everyone else, choosing a name different than my own: Elsie sounded like a good, straight, divorced, middle-aged woman to me. I had even known one, once.

There was one group of five men all huddled close to the start of the buffet line. Two wore regular suits, two had their jackets off already and were wearing dress shirts, and one wore a vintage beige plaid jacket. He even had the '70s moustache to go with it.

I knew these people: though they weren't software engineers, they were still geeks. I worked with geeks every day. I hung out at the edge of their circle, finally slipping in when they started talking about autopilot.

"Will there be pilotless airplanes someday?" I asked. "Like those driverless cars?"

"There's too many variables," said one of the men, who, according to his nametag, was called Eric. "Particularly the weather."

They all shared a shudder over that ominous creature called *the weather*.

"And you can't make the software foolproof, which the regulators would insist on," added Floyd, the one in the plaid jacket.

"Yup. Fools are too ingenious. Particularly trained fools, like pilots," cracked another one of the men.

I rolled my eyes, but I understood what they meant. It was an old joke that translated into software engineering as well. Instead of making software foolproof or bulletproof, the focus now was on making it resilient.

I opened my mouth to make a comparison between the two industries. I shut it quickly, though, remembering the part that I played. "How about drones that carry passengers or something that's remotely controlled?" I asked. When I got a curious look from one of the men, I hastily added, "My dad built RC planes when I was a kid."

The men nodded and Floyd started explaining to me in very small words why that wouldn't work.

I tried not to bristle. While I wasn't in their industry, I wasn't an idiot.

But I was a woman. Beautifully dressed and wearing makeup. Even though the software industry didn't have that many women, it appeared that the field of aeronautical engineering had fewer.

Again, I stopped myself from putting Floyd in his place. I wasn't here as a brilliant software person, I was here to gather information. So I took a deep breath, batted my eyelashes, and at the appropriate times sighed a soft, "Really?" I may have even straightened my back and thrust out my boobs occasionally.

Inside, I continued to squirm.

This reminded me too much of when I'd been much younger and playing the part of a straight woman, pretending to be interested in guys when all I really wanted to do was just to make out with my best friend Amy.

I still kept to the script, thankful when muted bells rang and we were seated at our tables. The tables all had white linens, heavy silverware, and pressed crystal glassware. At least Patty and I were seated beside each other. None of the men I'd been talking with earlier sat at our table of six: two men and a couple sat there instead.

Patty did her best to interview them, getting them to talk about their jobs and what they were working on. I had no idea if she learned anything new from them—it sounded to me as though they all had their own scripts they were working from.

The chicken with Brussels sprouts that they served was as bland as I expected it to be: the caterer probably thought garlic was an exotic spice. At least they served good coffee (it was Seattle, after all —their caterer's license might have been revoked if they didn't).

As dessert was being served (delicious cinnamon, walnut, and raisin mini-cupcakes with vanilla buttercream frosting) the organizers of the event got up and started their speeches, intermixed with handing out the various innovators' awards. The acceptance speeches from the winners were long and dry and I truly needed the caffeine to stay awake.

Once all the awards had been given, the organizers thanked us and finally sent us on our way. I needed a bathroom and probably two more cups of coffee if I was going to stay awake for the "debriefing."

Patty found me as I was leaving the restroom. "This way," she said, indicating the northern wing of the museum.

This wing held all the WWII planes. We stopped beside the Supermarine Spitfire, still looking dangerous and ready to fight. Dark sky lay beyond the glass windows surrounding us, and I could hear the soft spray of rain. The air in here still smelled of machine oil. I slipped my jacket on over my bare shoulders.

"Did you learn anything?" Patty asked softly as she pretended to admire the plane above us.

I told her my suspicions about how at least one of her competitors appeared to be working on improving pilot-assisted takeoff and landing, again, difficulties primarily due to that monster called *the weather*. (It wouldn't have surprised me if most of the men in the industry didn't have a private altar where they made sacrifices to rain and storm gods, pleading for mercy.)

She merely nodded. "Yes, I've seen that in the literature. Thank you for verifying that for me. I'll dig into it more next week." She paused, then asked, "Anything else?"

I decided to be honest with her. "How do you stand it?" I asked. "Pretending to be something you aren't?"

"I was wondering if that would bother you," Patty said. She gave me a sad smile, like a teacher pronouncing that her star student had only achieved a B on their final test. "I've always played roles. Dutiful daughter despite my abusive dad. Poor college student even after the inheritance from dear old grandpa came through and made me rich. Asking stupid questions so teachers didn't expect what I tested at. Like that."

I shook my head. "I can't do it. Not anymore. I did it for too long when I was your age. Pretending to be something I wasn't. Never again." I shivered, hearing the hard edge to my tone.

The evening had unsettled me more than I had realized.

Patty, however, giggled. "That's okay. You did help. And I got some interesting leads. We should go home, though."

I followed her out of the darkened wing, still uncertain of myself.

Patty's next words didn't surprise me at all. "Oh, and I won't be taking any more yoga classes," she told me.

"Why not?" I asked, expecting to hear a lie.

"The physical part is great," Patty admitted. "I love all the stretching. But the meditation part, and truly studying the path, that's trying to change my soul."

I didn't say it, but I still thought it: *and you don't have one.*

That was how she was able to be a spy. To play a part. To delight in pulling something over on everyone.

I still had my story to tell at the end of the night. And a sweet kiss from Patty at the very end, though I knew it was all calculated and not real.

Like I said, Patty wasn't what you expected.

Or maybe she was.

TURKISH COFFEE

JOHANNA ROTHMAN

*Johanna Rothman's character Mira in "Turkish Coffee" goes out for coffee as
well, but in a more spy-like manner. Although Mira isn't quite what most of
us expect when we think spy.*

This is Johanna's first appearance in Fiction River, *but it won't be her
last. She has published fourteen nonfiction books on management. She is an
in-demand speaker worldwide, and as such, she's visited Jaffa. The city
became the inspiration for the story. She writes: "Jaffa is an anti-grid city,
which makes exploring fun. You never know what you'll find around the
corner: a fine restaurant tucked inside a courtyard; a school marching band
practicing; or a family-owned nut roaster."*

There's no marching band here, but there are plenty of surprises.

M ira was almost at the *shuk*, the open-air marketplace in Jaffa.
She'd walked down from the bluffs overlooking the crescent
beach and the openness of the Mediterranean Sea.

The sky was a brilliant light blue over the darker green-blue of
the Mediterranean. There were some high thin clouds, but that was
it. When Mira had started out, she could see four sailboats inside
the crescent of the Jaffa beach. They had been beating toward the
wind and running away from it. By now, the local races were on.

The sun was high and hot. On the bluffs of the shore, the wind
was a bit brisk. Just enough to take the edge off the sun. Here, closer
to the *shuk*, the wind was very light, just enough to cool off her neck.

Mira had visited the *shuk* each of the last two mornings, ever
since she arrived. She enjoyed the slight downhill walk, the buildings
close together and her feeling that she would discover something
momentous at every corner.

The street had sidewalks only on one side, a testament to Jaffa's
age and the narrowness of the streets. Some of the sidewalks had
cobblestones, almost matching the color of the red bricks of the
sides of the buildings.

Mira was surprised when she first got to Jaffa. Tel Aviv was all white and concrete. Just south of Tel Aviv was Jaffa with its old brick buildings. Sure, there were some white stucco buildings, but nothing like Tel Aviv. Here, there was more color: red brick, yellow stucco, and yes, some white apartment buildings. Those were new.

Everything was a big change from the wide streets in Virginia, where she was based. Virginia could trace its roots back hundreds of years. Israel kept time in the thousands of years.

She'd expected the older brick buildings to be low, maybe one- or two-stories. But no, some of the buildings were four or five stories high. The higher buildings provided more shade over the sidewalk, and shaded the courtyards between some of the buildings.

Yesterday, on her way to the *shuk*, Mira had made an impetuous left turn into an alleyway.

That alley brought her into a courtyard between two buildings. She'd seen four parked cars and a riot of flowers. Mostly, she'd seen bright pink bougainvillea flowers. There was a sign that said "Noah's" with a menu. Maybe she would be here long enough to have dinner there one night.

She'd eaten a small breakfast, just a hardboiled egg and some salad to take the edge off. She knew herself well. She would end up eating a chocolate rugelach, the rolled-up yeast dough treat. She knew she would eat some of the freshly roasted nuts and probably some dried fruit. Maybe she would treat herself to some Turkish coffee.

Mira had first tasted what the Israelis called this Turkish coffee when she'd arrived in Israel a few days ago. It was the kind of coffee that woke you up just by smelling it.

Mira had discovered why the locals called it mud coffee. The grounds were in the bottom of the cup. The coffee did look a little like mud.

If you tried to drink the grounds, yes, you might chew it. Mira had learned to not drink the grounds the hard way. Great Turkish coffee smelled of cardamom, a smell that permeated the Middle East stores and cafés.

Jaffa's *shuk* had small storefronts, just as Tel Aviv's *shuks* did. But, it seemed to Mira that Jaffa's *shuk* wound around more. The streets here were really alleys—and some of the stores went on forever.

Yesterday, Mira had wandered deep into the *shuk*. One store had pillows, sheets, and towels. All next to televisions. The store was maybe twelve paces wide. But, it went on and on and on, for what felt like a quarter of a mile. Behind the bedding and televisions, it had ovens and kitchen supplies. The organization didn't make sense to Mira, but she could appreciate the variety.

In the next store, Mira saw touristy scarves, all different colors of the rainbow, some with overlapping jangly coins sewn in. She'd walked past the scarves and other tourist jewelry onto the carpet part of the store. The carpets were a jumble of colors: primarily reds with some blues and purples.

When she turned to leave the store, she wondered about those scarves. No Israeli—or a spy—would wear a scarf like that. It made too much noise. They were pretty, though. Not useful. Just for tourists.

The next store had electronics of all kinds, including dead radios. What was the fascination with all the dead electronics? Mira had no idea. It did make for stores that beckoned you like the old woman in the story about Hansel and Gretel. All these stores beckoned to Mira. She was happy to explore the *shuk* every Friday morning.

The food stores in the *shuk* were the best. Some of the stores had dried fruit and roasted nuts. Others had gorgeous fresh fruit and vegetables.

The eggplants were bright purple. The cucumbers were a deep green, almost as green as a zucchini. The tomatoes were bright red. And the spices. Oh my. Bins of spices that you could sniff and then buy as much or as little as you needed.

Still others had baked goods. The rugelach, the croissants, the challah for Shabbat, all of it smelled like heaven. And, the roasted nuts and dried fruit. She couldn't wait to taste it all.

Mira didn't want to draw attention to herself, so she dressed modestly. Today, she wore a long denim skirt and a short-sleeved white blouse, along with her ever-present black sneakers. She was covered enough to be modest and not so hot that she would swelter.

She fit in just fine, she thought. Except for one minor detail.

Mira had green eyes, curly red hair and freckled white skin. She didn't look Israeli or Arab. She looked American.

Well, there were some—very few—Israelis with red hair. They were either from Europe or descendants of European immigrants. She'd been telling people she was a real estate agent. That would have to do. She strode to the *shuk*.

Mira didn't like to think of herself as a spy. No, she called herself an analyst. She investigated. She took all the data and created a picture for other people to understand.

Her job was to discover people's secrets. What everyone called "human intelligence." She discovered humans all right. But intelligence? Maybe, maybe not.

Sometimes, she discovered the secrets through investigating who the subject's friends were. That six degrees of Kevin Bacon thing. Sometimes, by looking through financial statements or real estate records.

Mostly, she made friends. She was the kind of person people liked to talk to. It didn't hurt that she liked to talk back.

Some of her fellow investigators were big-time introverts. They were terrific at manipulating the data. Mira felt she was okay at the data part. But, give her a coffee meeting, a lunch, or even a cocktail party, and she was in her element.

Her job on this trip was to discover who was trying to infiltrate research nuclear reactors around the world. She'd first learned about the problem at the MIT research reactor, where the local security analyst had called for help.

The local analyst had realized someone was trying to hack in. The hacker hadn't succeeded yet. Mira had worked with the local analyst to create more traps and triggers. The reactor was as secure as she could make it right now.

Nuclear reactors always had a problem with potential hackers. This research reactor was no different.

Mira had contacted her counterparts in several other countries, including Israel. Her colleagues now had triggers set to trap unwanted visitors. Yes, Israel was tracking this hacker, too. No, they hadn't caught him yet. The Israelis offered her the chance to work here to understand what was happening.

For two days, she'd worked in the Negev at the reactor with Ofer, another security analyst.

Mira was sure Ofer was not an analyst in the same way she was. Ofer looked ordinary, from the top of his short black hair to his beige boots. He was a little predictable in his clothes: beige shirt, beige pants and the ever-present beige boots. He looked just like any other desert-based Israeli, but he didn't act like one.

Mira had seen him work out, doing some sort of martial arts. He had disarmed a guy who was taller and weighed more in about eight seconds. The guy was on the floor, cradling his wrist.

Ofer had apologized and helped the guy to the infirmary.

Mira had defense training, but she was not capable of disabling anyone inside of a minute, never mind eight seconds. Ofer might be handy to have around. She hoped she wouldn't need him.

Together, Mira and Ofer had traced all the IP addresses this hacker had used. By the time they untangled the pings, many of them led here, to a small café in the *shuk*. They'd both visited the café several times, separately. Once, Ofer had left a small camera embedded into the wall.

It was a special camera, of course. The camera was no larger than a pin and had a 360-degree view. The battery lasted for up to a week. It transmitted over the local network.

The camera had transmitted pictures of the café so they could see the people and run facial recognition on them.

One guy had consistently evaded any clear pictures. He kept his head down and always wore a red baseball cap. Mira and Ofer called him RBC, for Red Baseball Cap.

Mira and Ofer were pretty sure he was their guy. Not positive, so Mira's job was to engage him in conversation.

Mira stopped at the first stall to buy her fruit and nuts. She spoke with the woman behind the counter.

Every day, the woman asked her how her holiday was going. Every day, she said it was "tov," good. Today, she said, "gadol," which meant greatest. It was the closest she could come to "great."

The woman laughed and handed her the box of dried apricots and dates, along with several small bags of nuts. Mira put the food into her cross-shoulder blue bag.

Next, Mira stopped at the bakery. She bought a dozen rugelach and two challot. She added them to her now-heavy bag.

She was ready for Shabbat and for breakfast the next day. Time for her coffee and investigation.

She stopped at the café and ordered a Turkish coffee and a chocolate rugelach. She looked around to find a table. There, on the other side of the café, was a table that would be perfect.

She snagged her table, and settled down to wait. She slowly drank her coffee and ate her ruglach.

Over on the other side of the café, Ofer was drinking coffee. Waiting, just waiting.

Mira took out her phone so she had something to do. She'd been in this business for several years and it never failed. She got bored when she was waiting. Not a good idea for a spy. She carried an extra phone—not a secure phone—just for the waiting.

She noticed the man in the red baseball cap when he arrived. He took a seat at the next table. Mira remained busy on her phone.

He looked different this morning. He drummed his hands on the table. He leaned back and then leaned forward. He shifted in his chair.

Mira turned to him and smiled. "Waiting for a date?" she asked.

"Not really," he said.

"Oh, you looked like my boyfriend when he was waiting for me," she said, and turned back to her phone.

RBC asked, "Where's your boyfriend now?"

"Oh, at home," she said. "I'm here on vacation. I've been eating my way through Israel."

Mira pointed to the bag.

"How long is your visit?" RBC asked.

"I only have another week here. Then I have to return," she said.

RBC nodded.

"Can I tell you a secret?" Mira asked.

He opened his eyes wider. "Sure," he said.

"I love it here," Mira said.

"Well, most tourists do," he said.

"I'm thinking of relocating, that's how much I love it," she said. Out of the corner of her eye, she saw Ofer leave.

"What do you do?" he asked. "You have to be able to make a living here."

"I'm a realtor. I buy and sell real estate," Mira said.

They spoke for a few minutes about real estate. Then, Mira asked, "Do you live around here? I really like Jaffa."

RBC looked at his watch. "I've been stood up," he said. "Shalom." He walked out.

No answers there. Now what?

Mira and Ofer met again at the secure house. Mira walked in, and turned left into an interior room. The room had a secure satellite hookup to the different systems, both Mira's and Ofer's. No one else was in the room now.

There were three wall monitors, with surveillance cameras receiving feeds. One was the café, one was the clock tower in Jaffa, and one looked out onto the beach.

"Mira, come look at this," Ofer said. The setup was three computers, each with a chair at one table, with two monitors per computer.

"I ran him through our database and came up with this," he said.

Mira saw a picture of RBC. "Yup, that's him. What's the scoop?" she asked.

"He's a low-level low-life, name of David Orenstein," Ofer said. "He's a grunt. Okay skills. Never done anything like this before. He must be working with someone else to hack into the reactors. The question is who?"

Mira thought for a few seconds. "Okay, what kind of information do you think they want?"

"I'm pretty sure they want access to the highly enriched uranium," Ofer said. "The research reactors have highly enriched uranium."

"I suspect your place in the Negev has highly enriched uranium, too?" Mira asked.

"Sorry, you don't need to know that," Ofer said.

Mira smiled thinly. "Of course I don't."

Mira paused for a minute.

"Okay, how can we find the brains behind this outfit?" she asked. "We're sure David is not the brains. What do we need to do?"

"Tell me this," Ofer said. "How long did you talk today?"

"Just a few seconds longer than when you were in the café," Mira said. "I started asking him where he lived and he practically jumped out of his seat to leave."

"Ah," Ofer said. "Time to tail him. Whatever's happening is happening near or where he lives."

Mira and Ofer spoke for a few minutes longer. They decided on a plan, based on when David showed up at the café again.

While they spoke, the beach monitor showed a sailboat coming in to dock with three guys dressed in black.

"Hey Ofer, isn't it a little surprising that these guys are wearing black to sail?" Mira asked.

Ofer grimaced. He zoomed into their faces and shook his head.

"It figures. We've been watching these guys from Yemen. They are affiliated with ISIS, but not part of it. I'm not sure we can get an entire operation started today."

Mira said, "Well, we'll have to stop them, won't we?"

Ofer looked at her and said, "We will and we'll get help. Let me make some calls."

While Ofer made his calls, Mira changed into a dark blue shirt and checked her supplies.

They had a simple plan. Intercept the guys from the beach. Ofer suspected they were going down to the café. Intercept David and prevent him from making contact.

Ofer had "colleagues" as he referred to them, who would be in Jaffa momentarily. They were driving down from Tel Aviv, just 6 km. Of course, those 6 km could take them half an hour in traffic, but it was after lunch now. The traffic should be better.

If necessary, Ofer would intercept the beach guys.

Mira would meet David at the café again, and make sure he didn't provide any data to the beach guys.

Ofer had wanted a few people stationed at the clock tower and someone running a drone on the operation. He didn't get the people at the clock tower. He did have someone running the drone, Avi.

Mira said, "Well, it's simple, okay. I hope it works."

Ofer shrugged. "Me too."

Ofer took two ear plugs and handed one to Mira. "Use this, so we can stay in contact," he said.

"An ear plug?" Mira asked.

Ofer laughed. "Not just an ear plug. This is a transmitter and receiver. We have a secure frequency. We'll be able to talk to each other and hear each other." He paused. "The drone operator, Avi, is tied into us, too. She'll tell us anything we need to know."

Mira pushed it into her ear. It was a surprisingly comfortable fit. "I think we should test it," she said.

Ofer turned around and whispered, "I can hear you just fine."

"Hey, so can I!" Mira said.

A third voice said, "Avi here. I can hear both of you," she said.

"Okay, now we can all leave," Mira said.

Every other time Mira had gone to the *shuk*, she'd ambled. Not this time. The stores would only be open for another hour. The café might close at 2 p.m. also. She walked fast.

She got to the *shuk* in record time. Now what? If she went back to the café, that might be too obvious. She decided to look at some of those scarves she'd seen earlier. Maybe they had a scarf with no sound.

She whispered, "Hey Ofer, what's going on with you?"

Avi replied, "I can see him running up to the bluffs. He'll run down the stairs. He doesn't have much time before the guys are docked and free to roam around town."

Out of the corner of her eye, Mira saw David return to the café.

She decided to buy the scarf she'd been playing with. She didn't want to, but she haggled a little bit with the shop owner.

She wrapped the scarf around her head. She didn't expect the scarf to be a disguise. It would make her look just a little different. And, it kept her hair off her neck.

She entered the café again. She ordered a coffee and sat down at the table she'd been at before.

David sat down next to her, drumming his hands on the table. He looked left and right. He looked right at her, but didn't seem to recognize her.

Mira pulled out her phone and appeared to be busy.

A man in black showed up and sat down across from David.

"Here," he said. "Take this and introduce it to your systems." He put a USB stick on the table.

"I don't want to," David started.

The man in black said, "Lower your voice. I don't care what you want and what you don't want. Take it and introduce it."

David slowly extended his hand to take it.

Mira put her phone away and started to get ready to stand up.

David pulled his hand back.

Mira grabbed the stick and ran out of the café.

She heard footsteps behind her. She started up the hill back to the secure house and realized she needed to lose them.

She turned right at the next corner, and heard Avi in her ear. "Go one block straight and then turn left. I'll get you out of there," she said.

Mira didn't waste any breath talking. She kept running. She turned left.

Avi said, "Okay, two blocks straight. They're behind you by a block. Ofer is on his way."

Mira had almost reached the end of the second block.

"Okay, turn right, now!"

Mira turned right into that courtyard she'd seen earlier in the week. Except, she used a different entrance.

"Mira, stay with me," Avi said. "See the steps built into the wall right ahead of you?"

"Yup," Mira whispered.

"Okay, go up the steps. You'll see another alley and then turn right."

Mira followed Avi's directions. She went up eight steps and turned right. Another courtyard.

"Okay, you're in our courtyard now. See the door on the left?" Avi asked. "I have someone opening it now."

The door opened and Mira ran through. Ofer closed the door behind her and bolted it shut.

Mira took a minute to catch her breath. Then she said, "I thought you were going to meet me?"

"It was faster to come here and make sure you had an open door," he said. He smiled. "Okay, let's see what you got from these guys."

Mira handed over the USB stick.

Ofer and Mira walked into the secure room. Ofer selected a computer and unplugged it. Then, he turned off the wifi. "Okay, it's not connected to anything at all. Isolated. Let's see what's on here."

Ofer inserted the stick, and clicked to open it.

Mira took one look and said, "Wow, these guys don't know how to delete files, do they? I bet we can recover those ghost files."

Ofer looked positively gleeful. "I bet we can." Then he laughed. "Oh my, these guys don't know what they gave us!"

Mira and Ofer discovered spreadsheets of contacts, aside from the hack David was supposed to insert.

"Hey, what about David?" Mira asked. "Did we just leave him to be killed by these guys in black?"

Ofer smiled maniacally. "Hehe, we should have," he said. "Remember the help we asked for, especially at the clock tower?"

"Yeah, I didn't see them," Mira said.

"Well, they showed up just as you left the café. They got David and the guy in black, the one guy who escaped me at the beach. Our friends are interrogating them as we speak."

"Good," Mira said.

"Early reports are that they did want the highly enriched uranium. You don't need as much, especially if you want to build a weak bomb," Ofer said.

"You know, that's the kind of thing that makes me really nervous," Mira said.

"That's why we do what we do," Ofer said.

THE PATH

DAVID STIER

David Stier's astonishing short fiction has appeared in four different volumes of Fiction River *so far, with more to come. He will also be published in an upcoming issue of* Pulphouse *and a few other publications. Dave, a U.S. Army veteran, specializes in history, and has traveled extensively around the world.*

His experiences with other cultures informed "The Path." He writes: "I had a very strong reaction to how many people here in Twin Falls [Idaho] treat the Somali and Afghan refugees [poorly], where there is a refugee center."

He imagined what impact that treatment would have on the refugees receiving it, and wrote this story.

A isha Nawabi studied the sentence written on the blackboard which she had been asked to read.

"Can tell me how find bus to Market and Fourteen Street?" she said to the teacher who stood in front of the classroom at West Oakland Middle School.

Aisha and her older brother Ebrahim were the last survivors of their family. An infidel devil drone had seen to that when their house had been hit by mistake. She tried very hard to not hate Americans and many helpful people she had met since her arrival had aided in this desire. Her brother had forbidden her to take this nighttime English class but the women at the Refugee Center had said that this was most important in achieving success in this country.

They had arrived from Abdul Afghanistan three months ago. Her father, before he died, had made her promise to obey Ebrahim in all things and to obey *The Path*. She did her best to do so, but as the months passed Ebrahim's rage continued to grow. He despised all Americans as infidel Crusaders and Oakland as a den of iniquity. While she tried to embrace this new life, her brother could only embrace hatred. She would not obey his command that she not attend this class. She tried to follow *The Path*, but had started to question much. Perhaps what was proper in Afghanistan was unfitting here in America?

At the surrounding desks sat other refugees—mostly Afghan women, for Oakland California had a large number of Afghans, and like Aisha, they wore the hijab. One woman was fully veiled. During the day this room was filled with American students, but at night the local Refugee Center used it to teach English. The desks were scratched and the walls were stained in places and the floors were gouged and scuffed, but compared to the earthen-built madrasa in Abdul, it seemed a golden palace.

"You head down Market Street toward 14th Street until you see the bus stop sign, then look for the correct route number," the teacher, an Afghani American woman, dressed in stylish western clothing said. "Can you explain to me in English what I just said?"

A lump of fear rose to her throat, for she only partly understood. She felt her face get warm with embarrassment, but she forced herself to give a correct answer—or at least as correct as she could manage.

"You say to follow street name Market to... *tmdzy*—bus!—then find...*wat*—road?"

Aisha looked down at the desk to hide her shame. She tried to study more but her brother would get angry whenever he saw her doing so. She was surprised not to have heard laughter from any of the other students.

"That was very good!" the teacher said to her in Pashto.

She looked up in surprise then she looked at the students nearest to her. None of them looked upon her with scorn. In fact several nodded to her and smiled.

With much relief, the teacher moved on to another student, then the next and the next. Aisha listened carefully and took many notes and soon—too soon she felt—the class came to an end. As she prepared to leave the teacher came to her desk.

"Aisha," she said in Pashto, "may I speak with you for a moment?"

Aisha took a step back and again looked down, this time at the floor. Fear weakened her knees and her stomach. Was she going to be told not to come back? Often, on her way home from work or in the grocery market that understood Pashto, she would see this Afghan woman who dressed in western garb and looked and acted like a confidant American. Several times, Sahar—Aisha knew her name because Sahar would write it on the blackboard before the start of every English class—would smile and say hello in the market or on the street as Aisha walked home from her job. But outside of a hurried *salaam* in return, Aisha had not yet found the courage to say more.

"Please Aisha, look at me. I think your progress is going very well. In a few more weeks I think you will be ready for a more advanced class."

She looked up at Sahar in surprise who smiled in encouragement.

"My name is Sahar and I am from Afghanistan too. My family escaped Kandahar after 911."

Sahar always dressed as an infidel would dress, and secretly Aisha wished she could wear American clothes and look straight ahead like the American women she saw on the street. But her brother had also forbidden this, saying that Americans were not only decadent infidels but also the murderers of their family and that as Afghans, while they would have to endure life in this sinful country, that did not mean that they had to adopt its ways.

When she had asked him why he agreed to come to America if he hated this land and their people so much, his answer had been to strike her face with the back of his hand.

"It is of no concern of yours. You will not ask me this again."

She rubbed the spot on her face where he had struck her as she did often whenever she thought of Ebrahim.

"How did you learn English so well?" she asked.

Sahar, smiled and touched Aisha's shoulder gently.

"Like you are doing now. By coming to classes like this and by speaking to other Americans that I meet."

Aisha looked down again and took another step back.

"My brother has forbidden me to speak with infidels. He has

forbidden me to learn English. He says we are Afghan and will always remain as such."

Sahar's eyes sharpened in anger which she quickly masked.

"I urge you to return, Aisha. Learning English can be difficult, but you are doing very well. More than anything, it will supply the means of escape should you ever care to grasp it."

An ocean breeze ruffled her hijab as she stepped outside the school. The salt tinged air smelled refreshing. It also smelled of oil and gasoline, but still it was pleasant. And she did not have to cover her eyes from the desert dust and sand as in Abdul.

It was just a short walk to their apartment but it was also after dark. So far there had not been many problems with infidels because of the distance. Her job as a seamstress was in Old Oakland and while she had a monthly bus pass it was faster to walk home from the class. She could always tell her brother that the bus was late or that she had to work late. She walked quickly, staring at the sidewalk and staying close to the building's walls. Tonight she wore a dark dress which would make it easier to remain unseen.

"Hey karina-girl, how about we make us some babies?" an infidel said from across the street, followed by laughter.

Three dark-skinned men stood on the corner, smoking cigarettes. One of them made lewd motions with his body and another blew her kisses. She quickened her pace, glancing across the street several times to keep them in sight.

"Damn, homes, broad waxed your sorry ass on that," one infidel said.

Another infidel started to cross the street.

"Hey sexy mama! Nix the gargoyle hooker act," he said. "Ya'll look like a real sausage jockey to me, babe."

More laughter followed. Her heart began to pound and again her stomach tightened up. She clutched her backpack straps tightly with her hands, looked at them once more and for an instant they all appeared garbed with the black and white checked keffiyeh common among foreign fedayeen. She gasped, bit her hand to prevent it from happening again, purposely slowed her pace. Fedayeen could smell fear, as she believed possible of these three infidels.

Her apartment building was visible, but to her at this moment it looked very far away. As she neared the intersection a police car turned the corner, slowed as it approached the three men, almost stopped. They began to walk in the opposite direction. The police car backed up until it neared Aisha.

"You should be careful, Miss," the light-skinned officer said. "Where do you live?"

She struggled to understand. Did he say something about where she lived?

"I live there," she said, pointing to her apartment building.

"Okay, Miss, I'll keep watch until you get home."

She smiled nervously, bowed. "Thank you."

In this part of Oakland there were more police officers present. And unlike Afghanistan, American police were more interested in upholding the law and not looking for bribes or for engaging in other less savory pursuits.

As Aisha entered the apartment after leaving her shoes at the door, she heard voices from her brother's bedroom as was often the case. This secrecy worried her but she did not know what to do.

Their home was very strange. The walls were painted different colors and were scuffed in places. The toilet was different but they had their own shower and both were in the same room. Some Americans feared or hated them, but compared to Afghanistan, Oakland was a paradise.

She took her backpack into her bedroom, slid it under the bed

"*Allahu Akbar!*" someone cried, followed immediately by her brother's voice.

"Be quiet!" he said in Pashto loud enough to be heard from the other side of the wall.

She left her hijab on since there were other men in the apartment, set the table then worked at the stove making pilau, the lamb and rice dish her brother preferred. Soon, the pleasant aroma of cooking rice and meat permeated the apartment. Next she took three loaves of naan bread and placed them in the oven.

She waited in dread for Ebrahim and his friends to emerge. Mostly they were the same three men and the calculating expressions—identical to those of foreign fedayeen in Abdul—left her feeling with a great sense of unease. It was obvious that they wished her for a wife. She had promised her father to obey Ebrahim, but she would resist this edict of *The Path* just as she resisted his order not to learn English.

The door to his room opened followed by the loud voices of his friends.

"*Allahu Akbar!*" the same voice from earlier said. "We will surely strike a blow—" but the words stopped immediately with a grunt, as though someone had elbowed this man to silence.

Aisha's stomach again tightened up. While she concentrated upon the meal, her eyes filled with tears. Daily she prayed that this escape to America would deliver them both, but events only seemed to worsen. Her brother's anger continued to grow. Whenever she asked him about it his usually handsome features would twist into a scowl.

"Such matters are not for you to understand," was his most common answer.

She took a dish rag and dried her eyes.

Purposely she had prepared only enough for two as a convenient excuse should her brother invite his friends. It may have been inhospitable, but it was also practical for they had little money. Life may have been hard in Abdul, but food had been plentiful because they had grown much of their own. Here everything cost money.

She kept her back to them, as an obedient Afghan woman should until spoken to and prayed that this would not happen. This time her prayers were answered for after they put on their shoes the front door opened then closed. All had left, including Ebrahim, but the sounds of soft spoken voices continued outside the door. She set the table and placed the pilau into a bowl which she set in the middle. She spread butter upon the heated naan bread and awaited her brother's return.

Aisha spooned pilau onto her plate and began to eat it with a fork as she had seen Americans do. Her brother sneered at this, took some in his hand and rolled it into a ball then popped it into his mouth, repeating this action several times.

"So easily you forget our ways," he said, as he took more pilau in his hand and spread it on a piece of naan bread then angrily chewed the food.

She watched his actions for a moment, his rage now directed at the meal.

"Have you found a job?" she asked.

He reached for the naan bread again, tore off another piece, pointed it at her from across the worn metal table. "You did not use enough butter," he said, "and why do you ask this?"

She took the butter from the refrigerator, placed it upon the table.

"You spoke of meeting your friends tomorrow at a garage where you have sought work."

He said nothing more, continued to shovel food into his mouth with an occasional gulp of tea. After finishing the meal he poured himself another cup of tea, added some honey.

"You need to learn your place in this house," he finally said.

She set her fork down with a loud clatter.

"And what is that supposed to mean?" she asked.

Ebrahim slowly drank his tea. He smiled but with little humor.

"What I mean is that as the head of this house, it is your duty to obey me. You have forgotten the ways of *The Path* so it is now my duty to enforce it. You will stop going to these English classes—immediately!" he said. "It is also proper that I find you a suitable husband."

Aisha shook her head, started to clear the table. "I promised our father to obey you in all things but that was before your heart had filled with hate and before Allah answered our prayers and we escaped to America."

He stood, grabbed her arm and shook her hard enough to dislodge her hijab. Finally she was able to break free.

"We are in a new place, Ebrahim. A place of opportunity. While the devil drones killed our family these infidels did not. Unlike you, I will not allow myself to be consumed with hate." She took one of her brother's hands, which he reluctantly allowed. "Please my brother, tell me how I can help."

Ebrahim's face darkened in the manner she saw so very often now. His mouth curved downward, his eyes drew together and his forehead creased in rage. He yanked his hand free and for an instant she thought he would strike her.

"You will obey me, my sister. And you will keep out of matters not of your concern."

She picked up her hijab which had fallen to the floor then started to clean up after the meal.

"I will keep my own counsel in these two matters," she said.

After a few moments, Ebrahim went to his room, then left the apartment shortly after.

Aisha had to work late the following day and it was well past dusk when the bus reached her stop. This was a good thing because the Pakistani Muslim she worked for did not take advantage by forcing her to work without pay. Her mother—an expert in needlework—had taught her the craft. Her designs and clothing were prized by Afghan and infidel alike. It was Aisha's desire to one day open her own shop.

As she neared the apartment, she saw her brother and his friends walking in the direction of the garage that Ebrahim had applied to for work. It was one of the few acceptable places of business in his mind because it was owned by Sunni Muslims. She watched them briefly with growing unease that in truth had not left since the previous night. All through the day her fear that Ebrahim and his friends were planning to do something foolish—or worse—would not leave. She hurried toward the apartment, quickly changed into her black dress and hijab then left in pursuit.

The bus pulled up to its stop across the street as she left the apartment. She ran, waving her hand and calling out. It started to pull away but luckily the driver saw her and waited. Usually she did not mind the stop-and-go progress. It allowed her to study the people and different parts of the city and take in the foreign strangeness. As they moved closer to the garage the buildings began to look less cared for. Unlike Abdul, the bricks used here were smaller and red in color and they did not need constant care as the mud bricks used in her homeland. Much of the buildings were painted with graffiti—a word she had learned soon after her arrival. Some of this graffiti had been crafted with great care by people of obvious talent while some of it was just crude words she could not understand. More and more windows were cracked or broken and there were fewer streetlights.

She checked her watch. Finally they arrived at her stop. As she left she thanked the driver, a dark-skinned middle-aged woman who smiled thanks in return.

"You be careful, honey," she said. "This a nasty part of town."

Aisha smiled again, understanding little except that she should be careful. As she crossed the street, she despaired that her brother could not see the good in many of these infidels.

It was nearly dark. Some of the street lights were broken, so chances of being discovered were less. She turned the corner onto the street leading to the garage. Something hard and wet struck the side of her head. Laughter immediately followed.

"Fucking sand nigger," a younger male voice screamed from

across the street. At her feet she saw a broken egg, raised a hand to her sore ear where it had struck. Her hand came away sticky and wet. She looked up in time to dodge a second egg which hit the brick wall behind her. For an instant she was back in Afghanistan and a spray of *Kalashnikov* bullets had replaced the thrown egg. She fell to the ground to even more laughter.

The two light-skinned teenaged boys laughed even harder. "Get the fuck gone you fucking terrorist!"

With their middle fingers raised in mocking salute, they turned and ran down a side street. "*USA! USA! USA!*" their screaming voices echoed up and down the street.

May Allah curse you both!

She removed the hijab, rubbed her sore ear then wiped away what of the egg yolk she could.

Aisha studied the garage from the corner of another building across the street. It was lit on the inside. Also, the smaller door next to a large sliding door had an overhead light. The far corner of the garage was cast in shadow, so she raced across the street to the garage's darkened corner.

She waited, her heart pounding. She heard voices from within but not well enough to understand them. Slowly she moved closer to the large sliding door.

"—must act tomorrow, my friends. The Crusaders may discover the missing fertilizer at any time."

Ebrahim, what have you done?

Aisha crept to the long narrow window on the sliding door. It had been painted over on the inside, but one corner had been scraped clean. Four men stood with their backs turned, facing a large truck that was parked at the back of the garage. Also, she smelled something that she remembered from Abdul. Something that usually meant the presence of some kind of bomb. As she watched, two men rolled something to the back of the truck. When they stood it up she saw that it was a large container like those used to hold gasoline or oil. Ebrahim and another man she remembered from the apartment rolled a similar container to the truck then stood it up as well. Together, they raised each container in turn into the back of the truck. Then another man she recognized went to a cluttered workbench and returned with a spool of wire.

Aisha moved away from the window but stayed between the sliding door and the corner of the building in hopes of hearing more. The smaller door opened. A man stepped outside, illuminated fully in the light—the one who most often looked at her as many fedayeen had done in Afghanistan. She froze in place, praying that he would not turn in her direction.

A voice from inside called out. He turned away from her, stepped back into the garage and closed the door.

Aisha scurried backward and slid around the side of the building. She fell to a sitting position and wiped the sweat from her brow then peered around the corner. A few minutes later the light was turned off and the door opened. She moved farther along her side. The sounds of whispering voices slowly receded. After they had faded completely she stood, peered around the building to make sure they had gone then left in the opposite direction.

Aisha had gotten lost. But she had learned from her father to follow the stars and while much of this night sky was strange, she did see the star that always pointed north. There were also brighter city lights in the distance, so with the star and these lights she walked slowly back toward her apartment. The tears would not cease. She wiped her eyes often in order to see clearly.

What am I to do?

Save for Ebrahim, the foreign fedayeen and infidel devil drones had destroyed her family. Only through the intervention of a United Nations relief worker had she and her brother avoided a similar fate.

How can I betray him?

Would they both be thrown into prison, or would her brother be shot down in the street like a dog as she had seen fedayeen do in her homeland? Not only her family but so many of her people had been murdered by infidel devil drones and *Daesh* terrorists.

Did not he have a right to his rage?

The American fedayeen she had seen last night would surely have attacked her had not the police car driven by, and the young egg throwing hoodlums also wished her nothing but ill will.

Why should I care?

Ebrahim wanted to die and his hatred was at least partly well founded and it would atone for the murder of their family and so many of their people.

But there were also infidels such as the bus driver of tonight and Muslims like Sahar her English teacher and the Pakistani she worked for and the police officer who protected her. They all had enriched her life. If she tried to stop Ebrahim herself he and his friends would probably kill her then martyr themselves. Since they had found sanctuary here she had seen several such attacks on the television. And while fewer innocent people had died in America, they were still innocent of any wrongdoing.

She had sworn to her father that she would follow *The Path* and following *The Path* was to obey her brother as father had commanded. But was it right to obey when in doing so she would make her life a lesser gift than what Mohammed had taught? One Pillar of Islam was that of *zakāt*. Would not it be a charity to prevent the taking of innocent lives with the saving of her brother?

She gazed upward into the night sky. Fewer stars were visible here than they were from her homeland but these stars, this world, and her presence, while insignificant within the universe, were meaningful in that none directly opposed life.

"Aisha, what are you doing out so late? This is a very dangerous part of town."

Sahar, her English class teacher, stood at her side, a look of concern upon her face.

"You look troubled, my dear. Is there something I can do to help?"

Aisha looked back up at the night sky and then back down to this, her friend.

"Will you help me talk to the police?"

TRAFFICKING STOPS

LISA SILVERTHORNE

Lisa Silverthorne also set her story in the here and now, but there's no clash of cultures. Just closed eyes to the actual culture around us. Her spy is monitoring a world that exists under all of our noses.

You'll find Lisa's work in many, many Fiction River *volumes, both in the previous issues* How to Save the World, Christmas Ghosts, Hex in the City, Moonscapes, Past Crime, Recycled Pulp, No Humans Allowed, Justice, Wishes, Editor Saves, *and* Pulse Pounders: Countdown. *But the stories in* Fiction River *are a small part of her oeuvre. She has published nearly 100 stories in a wide variety of anthologies. Her novel* Isabel's Tears *appeared a few years ago, and her second book,* Rediscovery, *just came out.*

About "Trafficking Stops," she writes, "I felt overwhelmed by 'Spies.' What could I possibly add? Then I read a local news article about a restaurant being a front for a human slavery ring. Everyone I asked about the article reacted the same way. 'That happened here?' Right here. To refugees desperate for a better life."

The resulting story is one of the strongest in the volume.

S liver of moon was lost in the dark Illinois sky, truck stop's blinking signs polluting the cool June night as Sawyer Smith bought her first heroin balloon. From the truck stop's dark side where all the truckers parked for the night. Where anything—and anyone—under the moon and a blind eye could be bought, sold, or traded. And it was. Every. Single. Night.

Like the night her stepfather brought her here from Ohio and sold her to some monsters in Iowa. She had been fourteen.

Sawyer passed the rail thin man with wild eyes a twenty. He grabbed her arm, his hand grimy and pocked with track marks, fingernails caked with dirt. His breath reeked of alcohol, his body odor almost knocking her to the ground.

Sawyer froze, the memories of eleven years ago trickling back. The violence was as normal as the drinking and drugs and secrets she'd tried to keep. From the family that didn't want her. From the *boyfriends* and *brothers* offering her *help* as they passed her around like a broken thrift shop doll. From the lies she told herself, that all of this was normal, that she deserved it because she was worthless. And afraid. Until a night like this when she just—walked away. Bought a bus ticket to Pittsburgh and got off at the YWCA.

And told someone.

"How 'bout we do a trade, honey," he said, his gap-toothed leer unnerving.

She jerked free of his hold. "Not happenin'," she said with a growl and held out the twenty again.

He glared at her and yanked the bill out of her hand. "Fucking bitch."

And he was gone into the darkness and tangle of people working the night shift.

"You get all that, Radwell?"

Sawyer whispered into the night vision camera sewn into her blue hoodie, its lens pointing out of an eyelet where the drawstring used to be. The earpiece was tiny and fit into her ear. She wore torn-up skinny jeans, a ripped white V-neck T-shirt, and sneakers, looking more like seventeen than twenty-five with her short black hair highlighted blue to match her eyes. She slid the little red balloon deeper into her hoodie pocket.

Couldn't lose the evidence.

"That was too dangerous, Sawyer," said Corbyn Radwell in her ear, his voice deep and raspy, all business.

She didn't want a partner on this assignment, but her employer, Trafficking Stops, insisted. Hadn't five years of investigative work proven that she could handle any job thrown at her? Her evidence and information helped bring down dozens of human traffickers. Every conviction healed part of her pain. Every rescue cut away at the deep, cancerous fear that had always ruled her life. She loved her job.

She was a good spy.

"You got that, didn't you?" she said as she walked through the rows of parked trucks.

"Sure did," said the deep, raspy voice in her ear.

"Then get this. This isn't my first investigation, Radwell. I don't need a partner."

She'd lived this life. There were places like it all over the country. Where polite, trusting people followed their dreams and disappeared. Every. Single. Day. At fourteen, and the oldest of six siblings, she had left Gallipolis, Ohio (and horrible stepfather when her mother died) dreaming of being a singer. When she met her *boyfriend*. Who just wanted to *help*. Introduced her to heroin and meth. A dependent zombie, she was passed around to other *boyfriends* and *brothers* pimps. For four long years. Until she ended up as some bastard's sex toy in a tiny Nebraska town that tried to pretend she (and others like her) didn't exist. After she'd escaped.

We're all good people here, the mayor of that town told the media. *This kind of thing just doesn't happen.*

Too bad all the good people were out of town the night they sold her to a man and his son for four hundred bucks at the only gas and sip. They all turned a blind eye to her desperate looks and signals for help.

"Who's running your wireless hardware?" Radwell replied. "Backing up your information. And who's got your back if this all goes south? I do. And that's a promise."

She remembered him from Trafficking Stops' Seattle office and from running hardware on a few assignments. Tall and blond. Thirty-something. Hazel eyes and cocky smile. All business in the field. He sounded sincere. For now.

Trust didn't come easily.

"So when's the big show?" she asked, changing the subject.

"Take out your TracFone. Pretend you're on a call."

Sawyer pulled the phone out of her hoodie pocket and put it to her ear.

"Slaver's Shopping Club starts at eleven thirty, 'bout an hour away," said Radwell.

Sawyer winced, fear a sharp stab to her belly. She knew this place well. Sales of illegals and young teenagers (even kids) to the highest bidder held in the backs of rental trucks. She'd been sold twice here. No questions asked.

Nothing would make her happier than bringing this place down.

"There's been a slight operation change."

"I don't like this, Radwell." She didn't like changes to the protocol they'd set up in the office.

"An informant came through with a seller's wristband. Remember, we talked about the possibility, but knew it was a long shot."

Sawyer chewed her lip. She vaguely remembered discussing it. Having that route inside open up was a huge break in this case. She'd gladly walk into that monster pit if it brought them closer to closing it down.

"So, you and I are going in together. In the meantime, gather faces and evidence on camera. I've shared my location to your phone, but meet me at a green Mercury Cougar parked near the lot at 11:15 p.m. With Pearl Jam and Blind Melon stickers on the bumper. South side of the lot."

"No Nirvana or Weezer? You savage!" Sawyer said with a smirk.

Radwell laughed. "My brother's the savage. It's his old car. Remember, Sawyer—no heroics. We're just taking pictures and gathering operations details. Getting one of these sales documented on camera. And then get out. Got it? Meet at the car. Hardware's in a truck labeled Midnight Sun Shipping with Alaska plates."

"How do I know you can pull this off?" Sawyer replied.

She knew nothing about Radwell and didn't like him giving all the orders. Why should she trust him?

His deep laugh echoed in her ear. "I've been a lot of things, Sawyer. Military. Police officer. Private security. Why should I trust you?"

"I lived this life for four horrible years until I escaped. Spent the last seven years learning to protect myself. And I get a personal high from taking them out."

"Four years? Damn—that's rough."

"Seeya in an hour. How will I know it's you? It'll be dark and I can't risk standing out in this crowd. I need to ID you quick."

Radwell chuckled. "Look for the guy in the Nirvana T-shirt, black hoodie, and military haircut."

"That I've got to see," Sawyer said with a laugh. "Not sure I'll recognize you without your suit and tie."

No way Radwell had a Nirvana T-shirt. She put her TracFone back in her pocket and faded into the dark.

Sawyer walked through the dark lot that eclipsed the bright, dancing lights of the truck stop store and restaurant. The smell of cut grass and diesel fuel tanged the air, wind gritty from the surrounding farm fields. She moved through rows of dark trucks, capturing footage of rampant, small-time drug deals selling anything from crack to heroin. Everything was for sale. Or trade. There were more prostitutes than truck drivers.

She bought more drugs and eavesdropped on prostitution propositions, capturing details, hoping to find a lead up the chain and into its infrastructure. To the people running things. Most were hand to hands, supporting a family or a habit. Some were small-time brokers selling domestics and beats selling fakes or pushing shorts. She wanted the cartel marks and the slavers.

"You cheated me, you bastard!" shouted a man with brown dreads, shorts, and a Phish T-shirt at a man in baggy jeans, flip flops, and white T-shirt.

Sawyer stepped back as the fist fight started, capturing all of it on camera. The lot policed itself, so any fights or arguments were immediately squelched.

She moved away from the scene, heading south toward the lot's edge. To find Radwell.

She was early, but she found him leaning against the driver's side of the old green Cougar. She'd already checked the bumper from a distance and found the Pearl Jam and Blind Melon stickers.

She glanced at Radwell's wrist, seeing the white silicone bracelet. It had the word Admission printed in black. And sure enough, he wore a black Nirvana T-shirt, jeans, and black sneakers.

"How'd you do that?" Sawyer asked as she approached him.

She didn't remember him being so handsome with his rugged good looks, sexy tousled blond hair and sad hazel eyes, like a scolded puppy.

"What? The T-shirt?"

He tried to keep a straight face, but the smirk slipped through.

"Okay, I traded it with the tech guy."

Sawyer couldn't help but laugh. He'd done that to impress her and dammit, it worked.

He moved beside her and leaned against her shoulder, whispering. "They've got security all along the perimeter, so we've gotta stay in character. Got it."

Sawyer nodded.

"There are sales in four trucks tonight," Radwell whispered. "Each one has black bear in the name."

He grabbed her arm and pulled her against him. "Move, bitch or I'll drag you."

For a moment, Sawyer froze, the voices from her past taking hold, fear burning in the pit of her stomach as he led her through the darkness and the rows of trucks.

They walked down several rows of semis and large trucks until Black Bear Moving appeared at the end of a row. It was a huge semi trailer with two burly men standing in back.

The men glanced at Radwell's wrist. One of them stepped toward him, glaring, ignoring Sawyer. To him she was just cargo. Something to be sold and used. She wanted to rip the burly guy's head off.

"How about those Bears this year?" one of the men asked.

"How about those Cubs?" Radwell answered. "Best season ever."

The man glanced at Radwell's wrist and then turned and nodded at the other man who opened the trailer door, motioning Radwell inside.

Radwell grabbed Sawyer's arm again and pulled her up the ramp, toward the door.

"Resist," Radwell whispered.

Sawyer pulled away. "No! I'm not going in there!"

Radwell grabbed her arm and jerked her forward, allowing her to get the two men on camera. And the name on the truck.

"Shut your mouth or they'll find you in a ditch somewhere!" he said in such an angry voice that Sawyer recoiled from him.

Holding her against him, he pulled her forward. Inside the truck's dim-lit trailer.

Cigarette smoke hung in the air, giving the trailer an eerie fog-like presence as Radwell moved her through the crowd of men (and some women). The air smelled dry and stale with cigarette smoke and motor oil, voices a dull drone that reverberated against the metal walls. Ahead, at the front of the trailer, were three men with clipboards. And a group of ten women, each one with large black numbers hanging around their necks, eyes red, faces streaked with tears.

Sawyer heard muffled sobs as Radwell moved her closer.

And then she noticed men turning their eyes toward her, sizing her up like a 4-H calf up for auction. Her grip on Radwell's arm tightened, but she pushed back her fear, standing tall. Until Radwell hung a sign around her neck. With the number 1019.

She couldn't control her shaking as she watched them sell a long-legged redhead whose eyes looked far away on drugs. Or maybe she'd just withdrawn to keep her own sanity. Sawyer captured the sale on camera. And the next one, two fourteen-year-old girls sobbed and shook as they held onto each other.

The betting sky-rocketed, becoming a tinny roar that reverberated through the hollow trailer. Two thousand. Three. Do I hear four grand?

At five grand they were sold to four muscled men in camo jackets.

"I can't do this, Radwell," she hissed in his ear. "Can't watch this."

Radwell held onto her arm. Made her look at him.

"Information first. Then the cavalry, okay?"

It took every ounce of strength she had to nod and stand there watching a fifteen-year-old girl screaming and crying as a man in a black shirt and jeans dragged her out of the trailer. Bought for a hundred bucks.

Sawyer felt sick. A hundred bucks. The price of a good set of headphones. An e-reader. Small tablet. A fifteen-year-old meth addict. Things we don't think twice about when we shop.

This had to stop.

Sawyer moved away from Radwell, edging along the side of the trailer as the next bidding started. Where three young girls cowered against the metal wall. She slid down beside them. The first girl was short-haired like Sawyer, auburn hair and about fifteen.

"I'm so scared," she said to the girl beside her. Long brown hair and big brown eyes filled with tears.

"Why can't I just go home?"

Sawyer leaned toward them. "First chance you get, walk away. Walk into a store, a restaurant, a health club. Ask for help."

Both girls' eyes widened as they turned to stare at her.

"It just makes things worse," said the auburn-haired girl.

"Not if you don't go back to them," Sawyer replied. "Believe in yourself. You're not worthless. Fight for your life."

She leaned toward the middle girl, but the words froze on her tongue as she stared past her, at a young girl with black hair and blue eyes, a younger mirror of her own face. Her number was 999.

"Tabby?" Sawyer cried.

The young woman turned around, tears flooding her face.

"Sawyer? Oh, my, God! Sawyer!"

Her little sister, Tabitha. Called Tabby. Sawyer threw her arms around her and held her tight.

Tabby was just eight when Sawyer left home. After Mom died and they were left with their horrible stepfather. Treated Mom's four kids like garbage. Sawyer hated him more than anyone in this world.

"How'd you get here?" Sawyer asked, brushing hair out of Tabby's face.

Tabby started to answer, but a stocky man grabbed hold of her and pulled her in front of the crowd.

"No! Tabby, no!"

Sawyer rushed back to Radwell.

"We have to do something," she said in his ear. "That's my little sister! Number 999."

Sawyer pointed at the young girl being paraded like a pony around the crowd. And there, standing on the side with a leering grin was her stepfather. In her head, he'd been tall and stocky. Fierce. Menacing with steely grey eyes, thick brown hair perfectly placed, and a heavy gait. But the monster had aged.

Seeing him now made her stomach churn, the old sour fear rising. But he looked grizzled, weathered, age hollowing his cheeks, brown eyes sunken into his face, still sharp and angry. Red and rheumy, nose and cheeks flushed. He lumbered with an uncertain shuffle, balding, unshaven, hands calloused and dirty, teeth missing from his leering grin, moving like an old alcoholic. Temper bubbling over, ready to explode. She'd seen it so many times.

"Get it on camera, Sawyer," Radwell said through gritted teeth.

"Buy her!" she shouted.

"But I—"

Sawyer grabbed Radwell's arm and pushed his hand up.

"What are you doing?"

"Justice," she whispered.

Radwell grumbled, but kept bidding. Winning the bid at $500.

"Make sure you get footage of him taking the money," said Radwell.

Sawyer nodded, her heart pounding as she turned her camera toward Radwell as he walked up to that thin, balding monster with angry brown eyes and explosive temper. She captured all of it as Radwell pulled Tabby along beside him, heading back toward her. Tabby sobbed, hands against her face, but when she saw Sawyer, her sobbing softened. Radwell leaned down to her and said something she couldn't hear.

He grabbed Sawyer's arm, pulling her close. "We're leaving. Now."

Radwell lurched into the crowd, Tabby on one side, Sawyer on the other as they pushed their way toward the back of the trailer. Someone ahead knocked on the trailer door. It opened and then closed quickly.

When they'd gotten through the haze of smoke and press of bodies, Radwell pounded the door with his fist.

A heartbeat later, it opened. One of the burly men held up his arm, but Sawyer was ready for him.

She swung under his arm and ran down the ramp. The burly man chased after her. She heard other footfalls and then Radwell in her ear.

"Keep running! To the restaurant."

Sawyer ran as hard as her legs would pump, slipping behind trucks, through groups of people until the truck stop lights burned her eyes. Until she saw the Midnight Sun Shipping truck drive up beneath the sliver of moon. She ran toward the truck, climbing inside the tech van when the door slid open. The IT crew inside grinned at her.

"We got it all, Sawyer. All the evidence you need to take that guy down."

"I made sure to get every girl's face on film. And the—auction-eers. We'll start IDing everyone in the morning. I'll focus on rescuing the girls while I wait for the arrest warrants on their captors."

Sawyer collapsed into a chair and waited for Radwell and Tabby. It seemed like forever until the door opened and Radwell leaped inside, Tabby beside him. He slammed the door.

"Go! Now!"

The truck lurched forward and sped away onto the interstate. Only when they'd put a lot of distance between them and the truck stop did Sawyer relax. She reached over and patted her sister's hand.

"It's over now, kid."

Tabby nodded and threw her arms around her sister. "I thought you were dead. That's what he told us."

Radwell glanced over at Sawyer and grinned. "That footage is going to put him away for a long time."

"Thanks, Radwell," Sawyer said, returning his smile. "I know we broke protocol, but I couldn't walk out and leave Tabby like that."

"It's okay," he said in a quiet voice, nodding. "I'd have done the same thing."

Eight months after the assignment, Sawyer flew from Seattle to Ohio for her stepfather's trial. It felt so good when the prosecutor played the evidence for the jury, showing her stepfather selling Tabby for $500. They took two hours to find him guilty.

A month later, Sawyer returned with Radwell and sat in the second row beside Tabby, listening as the judge sentenced that horrible man to life in prison. And Sawyer made sure that bastard looked into her eyes as they took him from the courtroom.

"Remember me, Eric?" Sawyer said.

Her stepfather glared at her. "I thought you were dead."

For the first time in her life, Sawyer saw that this man was only five foot nine at the most. The towering, explosive anger that had burned in his eyes had made them look so dark and menacing, but his brown eyes just looked cold. And empty. His shoulders sagged, a beer belly rounding over his brown pants. He looked like an old newspaper, yellowed and brittle, ink fading from the words so they had no meaning anymore. His soul was an ugly, sallow ashtray, crusty and stale with cigarette butts. Too cold to light even the memory of flame.

Sawyer stared through him, feeling like she towered over this grizzled monster.

"I'm sure you did," she snapped. "Too bad that the men you hired to sell me into—into hell sang like sparrows to the police. How ironic that selling Tabby is what sent you to prison?"

Sawyer turned away as they led her stepfather out of the courtroom, shouting and in cuffs. She moved over to Radwell. He put his arms around her and kissed her. They'd just moved in together after a few months of dating. She'd trust him with anything now.

"Nice work, Sawyer," he said.

Tabby hugged Sawyer and then Radwell. "Thank you both for everything."

"My pleasure," said Radwell.

The three of them walked out of the courthouse and out to a red Ford rental.

"Can't believe I'm going to live with you in Seattle," said Tabby, climbing into the back seat.

"Can't believe we're together," said Sawyer. "I'm still looking for Chris and Kayla."

She wouldn't turn a blind eye like the others. And she wouldn't stop searching until all four of them were together. Sawyer glanced at Radwell as he started the car. With Radwell as her partner, she could succeed at damn near anything.

THE SPY WHO WALKED INTO THE COLD

RON COLLINS

Ron Collins' story "The Spy Who Walked into the Cold" also examines a part of the United States that most people don't know about, only unlike Lisa Silverthorne's story or David Stier's, Ron's story takes place in the not-so-distant past. Like C.A. Rowland, Ron uses real historical events to make his story even stronger.

Ron has published stories and novels for years. He has two novels series running right now, Stealing the Sun, and The Saga of the God-Touched Mage. He's a regular in Analog SF as well as in eight volumes (so far) of Fiction River. His story, "The White Game" from Fiction River: Hidden in Crime was nominated for the Short Mystery Fiction Society's Derringer Award.

Along with his daughter Brigid Collins, Ron will edit a future volume of Fiction River as well. He's blogging about that experience at typosphere.com.

Be prepared to dive deep into a world you thought you knew, a world of spies and spying that is both true and heartbreaking at the same time. It's time to join Mr. Radner, in the cold.

I dreamed of the fight in A Shau Valley again.

Three years back and I still see it clear as day.

It's raining the kind of rain that only falls when you're on your own in an isolated camp out in the middle of the jungle, big drops that pelt your shoulders like bullets and make your helmet drum against your brain. Ten of us Green Berets from the 5th Special Forces and a couple hundred civilian irregulars are there to keep the Viet Cong off the Ho Chi Minh Trail. A couple NVA spooks who came over said they had four battalions in the area and after we asked twice the brass believed it enough to send us a MIKE company and a handful of new Berets, so we know they're coming.

Everyone understands Charlie needs to clear the pipeline.

Per the playbook, the VC begin at night.

By the time the first mortars fall, the whole place is a muddy slop sheened with whatever moonlight can cut its way through that thick overcast.

I fire the M-14 at places where the machine-gun fire comes from, and hightail from one defensive position to another.

A mortar shell drops ahead, then another behind. From the sound they're the smaller 107mm shells rather than the big 120 or 160 mothers.

I drop into one of our stations. The sandbags are already bullet-pocked, their frayed edges of burlap pucker and trail fibers. Wet sand is better cover, I think as the rain fades to a drizzle.

"They're coming from there," Dinh Lu yells and points to the field of tall razor grass east of camp.

Dinh Lu has an old Browning Automatic balanced on the bags. His uniform is covered in mud that clings to him in clumps and makes a base over his face that runs with lines of sweat and rain that glisten like spiderwebs over his cheekbones. He smells like too many cigarettes.

"Good," I say.

Both the grass and the claymores we laid in those fields should slow the VC down.

"Be advised to hold this position."

He yes-yesses me, and I'm running again.

Tracers. Explosions. Debris. In front of me. Behind me. Right and left. The smell of oil and thatch burning through the rain. C4. The ground shaking like the end of the world is here.

As always, this is when I realized I was dreaming. And, like always, knowing made everything worse. I watched myself run, feeling every step in my ankles and my knees. Pounding drove through my spine, and acid air burned my lungs. I was aware of my heart thundering inside my chest, aware of the sound of bombs bursting in the distance, and also aware that nothing I could do now would keep the mortar from falling on Dinh Lu's station, just like nothing I can ever do will stop anything else that happened that night.

Head down, both hands on the M-14, I raced to the control

point, a thatched hut raised on stilts made of tree trunks. Even in the dark I see the hut's shot all to hell.

Kendrick was kneeling, pressed up against one of those trunks. He looked at me through the rain.

We had trained together three years, Kendrick and I. He was from Saginaw, and had one of the worst poker faces in the 5th. He had a girl at home and was going to be an electrician when he got back to her.

His eyes were wide and open.

He screamed, "Be advised of VC down and eastward," and he waved his hand to the same patch of high grass Dinh Lu had.

The blast hit behind him.

The image froze like it always does: Kendrick lifted up in the air, his body silhouetted in orange fire, arms and legs cartwheeling like he's some kind of cartoon.

Then came the concussion, the wave of heat, the blistering pain that burned down my leg. Everything went hazy then. There was only rain and mud and gray images of movement happening around me. Eventually I heard voices, and then the chop of the H-34 that came to get me out.

The dream stayed with me that day, like it did every day. I was sitting in the basement of Kosmo's, a tavern on Chicago's South Side, not far from Bronzeville and not far from the lake. Special Agent Roy Mitchell was to my right, facing the door. It was June of 1969, just past noon.

Kosmo's is a dark place, a dive, really, owned by a Polish man and run mostly by his kid. It smelled like beer, cigarettes, and the burgers they would sometimes fry up in the back. A radio sat on the far end of the bar playing a tinny version of "Get Back" with Billy Preston on the keyboard.

Mitchell and I both had gin and tonics sweating into green napkins in front of us.

"Cigarette?" I said, waving a box of Winstons at Mitchell.

"No thanks."

I lit one while we waited.

As far as I was concerned, Special Agent Roy Mitchell was a star. He'd been in the Bureau for more than a decade. Did a stint in Korea before that. Like me, he was an Indiana boy growing up, but he worked in Mississippi before coming here to Chicago. So, yeah, he'd been around. The guy had a way about him, too. Quiet. Mostly calm. He thought a lot more than he talked, which was more than I could say for a lot of guys who'd trained me before.

I looked at my watch. "He's late."

"He'll be here," Mitchell said.

Right on cue, the black man appeared. He was tall and thin, a little awkward in the way gangly men can be. His cheeks were hollow, his eyes slitted but busy. A mustache covered his upper lip, and he walked with that certain air about him I had seen a million times—confident, tough, but paranoid all at once.

This was William O'Neal, Chief of Security of the Chicago chapter of the Black Panthers. I couldn't help but feel edgy at the idea of it. The Panthers were an openly militant, openly communist organization, and I'd recently spent a lot of time getting shot at by openly militant communists.

He sat to my left, across from Mitchell.

Mitchell waved at the bartender and a tall glass of soda, complete with a straw, appeared a moment later.

O'Neal read my expression. "Everything goes better with Coke, right, brother?" He picked up the glass and drank. When he put it down, I felt rebuked.

"How are you, William?" Mitchell said.

"I'm good, Roy," O'Neal replied. "Who's the boy?"

"Meet Detective Radner," Mitchell said, waving an open-palmed hand my way.

"He okay?"

Mitchell smiled and gave me a crosswise glance. "Greenhorn, but he's got promise."

O'Neal gave me the once-over. I picked up the box of smokes and offered him one. He took it, but didn't light up.

"What do you have for me?" Mitchell said, sipping his drink again.

"Lots of talk about Bobby."

"I suppose that would be," Mitchell replied.

Bobby was Bobby Seale, who was awaiting trial for his part in the riots at the Democratic National Convention last summer. Both he and Huey Newton, the original founders of the Panthers, were now behind bars, a fact that, combined with Eldridge Cleaver having run off to Algeria, wasn't helping the group any.

"We got maybe three hundred across town now."

"Members?" Mitchell clarified.

"Yeah. Three hundred brothers and sisters."

"Weapons?"

O'Neal proceeded to list off guns and ammunition stored in several places around town, but focused on Panther Headquarters. His tone of voice was controlled, his statements were made in a straightforward manner, like he was reading off a menu. There was no ideology there. No sense of concern and no clandestine whispering. Just recitation. Just the facts.

"They're all legal, though," O'Neal said at the end.

The twitch of Mitchell's lips said he didn't care for that part of the answer, but O'Neal just shrugged.

"New people?"

"No one big."

"Bobby Rush? Freddie Hampton?"

"Still here." O'Neal sipped his soda. "Deborah's still pregnant."

Mitchell looked at me. "That's Hampton's girlfriend."

I nodded. Given Hoover's total hard-on for the Panthers, the BBP org chart was among the first things I learned as I came up to speed with Chicago's inner workings. Bobby Rush was now minister of defense. Fred Hampton was the chairman of the Illinois chapter. Deborah Johnson was, as Mitchell said, Hampton's girlfriend. She was carrying their child.

O'Neal spent a few minutes discussing the training of new members—the Panthers took their ideology seriously, and constant discussion was part of their program. He described the Panthers' work on the street: meetings with the Blackstone Rangers, operations for the free breakfast program, and conversations Panther officers held about how to work with the Weathermen, the Young Lords, and several other radical left-wing groups.

"That's a lot of people," I said.

O'Neal gave me a doleful stare. "Chairman Fred's not afraid to work with anyone."

He finished off the soda.

"Anything else?" Mitchell said.

"Not I can think of."

Mitchell reached into his breast pocket with two fingers and removed an envelope. He placed it on the table, and slid it toward the black man.

O'Neal folded it over once, then put it in his pocket.

"Meet again in two weeks?" Mitchell said.

"Wouldn't miss it for the world," O'Neal replied as he stood up. "Nice to meet you, Detective," he said to me.

Then he left.

"What did you think?" Mitchell asked as he chewed a handful of peanuts.

"I'm surprised you paid him."

"Why?"

"He didn't give us anything on the Bradford case."

Mitchell finished his drink, then placed it on the table.

"We weren't here for the Bradford case."

I squinted at him and stubbed out my cigarette. I had already learned how to keep my mouth shut when I wasn't connecting all the dots yet, so I didn't say anything about the murder I thought we were investigating.

"And the other stuff?"

"What about it?"

"We already know everything he said."

"Yes, we do."

"So how was that worth $300?"

"You're Green Beret," Mitchell said, his eyes taking on a sparkle that felt oddly personal. "I would've figured you to be quicker on the uptake."

I stayed quiet.

Mitchell looked me square in eye. "Here's the deal, Carl. Chicago's no different from the jungles, all right? Sure, the streets might look civilized as shit to the average Joe, but that's a fake draw. This is a hard town, you hear me? Cops, gangs, crazy-assed hippies zoned on acid...it's a war zone out here. I know you saw your share of war zones, and you know I've seen mine. So you can trust me that I ain't shitting you on this. This city's full of assholes like the Panthers. Guys who got no problem putting a .45 upside your head any day of the week. So you keep your eye on the ball, right? You keep all your cards in the game because you never know when you're going to need something special."

"You're calibrating him," I said, understanding. "He's corroborated what we know."

Mitchell's smile told me I was right.

"It's worth a few hundred bucks every now and again to know young William tells the truth, don't ya think?"

Something in his eye told me that, yes, that was what I thought.

I got home late that night.

I was tired, and my leg hurt. My brain was on overload with how much I had to learn about the job: picking up a caseload on the fly, making connections within the office, learning how to deal with CPD. The assignment with Mitchell had been a huge boost to my ego, but the extra field work took so much time that by the end of the day I always wound up feeling deeper and deeper in the same hole I had been in when I first got to the office in the morning.

Had I screwed the pooch going civilian?

Maybe.

There was more going on tonight than pure fatigue, though.

I might be able to hide these kinds of things from everyone else, but I learned a long time ago not to pretend to myself.

"You all right?" Marjorie said as she put a beer and a plate heaped with meatloaf and potatoes in front of me. The smell alone made me realize how long it had been since lunch.

"I'm fine."

Our little TV was on the kitchen counter and had been turned to face her while she was cooking. She reached over, scooted it around, and sat down to her own plate. *My Three Sons* was on. It wasn't her favorite, but it was Thursday, so *Bewitched* would be next. She loved *Bewitched*. Neither of them were any *Bonanza* as far as I was concerned, and definitely not *Gunsmoke* or *Get Smart*.

"You don't look fine," she said. "Your leg acting up?"

"No, babe, I'm fine."

"Did the White Sox lose again?"

"I said I'm fine, honey."

She sat back with a sharp movement, and her face got clouded enough that even an idiot like me could see she was upset.

"I'm sorry," I said.

"I'm just trying to help."

"I know you are. I'm sorry."

Marjorie was one of the special kinds of women. She married me just before I shipped out, and dealt with all the things a woman deals with when her husband is off in the jungle. When I came back and told her I wanted to finish Bureau training, she was right there with me again. Now she was working at a legal office during the day, filing papers and getting coffee or whatever the hell else they do in a legal office. Then she came home and made dinner.

She deserved something more than I was giving her, but what was I supposed to say? *I met a Black Panther today, honey. Great guy. We should have him over for dinner sometime.*

Of course not.

First, I didn't know what to think about the Black Panthers to begin with. On one hand, this was America and I took a crap load of shrapnel to ensure that every American got to say whatever the hell they wanted to say. On the other hand, I worked in an organization that's about control. Control is peace. Militant radicals are, by definition, hard to deal with.

Second, there were some kinds of secrets you didn't tell anyone, not even your spouse—especially not your spouse.

And, third, this was a helluva dangerous secret.

The meeting with William O'Neal had gnawed at my gut all afternoon. I had walked into Kosmo's thinking O'Neal was going to be a garden-variety snitch, a guy who sold some stiff down the river to help us figure out the deal on Jonet Bradford's murder, a case we thought had ties to organized crime in New York and Philadelphia. I knew we were going to pay him, and I figured that money would flow right into some Panther program—which made me angsty in a totally different way. But that's not what was going down here. William O'Neal was, purely and simply, an undercover agent working for the FBI, a man who had infiltrated the Black Panthers, a spy who walked into the cold.

I knew spooks back in Vietnam, of course.

In certain situations good intel could be life and death.

But the FBI was in the law enforcement profession, not the spy business. We were supposed to be Melvin Purvis and Elliot Ness, not Boris and Natasha.

I was never any great lover of the Panthers, of course. They made me nervous as hell and caused no end of trouble. Clearly it was helpful to know what they were doing, and clearly it was easy to argue that spying on the Black Panthers could help us keep people safe.

Still.

This was America.

The thing that gnawed at me most was the way Mitchell went about the whole thing—as if running an agent to dig up crap on citizens in country was just something you did every day. I had heard of this kind of thing before. It was why I went to Vietnam. I didn't mind the idea of the Black Panthers disappearing, of course. Not at all. But the idea of the FBI doing the removing made me feel like I'd eaten something that had gone off.

On the other hand, I'd been in the jungle myself.

I'd done a lot of things I wasn't particularly proud of.

I took a bite of my dinner. The meatloaf was perfect.

"How was your day?" I asked.

Marjorie's face lightened up and she launched into a conversation about Lorraine, the paralegal at the office, and about John, who was an up-and-coming lawyer who everyone said was probably going to be a partner soon.

I drank the beer, and ate the meatloaf.

I told her about the training sessions I was scheduled for and I told her I would give her a rundown about my cases when it was proper.

All the while I hoped it would actually become proper sometime soon, because while I was used to dealing with security and classified shit, it was getting to be uncomfortable as hell to be doing a job that you just couldn't talk about at all.

By the time we finished dinner and cleaned up, *Bewitched* was on. We settled into the couch to watch it.

I was asleep before Elizabeth Montgomery twitched her nose.

The next time I saw William O'Neal was late July.

The Cubs were playing later that day and I was going to sneak out and do the businessman's special. They were on top of the Eastern Division—the first time there ever was such a thing. Five games better than New York, a bunch more over the Cardinals. I was more of a football guy, but a winner was a winner.

Larry Roberson, a Panther brother, had been shot down by a cop a week earlier.

"What do they expect?" Mitchell said to O'Neal after O'Neal described the anger that was flowing through the black community.

"They shot officers. You can't expect the police to take it easy when you bring out the guns."

"That goes both ways."

"Cops say the Panthers shot first."

"That's not how it went down," O'Neal said, his jaw actually clenched. "And you know it."

"Our reports are corroborated by witnesses."

O'Neal sat back, then finally shrugged and ate a beer nut, then pulled on his drink. "You're the one asking what's going down," he finally said. "I'm just saying what the brothers're saying."

He glanced at me with an expression that had a sense of distance to it. It felt like everything was disconnected, like William O'Neal knew he was living in a different place than the rest of us and there wasn't anything he could do to change it. All of a sudden it felt like I was sitting in some extra dimension of the *Twilight Zone*, floating away out in space.

"Why are you doing this?" I asked O'Neal.

"Doing what?"

The expression on Mitchell's face said he wasn't going to stop me in front of O'Neal, but that he wished with every fiber of his body that I would keep my goddamned mouth shut.

I wanted my world to make sense, though. I liked facts, and I liked facts that line up. That's why I came to the Bureau to begin with. O'Neal's reports were certainly "facts" in their own way. But the expression on his face came from a deeper place than the dry-bones voice he used to give us the basics. "Ain't like a witness ever lied," that gaze said. "Ain't like a pig ever stretched the truth."

He never said it straight out, though.

Just left it there like a grenade in a trench, time ticking until whenever it might explode.

So what was real?

Either Larry Roberson had attacked the cops or he had died defending himself. There wasn't anything here that said which was which except for the words of people, and maybe the feelings other people had for those words. The Panthers had their truth. The cop's report told something different.

Does it matter which one is true? I thought.

In the end, did it really matter which event actually happened, or did it only matter that a man was dead who shouldn't have been dead and two others were shot that didn't have to have been shot?

I looked at O'Neal, and I looked at Mitchell.

Doing what? O'Neal had asked.

"Nothing," I finally said. "Never mind me."

"When did William turn?" I asked Mitchell after the envelope was transferred and O'Neal was gone. "How did you make it happen?"

Mitchell looked at his Timex and determined we had a little time.

"Classic case, I suppose," he replied. "William and a buddy stole a car and got caught crossing state lines."

"Making it a federal thing," I said, trying to prove my chops. I drank the last of the gin and tonic, tasting the sour lime and cracking part of a rounded ice cube in my back teeth while Mitchell finished.

"Yeah. I called him up and offered him a deal. Offered to drop him a steady stream of envelopes if he would join the Panthers and tell me all about it."

"Simple as that?"

"William likes his bread buttered as much as the next guy, I suppose. But, then, I guess we all do, right?"

"Yeah," I said. "I guess we do."

On November the 9th, the Bears beat the Steelers 38-7. Bobby Douglass threw for two touchdowns. Gayle Sayers ran for 112 yards and added a pair of scores. Dick Butkus kicked ass because Dick

Butkus always kicked ass. It raised the Bears' record to a stunning one victory over eight losses.

I missed the game itself, but read about it in the *Tribune* the next afternoon.

The news about Butkus made me grin.

Before Marjorie and I came here, Dick Butkus was my image of Chicago. Tough. Mean. Territorial and borderline animalistic, but brilliant at the most important defensive position on the field. My favorite story about Butkus was that one time he called time out with ten seconds to go in the game merely so he could hit someone again. To me, Dick Butkus in his black "51" was Chicago, and Chicago was Dick Butkus. Nothing I had seen since we got here served to say any different.

Thumbing the pages, I saw another story, too.

By the end of the month, the U.S. military said the toll in Vietnam would crest 300,000 casualties, 40,000 dead.

I rubbed my leg as I sat at my desk.

The image of Dinh Lu came to me.

I looked at the headline and thought about the number: forty thousand. It didn't include the South Vietnamese, of course. Guys like Dinh Lu wouldn't show up in that count because it would never cross the minds of the people who made the report to consider them as part of the cost of the war.

Not that I was any better, really. Until we got over there I didn't think any different. I did now, though, and the number in the paper made me mad in ways I couldn't fully say.

I believed in those guys. They deserved to be there.

I remembered the group of idiot Army who came through A Shau camp thinking they were shit. They always talked big, and said the South Vietnamese irregulars couldn't cut it, when in reality it was the regular Army who wound up breaking under the heat, the mosquitoes, and the incessant tactics of an enemy they couldn't see or understand. The Green Beret understood, though.

We learned early that you had to be one with someone before they let you lead them. You had to sit with them. Eat with them.

Share stories about their kids and about the lessons they had learned about how the VC operated in the field.

The handful of us had made it work.

A glance out the office window showed overcast and wind.

My knee ached more when it got like this.

Kids were protesting the war, and others like Abby Hoffman and Bobby Seale were in prison for a more radical version of the same. Martin Luther King, Jr., had been shot a year and a half ago, Bobby Kennedy a few months later. What was it for? Was it worth it?

I flashed on the expression that had covered William O'Neal's face when I asked him what he was doing. I saw the man now. At least I felt like I understood him better.

O'Neal was a man in limbo. He wasn't really a turncoat, not in so many words, anyway. Not even a hired hand just out doing what he was paid to do. At the end of the question, William O'Neal was a man caught in the flow of a machine he didn't understand. He didn't owe the Black Panthers anything, and he didn't owe the nation anything, either. Roy Mitchell had offered O'Neal his freedom in return for information, but when the deal was struck both O'Neal's freedom and any chance at the actual justice society was owed for William O'Neal's crime of stealing a vehicle went away, just disappeared into the ether like it had never existed.

How did it come that Roy Mitchell had O'Neal's freedom to bargain with anyway? Did freedom belong to the president? Did it come from a judge? Was it paid for by J. Edgar Hoover?

Was war simply government asking you to fight for something they stole away in the first place?

Was justice merely a piece of property, free to be bargained and sold?

What did I get in return for the pain in my leg that I didn't have before I went to Vietnam?

I wondered about William O'Neal.

How did he rationalize what he was doing to the Panthers? When he was alone at night and all by himself, how did he feel about the fact that he was giving away their secrets?

It was a long trip home that night.

Marjorie rubbed my leg while we watched Carol Burnett.

I told you she was special.

Like any other office in the country, Chicago's FBI building feels different on a Friday. Everything is lighter because everyone's looking forward to the weekend. As I stepped into the office that morning, shaking snow off my shoes and pulling my dark toboggan cap off my head, all that was on my mind was that Marjorie and I were going to see a movie later.

I realized something was happening as I slipped my coat off.

The room was tense. Everything felt like it was sitting on edge.

"What's wrong?" I said.

"Guess you didn't see the paper," Mitchell replied.

The *Tribune* was open on his desk beside the initial police report. The headline was circled in red pencil.

No Quarter for Wild Beasts.

Several more cops had been shot by Black Panthers, two dead. I picked it up and scanned the story. It described an ambush and explained how the cops had been attacked with shotgun blasts from positions in an abandoned hotel on the South Side.

"Washington Park," I muttered as I read.

One Panther was dead, another shot and charged with murder.

The headline was a clear call for harsh and immediate justice, and the final paragraphs of the report made it clear that Panthers were armed degenerates who had now forfeited any expectation of due process.

This had gotten personal.

Deeply personal.

"Get your coat on," Mitchell said, his voice as strained as the rest of the room felt. "We're going to get something to eat."

We met at a place called the Golden Torch this time.

It was downtown. More formal than Kosmo's, though just as dimly lit. They had cloth over the tables and actual menus. Given the weather and the time of morning, it was no surprise we were the only ones in the joint.

Mitchell and I sat waiting with just coffee cooling in front of us. A notepad sat at the edge of the table—one of those thin folders bound in black plastic that came from the supply cabinet. The pad of paper was thin and white.

"You ever wonder why we're doing this?" I asked.

Mitchell pressed his lips together, then shook his head. "I know why *I* do it," he said. "How about you?"

I was going to answer him when I saw William O'Neal arrive. He came and took his traditional seat across from Mitchell.

"I need updates," Mitchell said, not offering coffee.

O'Neal nodded. He looked tired. "You know the story's different than they put in the papers, right? Brothers didn't shoot first."

"Where is Fred Hampton?"

"Wasn't him."

"That's not the question I asked, William." Mitchell's voice was calm and controlled, but it didn't take any special analysis to feel the difference in his demeanor.

"He's in California. Vacationing."

All three of us knew Black Panthers didn't vacation in California. Black Panthers went to California to meet up with other Black Panthers and discuss national issues. Los Angeles, Denver, New York, Chicago. The Panthers ran as intricate an organization as we did. We also heard rumors that the organization was planning to move Hampton up to take open positions they needed to fill due to the absence of Cleaver, Newton, and Seale. David Hilliard, their current National Chairman, was struggling with the law, too, so a trip to LA could mean a lot of things, none of them very vacationy.

"I'll give you one more chance," Mitchell said, grinding his jaw. "Where does Hampton live?"

"He and his girl got a place up on Monroe."

"West Side?"

"Any other Monroe you know?"

"Tell me about the guns."

"They got 'em there. But they're all legal."

Mitchell stared ice.

"I want types, William. I want calibers and models. I want serial numbers. I want to know what kind of ammunition they have, and how many people they got staying there, you got it?"

Mitchell flipped open the notepad, and pulled out a pen. He put the pen beside the page, and turned it around to make it easy for O'Neal to handle.

"Draw me a map, William. I figure you've been there. I want a map of the floor plan. I want details."

A chill ran up my spine, and I could tell O'Neal and I came to the same conclusion at the same time.

O'Neal drew a breath, then picked up the pen.

He rolled it between his fingers, and began to draw.

Mitchell drove us back to the office.

The roads were clear, but still slick in places. A dusting of snow swirled in the wind, and clouds of vapor came from manhole covers at each intersection. The vinyl seats creaked against the fabric of our overcoats. The screech of old wiper blades rocked back and forth every time he toggled them on and off.

"I don't know if I can do this," I said.

He stared over one shoulder as he guided the car, the question unasked.

"You're going to give the cops that map, aren't you?" I said.

"That's the game, Carl. You understand that, right? They took two of ours, we take at least two of theirs."

"Hampton didn't do it."

Mitchell grimaced. He knew I was right. He understood

251

completely the truth they were getting ready to embark on was one the cops and the FBI were going to create.

"You think that's important?"

"Of course it is."

"No, it isn't." He shook his head. "This is a war, Carl. Remember that. We're fighting a war here, and the Panthers are the enemy. If you don't get that, then maybe you're not the man I thought you were."

I sat in silence.

"Besides," Mitchell added. "Who's to say Hampton didn't order those killings? This is the Panthers we're talking about."

"If we can prove it he goes down."

"When they go hunting cops, the rules change."

"He's got a kid on the way."

Mitchell didn't say anything.

I watched the sidewalk roll past until we came to the office. He checked in through security and found a spot in the enclosed lot.

"I don't know, Roy. I don't think I can do this."

"I'm a good judge of character, Carl. I'm pretty sure you can."

"Let's try it another way," I argued. "Let's put everything we've got on proving Hampton ordered it. Or let's get William on it. You know he can find things if we give him some time. If Hampton made the call, he goes down."

Mitchell turned the car off, then sighed as we sat in silence.

He looked old in the light of the garage. The lines of his face were black slashes down his cheeks. His hair, cut regulation short, could still pass in the service but was shot with streaks of silvery gray that gleamed in the winter light. Folds of skin around his eyes grew soft, almost fatherly.

"Check the glove box," he said, raising an eyebrow.

I hesitated, then punched the button that released the box.

It fell open with a clunk, and there, on top of old maps and registration cards, on top of a tire gauge and a pair of honest-to-goodness gloves, was a thin manila envelope that bulged a bit in the middle.

I pulled it out, looked at Mitchell one more time, and opened it.

Inside were pictures.

Me and a girl that had happened when I was on furlough in Saigon.

My throat got dry.

It had been a stupid night. I was tired, and I was drunk. So drunk.

Heat rose to my cheeks and the tips of my fingers actually felt like they were burning where they touched the photos.

"I think you can do this, Carl."

Marjorie lit a cigarette and blew the smoke away while I ate the last of my pork chop. She was wearing a red turtleneck and had gussied up her makeup for date night. We were at a place on East Division Street, sitting next to the glass window where the chill of the night leaked in to put up a fight with the sharp sense of embarrassment I felt every time I looked at her.

No. That was a lie.

If I was going to get anywhere with this, I had to face it straight up. I loved my wife. A little bit of Chicago bitterness couldn't stand up against the pain of knowing what a dumbass I had been. Every time I looked at her I felt the sensation of the photos against my fingertips. Every time she smiled I got a shadowed image of the woman in them.

"Let's see *Easy Rider,* instead," Marjorie said.

"I thought you wanted to see that other thing with Burt Lancaster."

"And Deborah Kerr?"

"Yeah. That one."

"I do." She looked at me from across the table as the waitress brought our check. The girls in the office had apparently been going cuckoo over Burt Lancaster and Deborah Kerr getting together again for the first time since *From Here to Eternity*. It was all she had talked about for a week.

"So, what gives?" I said. "One of the girls say old man Lancaster keeps his shirt on?"

"You wish."

I looked at the check and pulled money out of my wallet.

Marjorie smoked. "I just thought you might like to see something more like *Easy Rider*. Everyone says it's good, too. Like someone might get an Oscar out of it or something."

"Can't beat that, I suppose."

"Besides," she said, giving me one of her more dangerous-looking smiles. "The Esquire is closer, and *Easy Rider* starts at eight, so maybe we'll get home a little earlier."

I raised an eyebrow.

"Well," she said, crossing her arms over her chest. "You don't have work tomorrow."

"That's true enough." Thank God.

Seeing me put my wallet away, she handed the smoldering cigarette across the table like she always did. I took it and smoked while I pulled my hat from the rung I hung it on earlier.

"I'm thinking of quitting," she said.

"Again?" I replied as I blew smoke toward the ceiling. There was something to her voice that made me stop though. "You mean your job, don't you?"

She smiled again and I understood where she was going.

"You're back for good, right, Carl? No more Army. And you've got a great job now. Steady."

I nodded. "Yeah, that's right."

She leaned in.

"Do you think it's time, yet?"

"You mean for a kid, right?" I said, probably too fast.

"I mean for a family."

I hesitated, this time probably for too long. "I don't know. I...I just...I haven't thought about it, I guess."

"Just like a guy."

That was the thing about Marjorie. She was good about this kind of thing. She knew how to bring issues up in an easy way, but was just as hard to figure out. I couldn't, for example, tell if she was hurt by this response or if she had been expecting it and was merely letting me have space to sort it out.

"Well," she said, "think about it, all right?"

"Yeah. All right."

"In the meantime, *Easy Rider*?"

"Sure," I said.

We did the eight o'clock show.

When we got home I took Marjorie out of her red turtleneck and we made love. Later, in the darkness of our room, I laid there and listened to her sleep.

"You sit and watch," Mitchell told me before we got out of the car. "It's important you get a grip on out how this shit works if you're going to make it. You got that?"

It was a Wednesday morning. Cold as sin, but no snow, yet.

The parking garage smelled of concrete and exhaust, which made sense because that's what it looked like, too. It was the essence of Chicago, I thought. The under-girder of a no-nonsense town.

On the outside, the city's skyscrapers stood tall and rugged, built with an architecture meant for a man with a certain kind of common sense. On the surface the people of Chicago went to work despite the wind and the snow and the powers of Lake Michigan just outside their doors. It's a city of action, a place where people came not to become anything, but to do something instead. Chicago was like the country's Grand Central Station, I'd decided. Walking the city could make a man feel connected to everywhere else if he wanted to be.

In practice, this means it was a place where waves of people crashed into each other. Negro, Irish, Polish, Italian, Greek, Chinese, German. Male and female. Christian, Muslim, Jew, Hindu, Buddhist. Somehow it all had to work, and on the outside it did.

The city's undercarriage, though, had its own sense of pragmatism.

Here, cause and effect were sometimes one and the same.

The Machine, political and otherwise, moved in ways that maybe no one liked or maybe they did, but in ways everyone just looked away from because to do anything else would throw a spanner into the works and bring the whole goddamned thing to a grinding, shuddering halt.

To understand this, is to strip the city down to its concrete and its exhaust.

Sitting in the car, I looked at Special Agent Roy Mitchell.

"Yeah," I said, blowing into my already gloved hands. "I got it."

The meeting was held in a small office of the Chicago Police Department's Gang Intelligence Unit, a room that reeked of cigarettes, body heat, and a familiar tang of military fervor cloaked in something that might or might not have been discipline.

The session was brief and to the point.

The men of the GIU were focused. They listened with intensity.

We gave them people. We gave them events and relationships. We gave them what O'Neal told us about weapons, though Mitchell redacted mention of whether they were legal or not. And, of course, we gave them the map, which O'Neal had conveniently marked to show where Hampton's bed was.

We gave them a date, too: The date when Fred Hampton would be back from LA, and when William O'Neal would be visiting—a date when O'Neal might well find himself able to drop a mickey into a drink or two.

Through it all, I sat in a padded seat with a squeaky wheel that was stuck in one position and watched the conversation go down, thinking about Marjorie and thinking about that night, that one stupid night when the CIA photographed me doing something I had never done before and had never done again. Could they have arranged it? Was it possible I had fallen into a Hoover ploy? A stereotypical FBI joke? Gin up dirt on everyone just in case it becomes useful someday later?

Roy Mitchell had been my hero since I met him, and the fact was that he was a good agent—good at his job, anyway. Did he have some kind of skeleton in his own closet that his superior was pulling on him, or was he doing this on his own dime because he thought this was how it should all work? What was the truth? Did it matter?

I sat there thinking about the Panthers, and about the team of cops who were going to visit an apartment on the West Side of Chicago at 4 a.m. I thought about Dinh Lu, and forty thousand dead. I thought about the expression on Joe Kendrick's face, frozen in time.

"Can you get the warrant?" Mitchell asked at the end.

"With the kind of firepower you say they got, I could get a warrant against my grandmother," one of the GIU men replied.

"Your grandmother a Panther?" another added.

"Nah," he said. "My granny may well want to shoot my ass, but she ain't dark enough to be a Panther."

Everyone laughed.

It was just over a week later. December 4th.

The office was buzzing by the time I got in. I didn't need to read the initial ops reports to know the details, but I did anyway.

The shootout had lasted ten or fifteen minutes, tops.

Nine Panthers had been in the apartment. Four were wounded.

The two dead were Chairman Fred Hampton and Mark Clark, a Panther visiting from downstate Peoria who had been shot through the heart. They were taken to the Cook County morgue.

The other seven were arrested and charged with attempted murder, aggravated battery, and armed violence. The wounded were taken to Cook County Hospital, the rest to the Cook County jail.

Later that night, I found William O'Neal to get more details.

"Chairman Fred wasn't dead at first," he told me.

So he was executed. Two shots to the head from close range.

That was the Panther truth, anyway.

The Cook County State's Attorney had another story.

"While serving a warrant to search for illegal weapons, our brave officers staved off a vicious attack by the Black Panthers," the statement said. "It was a miracle that none of our men was killed."

The next morning I rose early because I wasn't sleeping anyway. I was out of the apartment before Marjorie woke up. Now I was standing on an open street in the December cold. The smell here was bitter. Dead blades of wet brown grass clung to cracks in the sidewalk below my feet.

"What are you doin' here?"

The question came from a black woman standing at the end of the line when I joined.

It was a question I had asked myself a hundred times since I finished breakfast and came to my final decision. For whatever reason, hubris or simple ignorance, the police had left the apartment scene open. O'Neal told me the Panthers were giving public tours. Said people were lining up to see it.

What are you doing here?

The woman's voice sounded flat when she challenged me.

Her eyes were sharp and questioning.

She held her overcoat closed hard against her chest. She'd wrapped a blue and white scarf tight around her head. Her dress was long under the overcoat and had some kind of print to it, but her ankles were bare to the elements. Her shoes were snub-nosed and worn.

She shivered in the cold.

What are you doing here?

"I had to see for myself," I said.

For a moment it looked like she was going to say something else, but then her lips pursed together and a sense of resolution came over her face. She turned her back to me and pulled the coat tighter.

It was a long line. A single-file of people that snaked down Monroe Street like a line to a circus freak show, which I suppose it was. The front of the line ended at the doorway to 2773, where less than thirty-six hours ago Fred Hampton and Mark Clark had lost their lives.

Our conversation drew stares, though, and I realized that until then the line itself had been silent. The only sounds were wind and cold, the occasional cough and the shuffling of feet. A man several steps ahead lit a pipe, the lighter throwing a full flint click. A car drove by.

Otherwise, nobody said a word.

These were Fred Hampton's people come to see the truth, come to stand here in this silence that was covered now in a kind of electric tension that built itself up slowly as we stood in the icy cold.

They examined me, though. I felt it when they turned to me, their eyes sometimes guarded, sometimes defiant. I felt it in the color of my skin, which was too white now. I felt it in my hair, which was still cut Green Beret short, and I felt it in my shoulders that now were covered in an overcoat that screamed FBI better than any badge ever could. I felt it when Negroes took positions behind me.

Pig. That's what I heard, and that's what I felt.

The line stepped forward and I followed the woman.

The line was long enough it took over an hour to get in.

Later, I would learn Fred Hampton played football in high school and that his father worked for years at a corn plant. Over time I would come to see his ability to connect to people and his drive to serve the community he came from. When I did I would understand exactly why Hoover and the Bureau had targeted him. I would hear the core of what Fred Hampton was saying, and then this line of people and this feeling of tension that ran through it would all make sense. But until then all I knew was that there were a lot of people here and that it was cold as hell, but that there was no way I would leave until I saw the inside of this apartment.

Then, suddenly, I was there.

"Don't touch nothing, don't move nothing," a Panther said as my footsteps clomped up the wooden stairway. "We want to keep everything just the way they is."

I pressed my hands into my coat pockets and stepped through the entryway and into the bullet-blasted living area.

Words cannot describe it.

Pools of blood. Spattered plasterboard walls shot to shards. Broken glass. Tables overturned. Tattered posters flapping free. Record albums strewn across the floor. "Here's where brother Mark was killed," a man said, pointing to a dried red-brown pool. I stepped to the hallway, past one bedroom to the next. An armchair was ripped to shreds. A dresser drawer sat open and unhinged.

"Here's where they blew Chairman Fred's brains out," the guide said.

It was a tiny bedroom, maybe ten-by-ten.

The mattress was soaked in dried blood.

Soaked like the floor where Fred Hampton had been dragged away.

A chair and a reading lamp stood nearby, giving the whole thing a surreal sense of normalcy that pulled my brain into pieces.

Who are you?

What are you doing here?

I was struck by how small the place was. No more than forty feet front to back. Six rooms, including the kitchen out back, paperboard walls strafed to Swiss cheese by bullets.

There had been what, nine Panthers and fourteen policemen here?

I pressed my hands harder into my pockets, but leaned in to scan the bullet holes.

Sixty of them? Eighty? My eyes moved across the scene with a practiced ease. No. A hundred. Maybe more. A hundred bullets: Every one of them coming from the direction the police came, aimed low and toward the bed.

"This was no shootout," I said, speaking for the first time since I stepped into the line.

"No shit, brother," a voice echoed.

I had known what was going to happen, but the brutality here froze my chest. The room was suddenly colder than the line outside. I thought maybe my knees would buckle.

This was Chicago, I thought.

This was America.

This was murder. Cold-blooded, politically driven murder. In other countries, we would call it an assassination.

And I had been part of it.

Suddenly I knew exactly why I was here.

It was Thursday night at ten, a week after the shooting.

Marjorie had bought new Christmas lights. They sat in a pile on our table. We were going to put them up that weekend.

In the meantime, Illinois State's Attorney Edward Hanrahan was having problems in the press. He'd released a daily string of accounts of the operation, each more belligerent than the last. Despite a significant home field advantage, it wasn't working. People were calling for investigations into the Panthers' claims that Fred Hampton was murdered.

Tonight Hanrahan's officers were going to air an exclusive show on WBBM in which they would give a mock version of the shootout to the public.

Both Marjorie and I had been following it in the *Tribune*, and I saw the daily briefings in the office. I knew exactly what story they were going to tell.

She had been talking about watching the program all through dinner, but when it came on, I knew I couldn't wait any longer.

I got up and turned the television set off.

"What are you doing?" Marjorie said.

I sank into the couch beside her, and stared out the apartment window and into the blackness of night, wishing I had the ability to talk about things like she did.

"Are you all right?" she said.

For just a flash I thought about William O'Neal. I felt the struggle of sleeping at night beside my wife, knowing what I knew. Knowing *everything* I knew. I still didn't know how William O'Neal did it. He had even been a pallbearer at Fred Hampton's funeral. Maybe he was stronger than me. I didn't believe that, but maybe it was true. Maybe he had just given up. Maybe he didn't care. I didn't know.

But I cared. That's one thing I knew for sure.

Someday I hoped Marjorie and I would have a family together. Someday I hoped she would look me in the eye again and tell me she loved me and that she understood and that nothing had ever changed in that department.

But if I was going to be the father I wanted to be, I had to be the man I wanted to be. The man I thought maybe I had once been.

And if I was going to be that man, I had to tell her this truth.

"You're scaring me, Carl," Marjorie said. Her brow was furrowed.

"I did something a long time ago," I said, turning my gaze from the window. They were literally the hardest words I had ever said.

Her brow was furrowed. "What is it?"

"I'm sorry," I said.

Then it all came out.

Three weeks later, New Year's Eve.

The forecast was for snow.

I was back at Kosmo's, alone this time. It was late in the afternoon, nearly three. The drink was bourbon, straight. I liked the sense of fire it gave me as I drank it, liked the way it burned against my nostrils as I breathed in the smell of it.

O'Neal picked his way to the table. I had a soda already there for him.

"Where's Mitchell?"

I shrugged. "He's got other things to work on."

"I don't work for you."

"I'm not expecting you to."

The black man looked confused.

"I want you to give Bobby Rush something," I said.

Rush was the Panthers' minister of defense. He had been one of Hampton's closest associates and was running the show for at least as long as it took the chapter to figure out how to move forward. The cops had raided Rush's house the day after they killed Fred Hampton, but someone tipped him off. The office pool was running about three-to-one that Rush would keep control, others said it would somehow fall to Jessie Jackson, who had come to eulogize Hampton. On the whole, the Bureau was happy about how things were falling. Most said J. Edgar had finally gotten what he wanted and that the Panthers wouldn't be able to recover, but I wasn't so sure.

"What do you have?" O'Neal said.

I put an envelope on the table.

"What's that?"

"A map of the city," I said. "Marked up to show every house the FBI knows the Panthers are using to house weapons and other equipment. There's also a listing of surveillance programs our agents are working, and a receipt he might find has an interesting set of names on it."

"Those are dangerous pieces of information if they're real."

"Tell Rush I want to help."

O'Neal laughed then. His expression said I might be more than half-crazy. "You're joking with me, right? I mean, if you think the Panthers will ever line up with a pig you are more than certifiably insane."

"I'm not a pig."

"The hell you're not."

"I know what a pig is," I said, staring him down. "I'm not it."

I dropped about half the drink down my throat, then pushed the envelope further toward him. Then I shrugged.

"Tell Bobby Rush I don't care if he burns these things or uses them to wipe his ass. Tell him I got other packages going to the papers. Tell him that I catch a Panther breaking the law, that Panther's going down. But tell him that if I see a bad agent, he's going down, too. Best as I can do it, anyway."

O'Neal looked at the envelope like it was a snake. "You know you're gonna wind up dead, right?" he said.

I finished the drink, then stood up.

"Maybe. But this is how I play it."

I dropped ten bucks on the table. "Get yourself a burger if you want," I said. "Or give it to the breakfast program. Whatever."

Outside it was cold, but not bitter. I pulled the collar of my coat up as I walked out the door to stand under the restaurant's awning. The sky was overcast, and snow was coming down in the kind of flakes you see in the movies. Big, fluffy things flying around in circles. They gave me an image of a boy in the middle of a field somewhere in Indiana, looking up and laughing as he staggered around like some kind of mummified zombie trying to catch one on his tongue.

I fished my last cigarette out of the box, then popped the top off my lighter. The flint caught and the flame rose orange and blue. The smell of burning fluid was sweet in the chilled air.

Marjorie agreed to see me at the apartment tonight. We're going to talk about what happens next.

I looked at the cigarette, still unlit, then gazed over the fresh snow.

I closed the lighter, stepped out from under the awning, and tossed the cigarette to the gutter.

As I walked into the cold, my leg felt good.

ABOUT THE EDITOR

New York Times bestselling author Kristine Kathryn Rusch writes in almost every genre. Generally, she uses her real name (Rusch) for most of her writing. Under that name, she publishes bestselling science fiction and fantasy, award-winning mysteries, acclaimed mainstream fiction, controversial nonfiction, and the occasional romance. Her novels have made bestseller lists around the world and her short fiction has appeared in eighteen best of the year collections. She has won more than twenty-five awards for her fiction, including the Hugo, *Le Prix Imaginales*, the *Asimov's* Readers Choice award, and the *Ellery Queen Mystery Magazine* Readers Choice Award.

Publications from *The Chicago Tribune* to *Booklist* have included her Kris Nelscott mystery novels in their top-ten-best mystery novels of the year. The Nelscott books have received nominations for almost every award in the mystery field, including the best novel Edgar Award, and the Shamus Award.

She also writes goofy romance novels as award-winner Kristine Grayson.

She also edits. Beginning with work at the innovative publishing company, Pulphouse, followed by her award-winning tenure at *The Magazine of Fantasy & Science Fiction*, she took fifteen years off before returning to editing with the original anthology series *Fiction River,* published by WMG Publishing. She acts as series editor with her husband, writer Dean Wesley Smith, and edits some of the volumes, as well.

To keep up with everything she does, go to kriswrites.com and sign up for her newsletter. To track her many pen names and series, see their individual websites (krisnelscott.com, kristinegrayson.com, retrievalartist.com, divingintothewreck.com).

FICTION RIVER YEAR FIVE

Feel the Fear
Edited by Mark Leslie

Superpowers
Edited by Rebecca Moesta

Justice
Edited by Kristine Kathryn Rusch

Wishes
Edited by Rebecca Moesta

Pulse Pounders: Countdown
Edited by Kevin J. Anderson

Hard Choices
Edited by Dean Wesley Smith

A subscription to Fiction River saves you money and ensures that you receive the very best short fiction from some of today's best authors. Subscriptions are available in electronic and trade paper formats and begin with the very next volume. Don't wait! Subscribe today at www.FictionRiver.com.

Missed a previously published volume? No problem. Buy individual volumes anytime from your favorite bookseller.

Unnatural Worlds
Edited by Dean Wesley Smith & Kristine Kathryn Rusch

How to Save the World
Edited by John Helfers

Time Streams
Edited by Dean Wesley Smith

Christmas Ghosts
Edited by Kristine Grayson

Hex in the City
Edited by Kerrie L. Hughes

Moonscapes
Edited by Dean Wesley Smith

Special Edition: Crime
Edited by Kristine Kathryn Rusch

Fantasy Adrift
Edited by Kristine Kathryn Rusch

Universe Between
Edited by Dean Wesley Smith

Fantastic Detectives
Edited by Kristine Kathryn Rusch

Past Crime
Edited by Kristine Kathryn Rusch

Pulse Pounders
Edited by Kevin J. Anderson

Risk Takers
Edited by Dean Wesley Smith

Alchemy & Steam
Edited by Kerrie L. Hughes

Valor
Edited by Lee Allred

Recycled Pulp
Edited by John Helfers

Hidden in Crime
Edited by Kristine Kathryn Rusch

Sparks
Edited by Rebecca Moesta

Visions of the Apocalypse
Edited by John Helfers

Haunted
Edited by Kerrie L. Hughes

Last Stand
Edited by Dean Wesley Smith & Felicia Fredlund

Tavern Tales
Edited by Kerrie L. Hughes

No Humans Allowed
Edited by John Helfers

Editor's Choice
Edited by Mark Leslie

Pulse Pounders: Adrenaline
Edited by Kevin J. Anderson

PULPHOUSE FICTION MAGAZINE

Pulphouse Fiction Magazine is returning twenty years after its last issue. The first issue comes out in January 2018, and the magazine will be quarterly, with about 70,000 words of short fiction every issue. This reincarnation will mix some of the stories from the old *Pulphouse* days with brand-new fiction. The magazine will have an attitude, as did the first run. No genre limitations, but high-quality writing and strangeness.

For more information or to subscribe, go to
www.pulphousemagazine.com.